CLEMHORN

NIGHTFALL

Andrew J Harvey

A Novel of the Cross-Temporal Empire

DEDICATION

My thanks to Sally Odgers who provided a final polish to the manuscript, and Vincent Rospond at Zmok books who had faith in the Clemhorns.

This book is for my mother, who would have been so proud.

Nightfall by Andrew J. Harvey
Cover: 'Red Square in Moscow' by Fyodor Alekseyev. 1801
'Donald Clemhorn' by Jade of Steam Power Studios
'Airship' by Michael Mosskothen, Shutterstock image

This edition published in 2019

Zmok Books is an imprint of

Pike and Powder Publishing Group LLC
17 Paddock Drive
Lawrence, NJ 08648

1525 Hulse Rd, Unit 1
Point Pleasant, NJ 08742

ISBN 978-1-945430-67-1
LCN 2018966902

Bibliographical References and Index
1. Science Fiction. 2. Alternate History. 3. Military

For more information on Pike and Powder Publishing Group, LLC,
visit us at www.PikeandPowder.com & www.wingedhussarpublishing.com

twitter: @pike_powder
facebook: @PikeandPowder

PROLOGUE

After eighty years of total war the remnants of humanity on the Nayarit Line struggled to survive in sealed domes, surrounded by radioactive wasteland and genetically engineered viruses. It was in the last, desperate years of the war that the first trans-temporal portal was developed at Chiqu, a small research facility on the west coast of North America. As the domes finally failed and civilization collapsed around them, Iapura led fifty-three survivors from Chiqu to found a new empire on a parallel Earth; an Earth where, in 1884, Russian and English armies faced each other across America's Great Plains, totally unprepared for the technology of the invading Nayarit.

Over the next ninety years Iapura's Empire expanded steadily across a series of parallel Earths, absorbing and conquering until it included over fifty-four separate timelines. Finally, however, with its technology stagnant and its ruling Council riven by dissent, the declining health of Manet, First Leader of the Cross-Temporal Empire threatens the stability of the Empire.

CHAPTER ONE

Perusia — Etu Line
April 1979 (95AE)

Ivy swore as her boots slipped on the damp rock, the rope tightening under her arms as she scrambled to find a foothold. Unfortunately, cavalry boots were turning out to be worse than useless for rock climbing.

"How is he?" she called, trying to make herself heard over the sound of the waterfall, craning her neck to see around the overhang that blocked her view. The rocks were covered with moisture, making the descent doubly dangerous as she tried to keep as much of her weight off the suspect rope as possible.

There was a pause as one of her squad went to look and she took the chance to catch her breath, flexing her fingers which were turning blue with cold. It was freezing within the funnel, despite her jacket.

"Still there, Troop Leader," came the eventual answer from her Corporal.

"Onwards and downwards," she muttered to herself, wishing she knew how much farther she had to go.

"Leader, are you still there?" It was the squad's radio operator.

"Where else would I be?" she said irritably, her attention fixed on working out a way over the next outcrop.

"Don't know," he said, unfazed by her reaction. "I just got a message from the fort. A message came in for you from Continental Headquarters."

"And?" Not paying any attention. She'd finally worked out the path she was going to take and had carefully started to lower herself by her arms, her feet struggling for purchase on the slick rock. The rope tightened before she could get a foothold and she swore, wishing she wasn't so short. "Slack," she called. The rope was loosened and she almost lost her hold before her feet found the ledge.

"You haven't told me what the message is," she called when she was safe.

"Maybe this isn't the best time," came the reply.

"Just tell me what the damn message was," she snarled.

Why did life have to be so difficult?

"They didn't say."

Her hand slipped and her chin slammed into the rock. She swore again.

"You all right Leader?"

"No." Blood had started to ooze from the cut. At least the blood was warm, she thought.

"What?"

"Doesn't matter." She had to raise her voice to cut through the sound of the water. She hoped there wasn't anything wrong at home. Still, if she didn't get her mind back on the climb the whole question could become moot.

By the time she reached the bottom her hands were numb, and her legs shaking from exhaustion. The young goatherd lay on a narrow ledge, almost at her feet, half-in, half-out of the pool into which the waterfall dropped before disappearing into a thin crevice in the rock. The ledge, slippery with moss, had been worn dangerously smooth by the water, while the din from the waterfall made it difficult to think.

He looked about ten but could have been younger; kids grew up quickly around here. As she pulled him the rest of the way out of the pool she tried to check his pulse but was unable to feel anything through the numbness in her fingers. She was just straightening up when she was startled by the faint flutter of his eyelids.

OK, so he was still alive, but looking back up the funnel of rocks above her she realized that in their rush to get someone down here they hadn't exactly worked everything through. The plan had been simply to pull the two of them up together, but the difficulty of the descent had already proved that to be impossible. And then there was the rope. In theory 3/8th inch sisal should be able to manage their combined weight, but that was when new and this was anything but. Indeed it was because she hadn't wanted to risk anyone heavier that she was there. She wasn't going to entrust both their necks to a jury-rigged harness and a rope that should have been replaced years ago.

The obvious solution was to wait for the reinforcements she'd sent for from the fort, but she doubted the kid would survive that long. Looking up she could just make out the Corporal peering down at her from the top of the rocks.

"I need the other rope," she shouted, indicating the rope and holding up two fingers. The Corporal nodded, and a moment later the end of the squad's second rope came slithering over the edge of the cliff towards her.

"I hope this is going to work," she muttered to herself as she pulled the boy up into a sitting position.

Her fingers were too numb to undo the rope around her chest so she pulled out her knife and cut through the knot. Then, after tying both ropes about the boy's chest, she carefully worked her way around the pool as far as she could with the second rope. She got about a quarter of the way round before she ran out of ledge, but looking up she thought it might be enough. Pulling the rope she was holding tight she gestured for Macros to start pulling the boy up with the other rope. With Ivy guiding the ascent, and putting just enough pressure on the rope to keep him away from the face of the rock, they managed to get him to the top of the funnel without further damage. Finally, as she saw willing hands reach out to haul him over the edge of the cliff, she let out her breath, surprised to find how tense she'd been.

It wasn't long before the Corporal's head reappeared over the edge of the cliff, and a moment later the squad had taken up the slack in her own rope. Compared to the climb down the climb back up seemed to take almost no time at all, and it wasn't long before she stood on solid ground again.

"Well done Troop Leader," the Corporal said, as he handed her back her kepi.

Ivy nodded, pleased at the compliment from someone with five times as much active service as she had, and replaced the kepi over her short, blonde hair. "How is he?"

"He's alive. The medic is checking him over. Here, you better get out of that jacket," he said as she started to shiver. "Horus," he called, "we need a blanket here."

As she struggled to get out of the jacket she noticed a deep tear down one sleeve and wondered how she'd managed to do that. Accepting the blanket from Horus she wrapped it thankfully around her shoulders. "Where is he?"

"Up on the road."

She nodded and headed back to the road where she found the medic working to splint the boy's leg while his sister, who had flagged them down as they returned to the fort, hovered uncertainly nearby. There was a sudden clatter of hooves as Mathilda, the fort's second-in-command, rode up with the requested assistance.

"Troop Leader Clemhorn, it looks like you've been busy," Mathilda said with a grin, looking down on her. A full-blood Mohican, she wore her long hair in a plaited bun today.

"A bit of rock climbing," Ivy said. "Did you bring the ambulance?"

"They were just harnessing up when we left. I didn't want to wait for them though as your message sounded urgent. It looks like you didn't need us after all."

"It seemed better to be safe than sorry." Ivy's teeth started to chatter.

Mathilda frowned. "I think you should take the Troop Leader back to the fort," she told the Corporal. "I can finish off here."

"I'm perfectly all right," Ivy said.

"Maybe now, but in fifteen minutes it's going to be another question. And you might want to get that cut looked at." She leaned forward to inspect Ivy's chin.

Instinctively Ivy touched her chin, blanching as she took her hand away and saw the amount of blood on it.
The medic, who had just finished with his bandaging, looked up. "Leader?"

"I'm fine," Ivy snapped. Why was everyone trying to mollycoddle her?

"And just who's the medic in this squad?" he said, coming over to have a look. "Nope, needs stitches," he pronounced, turning her face to the light. "We'll wait till you're back at the fort though. In the meantime I'll put a couple of butterfly stickers on it to hold it."

Ivy fidgeted as he rummaged in his pack.

"Stop it," he told her sternly. Two stickers later he turned to Corporal. "She's all yours."

The Corporal snapped to attention. "Leader." He indicated her mount.

Ivy scowled, admitting to what was obviously turning out to be a full on conspiracy. "I'll see you back at the fort," she told Mathilda.

"When you see the ambulance, tell them to hurry it up," Mathilda said. "I'd like to get back before dinner."

"Will do." Irrationally, having a task to do made her feel a little better.

A fine mist had started to descend over-the-top of the mountains as they broached the last of the hills blocking their view of the fort. As the massive, pink limestone walls of Fort Perusia came into sight Ivy pulled her mount in for a moment to look down on the purpling Umbrian plain spread out below her, the sheer beauty of the scene almost causing her to catch her breath. Paradise on Earth. Unfortunately, like most paradises, this one had its snake. In this case it was her commanding officer, Force Leader Jules McKenzie.

Regretfully she turned her attention back to the thick, stone walls that enclosed the top of the hill. Built several hundred years ago by the Hallstatt, it now housed the 96th Mounted Infantry of the Clemhorn 72nd Battle Group. Despite its present owners, there remained clear evidence of its previous occupants in the form of the massive stone griffin crouched on top of the main gate's enormous, granite lintel.

"Leader?" the Corporal prompted.

"Sorry Corporal." Ivy kneeded her mount forward, and it was obvious from the horse's enthusiasm that it wasn't only the Corporal who wanted to get back.

She had almost finish unsaddling her mount when the fort leader came storming into the stables.

"Just what the hell did you think you were doing?" Jules demanded, almost apoplectic with rage.

"My job," she said defensively, noticing the quick departure of the Corporal through the stable's far doors.

"It's not your job to pull stupid stunts like that." Jules was almost bouncing with anger. "You're a Troop Leader not some bloody grunt."

Ivy had never seen him like this before. She considered apologizing, simply to defuse the issue - but stuff him, it was her job. Nona had drummed that into her enough as she was growing up. Pulling the saddle off she staggered under the weight. The climb must have affected her more than she knew.

"I didn't have any choice," she defended. "Someone had to make the climb and I was the lightest. If Mathilda had been there she'd have made the same decision."

"Mathilda's father is not the bloody World Leader," he said, failing to notice the stagger.

"I don't see why that should make any difference," she said, as she swung saddle up and onto the rail.

"Then you're even stupider than I give you credit for."

All right, she thought, perhaps her father being World Leader did make a difference, but it shouldn't have.

"I want you packed up and ready to leave tomorrow," he said.

She froze. "What?"

"Mathilda will look after your Troop as well as her own until I can get a replacement."

"Force Leader," she protested, tears pricking her eyes. "That's not fair!"

"No, it's not fair. There are probably hundreds of other Troop Leaders more suitable for promotion than you but Continental Headquarters in its infinite wisdom has ruled otherwise. From now on though you're going to be someone else's responsibility." He stared at her for a moment longer before, with a snort and angry shake of his head, turned on his heels and stalked out.

Ivy stared after him, furious tears stinging her eyes. What was she supposed to do now — how was she going to explain this to her father? Suddenly the effects of the climb, coupled with Jule's tirade, were all too much, and leaning back against the wall she allowed herself to slide to the ground.

Mathilda found her there fifteen minutes later, still propped up against the wall of the wooden horse box.

"I was wondering what you were doing," the senior Troop Leader said. "I thought you'd have been celebrating by now."

Ivy looked up at her through tear reddened eyes. "What?"

"Your promotion."

Ivy looked at her, puzzled.

Mathilda stared at her. "He didn't tell you?"

"Tell me what?"

Mathilda swore. "Just what did Jules say?"

"That he was shipping me out tomorrow."

For a moment Mathilda looked as though she was ready to turn and storm out of the stable to have it out with the fort commander, before realizing there was a more immediate priority. Squatting down she looked Ivy in the face, forcing eye contact.

"You've been promoted," she said. "That's why you're leaving."

"Promoted?"

"To Force Leader," Mathilda said reassuringly.

Promoted? Ivy replayed Jules conversation about life not being fair. So that's what he was talking about. "He said I was stupid," she said.

"Talk about the pot calling the kettle black."

"He hates me."

Mathilda started to open her mouth to argue that statement, then closed it. "More fool he. Just be thankful you're out of here then."

"Why?"

"Why what?"

"Why have I been promoted?" She'd dreamed about it, being able to leave this damn fort with the coveted two stars on her shoulder. But Jules was right, there were hundreds of others more entitled than she was.

"Because you're a damn good officer. The troops respect you and you get things done. And you're not a shirker; I mean look at that stunt you pulled today."

"Jules said it was stupid."

"I thought we'd agreed Jules was stupid."

Unable to help herself Ivy gave her a small smile.

Mathilda returned the smile. "That's better."

"It's not because of my father?" Ivy was unable to hide her fear that all the hard work she'd done for the past three years, the absolute crap she'd put up with from Jules for the past two years had meant nothing, that in the end it had all come down to who her father was.

Mathilda shrugged. "Does it matter?" She paused. "Ah, I see it does." She tilted her head. "Perhaps," she admitted. "But I don't think you'll find anyone in the fort who begrudges you the promotion."

"Except Jules."

"Except Jules," Mathilda amended. "You're bright, and you've worked twice as hard as any other Troop Leader I've ever met. You've never taken advantage of your position, and I know you aced the selection test. I'd say it was well earned."

Ivy tried another smile. It still hurt. "He could have just said."

Mathilda shrugged. “Forget Jules, we’ve got a party to organize.” Standing back up she offered Ivy her hand. “Come on Force Leader, let’s get you cleaned up.”

Ivy accepted the hand gratefully. “Force Leader’s got a nice ring to it,” she admitted.

“Tell me about it. I’m sure it will start to pall after five years though,” Mathilda said with a grin. “In the meantime Force Leader, let’s party!”

CHAPTER TWO

Cempoala — Etu Line
July 1979 (95AE)

Conrad watched the bedroom door nervously, waiting for it to burst open and for Papanzin to come storming through.

All he had said was that he had to return to Leolie for the Festival and wouldn't be back for a couple of months and she'd started throwing things. He considered the small cut on the back of his hand sourly. He was lucky she had such lousy aim, otherwise the damage could have been even worse.

At least one of his problems might have solved itself. He'd been wondering how he was going to end his relationship with Papanzin, and now it looked as though it had been taken care of for him. He gave a wry smile - if it hadn't been so damn serious it might even have been funny. Here he was; thirty-two, maybe three times her weight and at least a foot taller than her, and she had him cowering in his room.

The gods knew how Papanzin's father was going to react. He was fairly laid-back as fathers generally went, but as Tlatcani and head of Cempoala's city council he did have a certain standing to maintain. And a public screaming match between his daughter and the supposed Continental Leader for all of South American was going to have repercussions no matter how you looked at it.

Things seemed to have quietened down, so he cautiously stuck his head round the door to check the courtyard outside. No one was there, which was highly unusual in itself. At this time of day there should always be at least a couple of servants around. The broken pottery that littered the red brick floor when he made his escape had been cleared away, although they hadn't been able to do anything about the large stain that now marred the mural of the ball-game on the far wall. He winced when he caught sight of the empty pedestal standing next to the door; the vase that had stood there until less than thirty minutes ago had been over a thousand years old.

As he stepped out of the room, Achicauhtli, his personal secretary, appeared in the far doorway. "Do you need anything Leader Clemhorn?"

Conrad shook his head. "Has she gone?"

"Yes Leader."

"I'll be in my office then." He still had a lot of paperwork to catch up on.

"Of course Leader," Achicauhtli said equably, ever the perfect secretary.

An hour later Conrad was reading the latest report on the Tumbez railway extension, when Achicauhtli knocked on the door.

"Yes?" Conrad said, looking up, unhappy at the interruption. The report suggested the project was almost back on schedule, but he was concerned at some of the costings.

"Nezahual has asked to see you."

"He's here?" The thought of facing Papanzin's father was almost as bad as facing Papanzin herself.

"Yes."

"Show him in then," Conrad said regretfully, putting the report to one side.

"Leader Clemhorn?" Nezahual said uncertainly.

"Come in Councilor," Conrad said, standing up to greet him. "Can I offer you a hot chocolate?"

"Thank you," the small Campaolan said.

"Achicauhtli, two chocolates. Please, take a seat," Conrad told the Councilor.

Nezahual waited until Conrad had resumed his seat before sitting down. As they waited uncomfortably for Achicauhtli to reappear with the chocolate Conrad wondered if the Campaolan had any rules for this sort of situation. He suspected they had; they had rules for almost everything else. It would be helpful to know what they were though.

It was so unfair, he thought. Generally his relationships came to an amicable and often profitable conclusion for the other party. This was the first time a breakup had involved such. . . passion. And it wasn't as though he had ever lied to Papanzin. He'd always told her their relationship wasn't permanent. Where had she got the idea that he loved her? He had never told her that. He'd told her he liked her, enjoyed her company, but never that he loved her.

To cover his thoughts Conrad took a cautious sip of the bitter, spicy chocolate Achicauhtli placed on the table in front of him. Laced with vanilla the froth on its surface coated his moustache, and he wiped it off on the back of his hand.

"Thank you," Conrad told his secretary.

With a nod Achicauhtli backed out of the room, closing the door behind him.

Nezahaul cleared his throat nervously. "My daughter has asked me to apologize for her outburst earlier today."

Caught by surprise Conrad felt some chocolate go down the wrong way and it was a minute or so before he had recovered enough to wave off Nezahual's offer of help. "I'm sorry, Nezahaul," he said. "I was expecting her language to be more along the lines of - you can tell that fat prick where he can stuff it." Paraphrasing some of the language she'd used earlier that afternoon.

Nezahaul flushed, embarrassed, and Conrad almost burst out laughing. She had!

"Please, Conrad," Nezahaul said. "Perhaps we could at least pretend she had apologized."

"I understand." It was a question of appearance. From the outside Campaolan culture appeared quite macho. In reality, however, the city's females had a lot more freedom in their personal relationships than one might suspect. But still appearance was important. "How is she?"

"Still furious. Her mother is with her."

"I'm sorry."

"She is extremely passionate, is our Papanzin, very like her mother in that respect. And I suspect there is also the matter of pride."

Conrad nodded. "Will she be all right?"

"In time." Nezahaul took a sip of his own chocolate. "I understand you are returning to Leolie for a couple of months," he said, referring to line's capital.

"Yes, for the Festival of Livas. I leave next week."

From his expression it was obvious Nezahaul wanted to say something and Conrad raised any eyebrow. He had never met a more astute politician than Nezahaul, perhaps even better than his father, and he wondered what his concern was. "You have a problem with that?" he asked.

"Not a problem as such, but I was thinking it would be useful for you to visit Papantla on the way. Vanilla production is well down on last year's output."

Conrad nodded thoughtfully. Although vanilla was a significant income source for the fiefdom, it wasn't important that he personally check on it and he suspected Nezahaul was trying to get him out of the city as soon as possible; perhaps to prevent another confrontation with his daughter.

"If I were to do that I'd need to leave tomorrow to give me enough time to get to the Festival before it started," Conrad said. Nezahaul surveyed him levelly.

Conrad gave a pained sigh. "Very well," he said. "And you'll tell Papanzin?"

"Of course."

"Then if that is all Councilor, if I am to leave tomorrow there is a significant amount of work I still to do."

"Of course Leader," Nezahaul said quickly, placing his mug on the side table as he stood up.

"I will see you on my return."

"If I could ask when that might be?"

Conrad shook his head. He wasn't going to let Nezahaul completely run his life. "I can't say at this stage, it will obviously depend on my father, the World Leader."

"Of course," Nezahaul hurried to agree.

Conrad watched Achicauhtli lead the Nezahaul out, before returning to the report he had been reading. At least that problem seemed to have sorted itself, and with luck, by the time he returned. Papanzin would have got over him.

CHAPTER THREE

Detroit — Mainline
Late August 1979 (95AE)

It was hot and humid as Donald climbed stiffly down onto the platform in Detroit. Outside the protection of the station canopy a thin, drizzling rain added to the humidity, while inside the air was heavy with coal smoke and steam. It had been a long fifteen hours on the train from Charleston and the shirt under his jacket stuck damply to his skin.

Checking the station's departure board he gave a groan. His connection was leaving in less than fifteen minutes, which didn't even leave him time for a coffee. Swinging the heavy duffel bag up over his shoulder he headed across the hall towards passport control.

The main concourse thronged with passengers, its cavernous space lit by sunlight that streamed in through dust shrouded skylights, creating pools of light on the hall's polished marbled floor. Luckily there were no lines in passport control, and with a sigh of relief he dumped the heavy bag on the officer's table and handed over his passport and ticket.

"Donald Clemhorn?" the officer asked, checking the photograph.

Donald nodded.

"Anything to declare, Sir?" the officer asked as he unzipped the top of the duffel bag for a perfunctory look inside.

"Nothing." Donald had often wondered at the bag check, there seemed any number of easier ways of getting banned technology through the portal.

"Thank you Leader" the officer said, and closing the bag up stamped the passport. "Have a good trip."

"Thank you," Donald said, as he swung the bag back over his shoulder.

Pushing through the double doors Donald paused as he caught sight of the massive locomotive in its Clemhorn livery of black and gold waiting impatiently at the end of the platform, steam shrouding its boiler. Almost home — just the portal to go, and he winced at the thought. No matter how safe Kaito assured him they were, he could never shake the thought that one day he'd simply step through a portal and simply disappear. No one ever had, but he'd never pretended the fear was rational.

He was the last to board, and even as he pulled himself up into the first-class compartment's vestibule the steward was already folding up the steps behind him. He'd barely managed to find his seat before there was a jerk as the train eased out of the station. Unfolding his newspaper he immersed himself back into the analysis of the present state of play in the Council of Leaders, which seemed to be becoming increasingly dysfunctional every day. He'd moved onto the crossword when a sudden lurch almost caused him to lose his pencil. Looking up he realized the train was slowing, a change in the tempo of the wheels letting him know they were approaching the portal.

He sighed and folded the newspaper neatly in half, folding it again and placing it on his lap just as the locomotive charged into the portal's flickering vortex. A sparkling maelstrom of light poured down the corridor towards him, consuming reality as it did so. Time hiccupped, and as chaos spat him back out again, he felt the train braking hard as it approached Lincoln Station. Outside the drizzle had disappeared, replaced by a glorious late summer's day. Same place, same date, different timeline. Once history had diverged the weather tended to quickly followed suite. Swallowing unsteadily he picked the newspaper up. Thank the gods he wouldn't have to do that again for another couple of weeks, he thought shakily.

The train had just pulled out of Lincoln, and was powering its way towards Leolie 175 miles away on the southern edge of Lake Erie, when someone slid the door open. Annoyed at the interruption he looked up from the crossword.

"What?" he demanded of the young, female Force Leader in the light blue uniform of a Clemhorn regular who'd opened the door.

"Is this compartment taken?"

"Yes," he started to say, then stopped. "Ivy?"

"Gotcha," his sister said with a broad grin, before a moment later almost suffocating him with a hug.

He returned the embrace before holding her out at arms-length to inspect her. The blond hair under her light blue kepi was shorter, and she'd lost some of the adolescent padding she'd had the last time he'd seen her, but then what could one expect after three years. Fine boned, classical features stared back at him, and she gave him a wink. Despite the lack of height, his little sister had definitely grown up.

"You're looking well," he said. "Europe obviously agreed with you." He tapped the two stars on her shoulder.

"It did," she said with a grin, studying him in return. He looked thinner than she remembered, though that just might be because Conrad, their eldest brother, was so. . . solid. With his roguish, good looks she couldn't imagine anyone who looked less like an academic than Donald. And unlike their older brother, Donald had never taken advantage of either his looks, or his position. He was just someone who. . . cared. Which after the last two years she was now only too aware of how unusual that was. It really was waste he wasn't in the army, she thought. She couldn't understand why he, or anyone else for that matter, would choose any other career. And if they had, why academia? It was just so boring!

"So what are you doing here?" he asked.

"I thought I'd take the train back with my favorite brother. I left the horses in Leolie."

"You want a drink?" he asked as the train suddenly swayed and they both had to grab for something to hold onto.

"If you're buying?"

He rolled his eyes. "And how could I avoid an invitation like that?"

His attention was suddenly caught by the window, as the train passed the sprawling buildings that housed Etu's Treasury and Military Headquarters. Squat and uncompromising, Donald had always thought the limestone buildings with their massive columned facade had resembled the woman who had designed them.

"What?" Ivy asked.

"Sorry, just thinking of Nona."

She nodded, her face clouding. It hadn't been that long ago their grandmother had died.

"Come on, let's grab that drink," Donald said, guiding Ivy out of the compartment. The carriage swayed around them as they made their way down the corridor, forcing them to fight to keep their balance. The lounge car was dim and almost deserted as the two took their seats at the bar.

"What would you like?" Donald asked.

"A whiskey thanks."

"Two whiskies," Donald told the bartender. "So how was Europe? Mama didn't think you'd be back for another couple of months."

"Good. The promotion was a bit of a surprise and Continental Command put me on furlough pending my next posting."

"Congratulations. What was it, three years as Troop Leader?"

"Two," she corrected him with a smile.

"So what, Corps Leader in five years?"

She grinned, refusing to be drawn. "And what about you? How's your PhD going?"

"Finished, I submitted the dissertation last week." He still couldn't believe he'd actually finished it at last, and that after three years an enormous weight had been taken off his shoulders.

"How long before you hear?"

Donald shrugged, taking a swallow of his drink. "A couple of months before I have to mount my defense. I know the Dean likes it though so I'm not too worried."

"And then what? Doctor Donald Richard Clemhorn, Alternate History. Sounds a bit of a mouthful to me."

"I suppose you'd prefer Force Leader."

"Well it does come with a snazzier uniform."

"I'm so glad my sister isn't shallow."

She snorted, the whiskey burning a passage to her lungs. "But seriously," she said when she could talk again. "What happens now?"

"I'm not sure," he admitted. "I really haven't thought beyond my PhD. I've had a couple of offers and the Dean has made encouraging noises about tenure. But for the moment I'm just taking some time off."

She gave him with a dazzling smile. "Clemhorn victorious," she said, holding up her glass.

Donald echoed the toast and both drained their glasses.

"Another one?" Ivy asked.

"Why not. So, how's the rest of the family," Donald asked, signaling the bartender for another round.

"Good. Papa's still at Naisre but he should be flying back tonight. The succession, or rather lack of it, is causing the Council quite a headache."

"It was a pity about Treik," Donald said remembering what he'd just been reading. "And now the First Leader's in hospital again."

She nodded. "I was at a diplomatic function in Europe when Treik's death was announced. It put quite a dampener on the occasion."

"And Mama?"

"Looking well, and happy to have us all home. Conrad's been back for a couple of weeks. Apparently he got himself into some sort of romantic entanglement and decided to leave early."

"Our elder brother certainly leads an interesting life," Donald said affectionately.

"He's going to have to settle down soon. Papa's starting to drop broad hints of marriage."

"Really?"

"Really."

"And Arnold?" Donald asked, referring to their other brother.

"Same old, same old. According to Mama he's started an artist's commune on the Mainline."

"What?"

"You know that's exactly what Conrad said. Nedo's with him."

"And what did Uncle Roland have to say about that?"

Ivy shrugged eloquently. "Probably a lot, but you know what it's like talking to Nedo sometimes."

He nodded. "Are the Perics all here?"

"Except for Nedo, he's coming in with Arnold."

"Oh," Donald said surprised. "This will be what, the first time in five years everyone's been able to make the Festival?"

Ivy nodded. "Probably the last for quite a while as well. It's just getting too difficult to get everyone together."

"That's a pity."

"You can't hold time back forever."

"No, I suppose not. Although I suppose it would be nice if we could."

From there the conversation fell into comfortable reminiscences as they brought each other up to date with what had been happening in their own lives over the past three years.

As they stepped down onto the platform at Leolie three and half hours later Donald had to steady himself on the handrail. Secure on the ground he tried to swing his bag up onto his shoulder and would have fallen if Ivy hadn't put out a hand to help him.

"I can take that," she said.

Donald drew himself up. "I have had three whiskies," he pronounced carefully. "I am not drunk."

"I didn't say you were," she said.

"You, on the other hand, have had four," he said, unwilling to ignore the obvious slur on his ability to hold his liquor. "However, I am exhausted, so of course you can carry it." He passed the bag across to her, and watched her stagger under its weight with amused tolerance.

"My god, what have you got in it?" she demanded.

"Books, and papers for marking."

She pulled a face.

Outside the station Donald paused and took a deep breath of the pine scented air. "You've got no idea how much I've missed that," he said.

"The horses are in here," she said, leading the way down the road and into the cool, shaded opening of the public stables. The stink of manure caused Donald to wince.

"I don't think I've missed this aroma though," he said, trying to breathe through his mouth.

The horses were quickly saddled, and they were soon on their way. Leolie's main street was well shaded by elms just starting to come into their full growth, and provided some relief from the heat. Donald quickly found himself relaxing into the gentle pace Ivy set for them.

As the buildings made way for the low, rolling hills that surrounded Leolie, glistening yellow with the stubble of harvested wheat, the old canal appeared beside them, cutting its way through the fields towards Lake Erie a short distance away. A bargeman waved lazily as they trotted past, while behind them a trail of moving smoke marked the departing train.

Despite Ivy keeping the pace down to an easy canter, by the time they rode down the dappled, oak-lined avenue to the house, and past the small waterfall cascading down the side of the hill and into a pool at its base, Donald's thighs were aching.

Ivy grinned, when she noticed him trying to adjust his position. "You're getting soft bro."

"And you're getting hard-hearted in your old age."

"Hey. I've only just turned twenty-two."

Donald snorted as they emerged from the avenue onto the gravel-lined terrace in front of the residence, blinking as he was almost blinded by sunlight reflecting off the windows of the three-story sandstone house nestling comfortably into the side of the small hill behind it. Nona had designed the house, which had been home to the Clemhorn family for over forty years, based on the Georgian mansions she'd seen during a visit to the Mainline. Its twin matching wings, that pushed forward to enclose the portico with its tall columns and deep balconies, gave it a certain harmony of appearance that to Donald would always mean home.

"I need a bath," Ivy announced as she dismounted.

"I wasn't going to say anything," Donald said, as he unbuckled his bag and handed the reins over to a waiting groom.

"Ever the gentleman."

"I try," Donald said with a grin as he followed her up the steps, one of the family's retainers holding the door open for them as they passed. He barely had time to register the familiar smell of lemon-wax from the freshly polished parquet floor before he was engulfed in a swirling mass of dog flesh, eager to welcome them home. For a moment it was utter chaos as Donald struggled to keep his feet.

"Down!" Ivy commanded loudly.

The three otterhounds immediately dropped to the ground, tongues lolling, eyes plaintively complaining their fun had been taken away from them.

"Thanks," Donald said dryly. One otterhound was large enough, but three. . . Then Conrad arrived, and Donald wondered why they'd ever seemed large.

"Donald," his brother said pulling him into a hug.

Donald returned the hug, and once released looked him up and down. The crew-cut was new, but Conrad was as large, and as overpowering as ever. One of Donald's friends had once described Conrad as 'built like a brick shithouse', and Donald hadn't seen fit to argue the description.

"It's good to back. And congratulations, I hear you might be getting married." He gave a sly grin.

"Now who told you that I wonder?" Conrad said, looking at Ivy. "I don't know what the rush is, I'm only thirty-two."

"Thirty-two!" Ivy rolled her eyes. "Listen to the boy."

"I know, I'm ancient," Conrad said gloomily. "Come on Mama is in the conservatory with Aunt Isobel. She said I was to take Donald out to her as soon as you arrived."

"I'll see you boys later then," Ivy said starting up the staircase towards the bedrooms on the third floor.

Donald barely noticed her departure, his eye caught by the massive mural on the far wall. "Papa's had the map updated?"

Conrad nodded. "Mama's been nagging him to have it done for a while."

Donald's eye worked its way up the Andes, measuring the progress of their control over the line by the slightly pinker hue to the painting. Here and there a gold star marked a major city or port. Clemhorn control now extended to most of South America, almost all of Central America, and the entire North American continent. Across the Atlantic the tide of pink now lapped against the foot of the Alps.

"It looks impressive," Donald said, moving towards it for a closer look.

The dogs whimpered. "Stay," Conrad ordered, as he followed Donald across to the map, his own eyes possessively surveying the area around Cempoala, Mexico's coastal capital.

"How are you finding South America?" Donald asked, catching his glance.

"Good. Ten percent annual growth, and once we get the railway through to Tumbez there'll be no stopping us."

"Sounds like you're enjoying yourself."

"I am. It's turning out to be a real buzz, building something that's going to outlast me. And," he paused for emphasis. "We're finally making some proper beer. I've brought a crate with me so you can try it."

Donald had never understood Conrad's fascination with beer, his own preference, as Ivy's did, tended to whiskey, but Conrad certainly knew his ales.

"Come on," Conrad said. "I don't want to keep Mama waiting."

The conservatory was built onto the north side of the house to take advantage of the winter sun. When the four of them had been younger it had served as their playroom, but now orchids and bougainvillea filled every space. Mama put down the pot she was holding as they arrived, pulling off her gloves to greet them. A small, dainty woman, her face showed the faint signs of sunburn.

"I'm glad you could make it Donald," she said, reaching up to kiss him on the cheek, before looking him up and down. Donald took the inspection uneasily. "You've lost weight."

"Leave him alone Elam," Aunt Isobel said, rising from her seat. "The boy's looking well."

"Thank you Aunt," Donald said gratefully.

His aunt held her cheek up to be kissed. As usual her makeup was immaculate, her hair a faultless mass of black curls. Donald kissed her cheek, trying not to smudge anything.

"Tea will be ready in an hour in the main dining room," his mother said. "I'd suggest a bath first though," she said, wrinkling her nose.

"Of course," Donald said, accepting the dismissal gratefully. Outside in the passage he couldn't help a sigh of relief.

Conrad grinned at him. "It is a little like that, isn't it?"

"You've got no idea."

"You forget I just got back from Mexico. I know exactly how it is."

Donald took his time in the bath, trying to soak away some of the aches, and by the time he was dressed for dinner the bell had just sounded. As he made his way down to the dining room the sound of an autogiro landing on the front terrace took him to the window. As he watched, the pilot climb tiredly out of the aircraft removing his helmet to reveal his long, gray-flecked hair. With a shock Donald recognized Papa - when had he got so old? His father paused, looking up at the window where Donald was watching, and waved.

As Donald returned the wave there was a burst of laughter from downstairs and turning away from the window he continued down the stairs to where the others were already gathered.

"Donald," Margaret said happily as he entered the dining room. "We were just about to send a search party out for you. Come and sit down." His cousin patted the seat next to her.

He blinked his eyes, surprised. "Your hair's red."

"I was tired of the black. Do you like it?"

Donald considered the question for a moment. "I'm not sure," he admitted finally. "It is different." With her long hair, distinctive green eyes, and statuesque build Margaret tended to turn heads when she entered a room. It had always surprised Donald how oblivious she was to the effect she had on any male over the age of fifteen. Donald wasn't sure if the red hair was an improvement though.

Donald nodded to his uncle and aunt as he took his seat next to his cousin. The table, a single, massive piece of redwood, ran the entire length of the room and was large enough to comfortably seat fifty. With just the two families, however, only the end closest to the door was occupied. A matching redwood sideboard ran along the long wall next to it, while the facing wall was covered by a huge tapestry. At the far end of the room French windows opened out onto the balcony overlooking the front terrace.

"Rajko," Donald said, nodding to his cousin sitting on the opposite side of the table. "Like the moustache." Rajko was sporting a new pencil-thin moustache.

"Donald, nice to see you again" Rajko half-rose to offer him his hand.

On the other side of Margaret, her two younger sisters now, what. . . nineteen and thirteen, were giggling at something and barely acknowledged his arrival. Conrad and Ivy were sitting on either side of Rajko, with his uncle and aunt further along the table. Only his parents were still missing.

"How was the trip?" Donald asked Margaret.

"Rushed. Rajko was late getting back from the World Leader's Court so we almost didn't make it."

"Talking about not making it, was that Nedo I heard landing?" Rajko asked.

"No, Papa. You don't need worry about Nedo and Arnold though. I've never known Arnold fail to achieve something he said he was going to, as Conrad learned to his cost." He grinned at his brother.

Rajko look puzzled.

"You know how Arnold can never resist a dare," Donald explained. "There was one time he'd just won a swimming marathon and Conrad got tired of his boasting, so he bet him he couldn't swim across Lake Erie, solo. Papa was furious with him."

"I remember that," Margaret said.

"Cost me a ten pounds," Conrad said with a grin. "And Papa made me man the support boat for the entire swim."

"Serves you right," Ivy told him.

Conrad shrugged, unwilling to argue the point.

Donald felt a hand on his shoulder and looked up to see his father.

"Good to see you again Donald."

"Papa," he said, half rising from his seat.

"How's your dissertation going?" his father asked, waving him back down as he held the seat out for his wife.

"Finished it last week," Donald said happily, as the servants appeared with the first course.

"So what did you end up doing it on?" his uncle asked, leaning across the table.

"My initial hypotheses was that the Empire was experiencing a period of scientific stagnation. What I found was that our technology had actually regressed over the last seventy years."

"Hardly surprising," his father said, "when you consider we lost seventy-five percent of our population in the Decimation. And then, when the new lines opened all our resources went into exploiting them."

Donald nodded, his eyes automatically drawn to the tapestry hanging along the long wall. The tapestry, modelled on the Mainline's Bayeux Tapestry, showed the battle for Leolie and the surrender of the Northern Lakes League in 48 AE, the final panel showing the effects of the Decimation on the native population. Donald had never worked out why Nona had hung it in the dining room, it was hardly the subject to improve anyone's appetite. The mass graves, funeral pyres, and the endless, circling flocks of crows had given him nightmares when he had been younger. Which might have been the reason — his grandmother had had a macabre sense of humor.

"The Edict hasn't helped," Donald said.

"No," his father agreed.

"What's wrong with the Edict?" Rajko demanded.

"It's the way it prevents any contact with a line with advanced technology. I can understand some restriction, but a complete ban? If we can't bootstrap ourselves we should at least be learning from others."

"Hmm," Rajko didn't look convinced. "It sounds risky to me."

"No more risky than the present situation if we don't do something about it. You've just got to look at the famines in Russia last year. If we knew how to tackle potato blight we could probably have prevented it."

Margaret, with her passion for farming, nodded her agreement to that statement.

"Well, if you're right, the situation may just get worse," Donald's father said. "That's why I was on the Mainline. Your Grandfather wanted to talk to me about a Bill Miro has before the Council to ban contact with any new lines, regardless of their ranking on the Hallow Scale."

Miro, head of the Conservative faction, was the Peric's World Leader so Donald wasn't surprised by the sudden look of interest on his uncle's face.

"What does Grandfather think?" Donald asked. The World Leader of Notway was the head of the Council's Progressive faction.

"He's opposed to the Bill."

"And who's got the numbers in the Council?" Donald's uncle asked.

"I don't know," his brother-in-law admitted. "The two factions are pretty evenly balanced at the moment. A lot of it depends on the First Leader, and that's a problem in itself. He still hasn't named a successor. I know he's afraid of causing a split in the Council, but this uncertainty . . . ."

"I heard he was in hospital again. Is it serious?" Donald's aunt asked.

"I don't know," the World Leader said, but his face showed his concern.

Donald retired early, tired from the trip, but was woken around one by the sound of an autogiro landing on the terrace. He lay there, half dozing, wondering who it was, until he heard Arnold's voice raised in argument with his brother, and rolling over went back to sleep.

CHAPTER FOUR

Leolie - Etu Line
August 1979 (95AE)

Ivy woke the next morning to banging on the door.

"Go away," she muttered.

"It's time to get up," Margaret called from the hallway.

For a moment Ivy simply considered burrowing under the pillow and going back to sleep, but the sound of others from the landing convinced her she wouldn't be allowed to.

"All right, I'm getting up" she called to avert another assault on her door.

She stretched luxuriously, enjoying the feel of her own bed, as Elizabeth, Emelia, and Eve watched her solemnly from the top of the wardrobe, as only toy-bears could.

It didn't take long to slip on the fringed, doeskin dress and bead choker she'd bought especially for the Festival, and applying her makeup was only a matter of minutes. By the time she'd finished, however, the landing had gone quiet.

"Boys - eat your heart out," she said and winked at herself in the mirror. Then, ignoring a disapproving glare from the three bears, headed downstairs.

Arnold and Nedo were talking at the foot of the stairs and looked up as she came down.

"Good morning Force Leader," Nedo said with a grin.

"And who have you been talking to?" she said with a smile, offering her cheek for a kiss.

"Donald," Arnold said. Her brother was wearing a caftan, his hair slicked back to his shoulders. He looked better than she remembered him, happier, but why the caftan? Sometimes Arnold simply didn't know when to stop.

"I hope we didn't wake you up last night," Nedo said. "Arnold was flying on instruments, and we couldn't see the house."

"I'm pretty sure you woke everyone," Donald told him good naturedly, appearing around the corner.

Nedo looked worried but Arnold simply shrugged.

"How's the commune?" Ivy asked.

"Coming along," Arnold said. "Show her your belt Nedo."

Nedo undid his belt and handed it to Ivy. A frieze of seagulls in flight twined themselves along its length. Somehow the artist had managed to combine five different blues into the leather so the white gulls glistened among an iridescent haze of blue.

"It's beautiful," Ivy said sincerely, passing it to Donald to have a look.

"Keep it," Arnold said.

Ivy looked uncertainly at Nedo.

"Oh do," Nedo said. "We've got about fifteen of them. Arnold thought it would be a good idea to bring some as gifts."

"Thank you."

"Good morning everyone," Conrad said coming through the door. "Nice caftan Arnold."

Ivy felt Arnold tense at Conrad's words, and wondered if he was really that sensitive to criticism, or whether it was simply because it was coming from Conrad.

"Have you had breakfast yet?" Conrad asked Ivy.

She shook her head.

"Well get a move on. Our cousins want to leave."

"Why don't you take them in now and I'll catch up?"

Conrad looked at Donald who shrugged. "Sounds good to me."

By the time she'd finished breakfast, however, her mother, father, uncle and aunt were all down and somehow she found herself agreeing to go in with them and by the time they finally ready it was already mid-morning.

"So what do you want to see first, Ivy?" her mother asked as they disembarked from the carriage. Around them the crowd spilled out of Leolie's narrow, twisting streets and alleys to the commons beyond the city's gates, where tents had been set up to handle the overflow.

Ivy tore her gaze from the row of flags on the far side of the field that marked where the drinking stalls had been set up.

"Oh leave her alone woman," her father said. "It's obvious she doesn't want us cramping her style."

"We haven't seen her for two and a half years Brian. I just thought it would be nice to spend some time with her."

"You'll have plenty of time before she goes back."

"Just so long as there is." The threat was bestowed equally on both husband and daughter.

"I'll catch up with you at the amphitheater for the ceremony," Ivy promised.

"Good. Just make sure you do."

"Come on Elam," her father said. "I want to have a look at the merinos. See how that new strain has bred up." As he led her mother away Ivy could still hear her complaining.

The crowd closed in around Ivy in a smorgasbord of color, with here and there the light blue of a Clemhorn uniform, and the occasional the darker tint of one of the specialist corps to leaven the dough. Most of the soldiers were from the barracks just outside of town, but from the Battlegroup tabs on some of their collars many had come from much further away.

The scent of roasted mash from the food stalls in the area made her mouth water. If she was going to do any serious drinking she needed to get some food into herself first. Most of the stalls seemed to be serving corn pasties; a mixture of corn and vegetables sealed into a thin corn bread envelope, although some were serving more exotic foods. The nearest stall, for example, was selling potatoes cooked in their jackets served with a thick dollop of cream, a combination of Peruvian and Mainline tastes.

She had just finished her pasty, and was licking the sauce off her finger when she spotted Donald being dragged through the crowd by Margaret. Before she could call out to attract their attention they had disappeared again, heading north towards the agricultural displays. Margaret was a fanatical amateur farmer and was obviously in her element, but she wondered how Donald was enjoying it.

Locating a tent selling home brewed whiskey Ivy headed in for something to fortify herself against the crowd, which seemed to be getting thicker. It was still too early for the serious drinkers and the tent was only half-filled. As she took a moment to let her eyes acclimatize someone walked past, and her eyes automatically focused on the muscles under his tight doeskin trousers. Nice butt!

The owner of the trousers reached the bar and looked round. Seeing her watching, he gave her a wide grin. Nice smile too, she thought, before realizing he looked vaguely familiar.

He mimed raising a glass to his lips. She nodded and looked round to claim a table for the two of them.

"It's Troop Leader Clemhorn, isn't it?" he said, as he placed two glasses and a half-pint bottle of pink whiskey on the table in front of her. He had dazzling white teeth, and a smile that seemed to light up his entire face. A large eagle's feather was stuck jauntily in his bonnet.

"Force Leader now, and call me Ivy," she said, trying to remember where she had met him before. She seemed to remember he'd been in uniform at the time.

"Force Leader Raincloud. Jon to my friends. We met in Europe."

"That's right, your Battlegroup was stationed next to ours. What are doing here?"

"I transferred to the Rangers a year ago. And you?"

"Between postings. I just made Force Leader a month ago."

"Congratulations." He poured a shot into her glass.

"Thanks." She rewarded him with a smile then took a swallow. The whiskey had a strange, rather fruity flavor. "Unusual taste," she said diplomatically.

"It's the cranberries. You won't notice it after your second glass."

"You sound an expert."

"My tribe distills it. Truth is they're probably the only ones prepared to drink it."

She took another sip. "It's not that bad."

"Thank you." He raised his glass in salute.

She studied the beaver motif that embellished his beaded jacket. "Oneida?" The tribe had been one of the six founding nations of the Iroquois Confederacy on Etu.

He gave a pleased smile. "I'm surprised you recognized it. There's not that many of us left. The Decimation almost wiped us out."

She shrugged, not bothering to explain that Nona had been a strong believer in them knowing the history of the civilization they had supplanted. "So where are you based?" she asked.

"Fort Lanegan."

She nodded, recognizing the name. Fort Lanegan was about a hundred and fifty miles west of Leolie. "Are you just here for the Festival?"

He shook his head. "My unit's going to be involved in the annual maneuvers. I thought I'd get here early."

"Really, I've been asked to help umpire. You know my brother is going to be commanding the Territorials? Any chance you'll be able to blood his nose?"

"We'll certainly try," Jon said uncertainly.

"Good, he can be an insufferable prig sometimes. I think that deserves a drink though," she said, pouring them each another shot.

Ivy emerged from the tent with Jon a couple of hours later, blinking warily as they emerged into the light of day. She was just turning to ask Jon if he wanted to join her at the ceremony when she heard her name called and turned to see Conrad and Rajko hurrying through the thinning crowd towards them.

"Conrad said you'd probably be here," Rajko said, slightly out of breath. "We've been looking for you for about half an hour."

"Sorry we lost track of time," Ivy apologized.

"Obviously," Conrad said. He stuck out his hand. "You'll excuse my sister's manners not introducing us won't you? I'm Conrad, and this is Rajko."

Jon took Conrad's proffered hand with only a slight hesitation. "Force Leader Raincloud."

"Jon's with the Rangers," Ivy explained. "His unit's involved in the maneuvers."

"The opposition," Conrad said with a smile. "And speaking of which Ivy, I don't suppose you could help out a bit do you? My Battlegroup seems a bit short of leaders with recent combat experience this year."

"Afraid not, I'm an umpire."

"Turncoat."

Ivy shrugged unapologetically.

"Can we discuss this on the way," Rajko indicated the crowd. "If we don't get a move on they won't be able to keep our seats for us."

"Have you seen Donald and Margaret?" Ivy asked as they joined the drift of the last of the crowd towards the amphitheater. "I saw them heading off to the agricultural display just after I arrived."

"They're already there," Conrad said.

The amphitheater overlooked the lake and was filling rapidly as they arrived, and the group paused uncertainly at the top of the steps.

"There they are." Ivy pointed at Margaret waving excitedly at them from down near the front. "Come on." She grabbed Jon's hand.

The rest of the family were already seated there.

"Everyone, this is Force Leader Raincloud," Ivy said. "Jon, my mother and father."

Her father studied him for a moment. "Second Rangers?" he said.

"That's right World Leader."

"Take a seat," the World Leader said, smiling at him.

Jon almost collapsed onto the stone as everyone squashed up to make room for him.

"I'll introduce you to everyone else afterwards," Ivy said, sitting down demurely next to him.

Jon nodded dumbly.

Conrad leaned forward so he could see Donald. "Donald do you still retain rank in the Territorials?"

"Infantry Troop Leader. My commission's still active, but only just. I haven't had the time to get the necessary training points together."

"The annual maneuvers are coming up in a couple of weeks, and I'm a bit short of officers. Any chance you can help? You'd be acting Force Leader for the exercise if you do."

"Sure, why not. Who's involved?"

The crowd had fallen silent, and Ivy looked up to see that while they'd been talking the competitors had filed into the arena. Both males and females wore only a brief loincloth, and carried a small brightly dyed ring of wicker, about three inches in diameter. There were twenty of them and they formed two lines, facing the entrance.

"Just the Third Clemhorn Territorials, and a couple of Group Units from the Rangers." Conrad lowered his voice to a whisper. "Our beloved sister is going to be an umpire."

Ivy gave Donald a broad wink.

"Just make sure I'm at the portal in time to get back to the university for the start of term," Donald told him, breaking off as the priestess followed by her two acolytes entered the arena.

The priest wore a long red robe, and a large, circular golden mask that covered her face and head. As she held up her hands in greeting the soft hum from the crowd died away to complete silence.

"We are gathered to give thanks for the harvest," she said in a voice that carried easily to the top row. "For the spirits of the field and the crop, and for the god of the sun."

An acolyte handed her a dish on which were twenty seeds of corn. "Here is the seed of life," she said, showing it to the crowd, before handing it back.

She accepted a silver goblet from the other acolyte, holding it aloft. "Here is the water of life."

"To our spirits, and to our god we give thanks. For what has been given us, and for what we have achieved we give thanks. For what we will receive we now pray, and offer our bodies as a sacrifice and as a symbol of our faith."

She lowered her head for a moment in silent prayer, then nodded at the first of those facing her to come forward. Placing a single corn seed on the applicant's tongue, she tipped the goblet foreword so that the applicant could take a sip of water.

The priest passed slowly down the two lines of applicants, giving each a single corn seed, and a sip of water. When she had finished she left the arena and the gate closed solidly behind her. The applicants reformed into a single line facing the gate, then, as a group, kneeled and touched their foreheads to the ground.

"What are they doing?" Louise, Ivy's youngest cousin, asked.

It seemed obvious to Ivy that Louise had never taken notice of the ceremony before. "They're supposed to be dedicating themselves to the spirits," she explained. "But a lot of them will simply be praying for success, there's a lot of prestige attached to ringing the bull, assuming they survive."

"Quite," Jon said dryly.

Something in his tone made Ivy look at him. "You've been out there?"

He shook his head. "My brother was, last year."

She winced, remembering reading accounts of what happened. "How was he?"

"Two broken ribs and concussion, five days in hospital. He was luckier than the two that died though."

Most of those in the arena had stood up now, and as the last one finished his prayer the gates were opened and the first of three bison trotted into view. It stood blinking uncertainly, bemused by the sound from the crowd. A moment later the other two followed it out. Their red coats gleamed in the sun, as different from the Northern Lakes' domesticated version as a tiger is from the house cat. As the gates closed behind them the first of the bison, seeing the thin line of his tormentors spread out before him, pawed the ground and charged.

The line broke as the bull went through it in a sort of loose skipping dance. As he did one of the contestants darted in and tried to put her ring over his horn; but the bull, sensing the movement out of the corner of his eye, turned and caught her on the tip of his horn, flipping her into the air. Ivy gasped with the crowd as she landed heavily on the ground. Two of the others immediately turned to help her; one to distract the bull while the other pulled her to the edge of the arena where helping hands reached down to lift her over the fence.

Ivy hoped she was all right, but already her attention had returned to the center of the arena where the second bull had entered the fray, charging at the fleeing figures in front of him. The third still stood there, uncertainly eying the chaos around him.

The crowd had quietened again but as another contestant escaped goring by the merest of slips they roared their support, stamping their feet, the sound reverberating around the bowl.

Two of the contestants cautiously approached the third bull, still paused uncertainly by the gate. The impudence of these two seemed to affect the bull, which pawed the ground and backed slowly away so as to keep an eye on them. Three of the other contestants now became aware of what was happening and arranged themselves behind the bull. Aware that he was boxed in the bull charged. The person charged hesitated for a moment, then throwing himself forward towards the horns, grabbed hold and somersaulted up over the bison's head, twisting at the same time to deposit the ring he was carrying on the bull's left horn. Yes! Ivy jumped to her feet as the crowd erupted around her.

As though slipping the first ring on the bull had been a signal the other two were quickly crowned and the contest was over. As the bulls were attracted out of the arena the three who had ringed them were carried shoulder high around the arena to the applause of the crowd. Jon was stamping his feet on the ground and Ivy grinned at his enthusiasm.

"Friends of yours?" she asked under her breath.

"Mother's sister's son," he said, unable to stop grinning, as the three clans represented by the winners started a spontaneous celebration on the bleachers.

"What now?" Ivy's uncle asked. "Are we heading back?"

"I am," her father said. "What about you lot?" He looked at his children.

"I think I'll grab something to eat and try the taverns for a while," Conrad said.

"Count me in," Ivy said. "Jon?"

Jon shrugged. "I haven't anything better to do."

"Rajko, how about you?" Conrad asked.

Rajko grimaced. "I'll pass. Last time I joined you on a pub crawl I ended up losing five hours of my life, and the gods know how many brain cells."

"Margaret?"

"I'm heading home. I think I prefer a more sedate evening than the one you're planning."

"I'll stay," Louise, her youngest sister, offered.

"No you won't young lady," her mother told her. Louise started to complain, but catching sight of her father's face subsided.

"Donald?"

"I'm in."

"Well don't drink too much," their father told them before turning his attention to Jon. "And Force Leader, I trust you to keep them out of trouble."

Jon gulped, and blanched. "Yes sir."

With a pleasant nod at the group their father led the others away, Louise casting a wistful look back over her shoulders as he did so.

CHAPTER FIVE

Leolie — Etu Line
August 1979 (95AE)

Donald woke with a pounding head. His mouth felt as though it was full of old socks and his feet were freezing. He was fully dressed apart from his shoes, and carefully he cracked his eyes open a fraction. He was lying on a bed, someone was next to him and cautiously lifting his head he recognized Ivy. Still asleep, Ivy seemed very young. Beyond her Jon was lying stretched out fast asleep.

Warily Donald swung his feet over the edge of the bed, trying not to move his head more than he needed to. As he did so Ivy stirred uneasily. Given Jon's presence that probably meant they were at his rooms; but he wished he could remember how they had got there. Most of last night was a blur, and after the second bar they'd visited a complete blank.

As he stood up, Jon opened his eyes.

"Bathroom?" Donald asked.

"Door on the left." Jon waved vaguely in the direction of the door.

When Donald returned he found Jon in the kitchen, lighting the gas for the kettle.

The table was covered with empty bottles, streamers, and a street sign, presumably souvenirs from last night. Jon had opened the curtains, and Donald winced at the light. It looked like it was going to be a beautiful day, which somehow just made his headache worse.

"Hangover?" Jon asked.

"Yeh."

Jon rummaged in the overhead cabinet and produced a small bottle of aspirin.

"What's the time?" Donald asked, as Jon filled a glass of water for him.

"About ten. I've got to get some milk, I'll be back in a couple of minutes."

The front door closing behind Jon must have disturbed Ivy because Donald could hear her stirring in the next room.

"How do you feel?" he asked, going in to check.

"I'm alive," she said carefully. "But couldn't you at least have made sure I took my boots off before I went to sleep." She raised her head and peered around uncertainly. "Where are we, anyway?"

"Jon's."

"Jon?"

"Jon Raincloud."

"Oh gods. At least I had a chaperon."

"Not much of one. I was so out of things I wouldn't have noticed anything happening if it had."

"Me too; I'll suppose I'll have to ask him."

"Ivy!" Donald shouted, shocked.

"Joking!" she said with a smile, as she disappeared into the bathroom. By the time she came out again Jon had returned.

"Does anyone know what happened to my choker?" she asked, gratefully accepting the mug Jon gave her.

Jon grinned. "You left it on top of a pole in exchange for the street sign."

"Couldn't you have stopped me? That thing cost me over a fifty pounds."

"I tried," Jon said. "But you were most emphatic on leaving it. You kept saying a swap wasn't stealing."

"God, I do the weirdest things sometimes."

"So I noticed," Jon said.

Ivy looked at him.

"In the nicest possible way I mean."

"Does anyone know where Conrad got to?" Donald asked.

"He headed off with Force Leader Lola sometime after midnight," Jon said. "She's with the Second Rangers," he said, in the face of their puzzled expressions.

Donald surveyed the bottom of his mug. His stomach felt distinctly queasy. "I think I'd better lie down again."

"Do you need a bucket?" Jon asked.

"Not yet."

"Well call if you do," Jon said, but Donald was already out of the room.

He relaxed gratefully back into the bed, closing his eyes as he did so. When Jon looked in on him a couple of minutes later Donald simply raised a hand to acknowledge his presence. He could hear Jon and Ivy talking in the other room, but their voices were little more than a gentle murmur. When eventually he felt well enough to get up again, and checked his watch, he found he'd been lying there for three hours.

Entering the other room he found Ivy stretched out on the settee, Jon curled up on the carpet at her feet.

"We better make a start," he told Ivy. "If we don't get home soon people will start worrying."

"I suppose so," Ivy said regretfully. "Eight o'clock tomorrow?" she asked Jon.

"I'll be there."

"What was that about?" Donald asked as they walked slowly down the apartment's steps.

"We're going riding. So what do you think?" she asked.

"About what?" Donald asked, purposely dense.

"About Jon."

"He's OK. I wouldn't be too obvious though, especially when Papa's around."

"What do you mean; obvious?"

He mimed a wistful look at the sky, and then had to dodge her swipe. He winced. "Careful, I'm still delicate."

The house was a subdued one that evening and Donald headed off to bed straight after tea. He awoke before dawn, however, and was out running before anyone else was up. He ran five miles without feeling any stiffness, and left it at that with the intention of building it up to ten miles over the fortnight. When he got back to college he promised himself he'd try and keep his standard up.

The next eight days were spent marking papers and generally spending time with his cousins. Finally, however, it was time for the Perics to leave, and as they piled into their coach Donald found himself promising Margaret to visit them on Dontfrey during his next semester break.

With the maneuvers now starting in less than two days, Donald wondered how he'd be ready in time. His uniform still hadn't arrived, and even worse he hadn't finished his marking. Somehow, however, everything came together and with his bag packed off to await him at the portal he rode out with Conrad on an overcast Sunday morning. Because of the weather both wore cloaks over their uniforms. Gas masks were attached to their belts, and their .303 Self Loading Rifles holstered in sheaths behind their saddles.

"Relax," Conrad said, sensing Donald's tenseness.

"That's all very well for you to say. This is the first time I've actually commanded Clemhorn troops and I'm doing it in a brand-new uniform. You've had ten years' military experience on the Mainline, plus all that staff training you had at the Academy. I've only had my two years compulsory service, plus what I've managed to pick up with my university regiment."

Conrad raised an eyebrow. "That just makes it worse. I'm actually expected to know what I'm doing. Just think what I'm supposed to be commanding. The Battlegroup hasn't trained together for at least three years. Sure everyone trains regularly, but it's all small-scale stuff. Put them into something as large as a Battlegroup and it's going to be an absolute disaster. There'll be people going everywhere. I'll be lucky if I don't lose an entire Troop. Plus I've got a real shortage of officers, most of those going 'career' end up retiring in Europe because of the land grants, which means the Territorial units have to make do with whatever is left."

Donald conceded the point with a stiff shrug.

"Just relax. You'll be fine."

The rest of the ride was taken in companionable silence and, as they rode into the organized chaos that filled the field that, until a week ago, had been used by the Festival, Donald looked around with interest. "I'm impressed."

Every Troop had its own assembly area marked out on the grass, and while there was a certain amount of confusion, hardly avoidable with six hundred troops and their mounts, the process seemed to be working well.

"That's because we've spent the entire week planning," Conrad said with a smile. "Unfortunately pre-planning isn't going to help once we're actually out in the field. And this is only two of the Battlegroup's three Groups; the other one is setting up camp on the other side of the lake. Come on," he said, dismounting outside the large marquee in the center of the field. "I better introduce you to your fellow officers."

At one o'clock the marquee was struck, and the two Groups moved down to the port to be ferried across to the other side of the lake. The three ferries provided were coal powered stern-wheelers, smaller versions of those the Clemhorns used on the Atlantic, and were limited to about sixty men and their mounts each. That meant four trips for each ferry, and it was nightfall before the last Troop had crossed. Camp was made that night about five miles north of the lake. The Battlegroup's third Group, whose members lived on the north side of the Lake, were waiting for them and had already put the tents up, so there was little to be done.

***

The initial briefing for the Battlegroup had been set for dawn, and as Donald and his three Troop Leaders made their way down the hill towards the main tent on the first day of the exercise the sun had just started to penetrated the pine forest's dense canopy. As the pine needles crunched underfoot their scent filled the air. It was a glorious day and Donald took a deep breath, releasing it slowly.

"It should be a good exercise," Troop Leader Bearclaw remarked. At thirty she was the eldest of Donald's three leaders and like most of the Battlegroup's officers a native Leaguer.

"I was just thinking that, although to tell the truth anything would be better than my last one," Donald said. "We were dropped into the Arabian peninsula to guard the oil wells. What with the sand, the flies, and the heat; it was the most uncomfortable three weeks I've ever spent."

"On the Mainline?" Bearclaw asked.

"Yes."

Troop Leader Wentworth, the youngest of the three at twenty looked at him with obvious awe. Wentworth was one of the few Anglos in the Battlegroup, a descendent of the Hraffor who had settled here after the inclusion of Etu in the Empire.

"You ever been off-line?" Donald asked the young Troop Leader.

"Wentworth's never even been overseas," Hanow, his third Troop Leader told him with a laugh.

"My parents died just after my term started and I had to leave to look after the kids," Wentworth explained regretfully.

"How many?" Donald asked.

"Four; two brothers, two sisters, all younger than me."

Donald nodded sympathetically. "Well Leaders, looks like

we're here," he said as they reached the marquee.

Inside most of the seats were already taken, and it didn't take long for the rest of the tent to fill up. On Conrad's appearance all those present came to attention.

"At ease," he said.

There was a soft rustle as those present resumed their seats.

"Leaders," Conrad began. "As you are aware, for the exercise, guerrillas have been raiding south into the farmlands from their base somewhere in the hills north of here. Our mission is to locate their base and to destroy it. So we can exercise as many tasks as possible, troops who have been declared dead by the umpires," he indicated two regular officers with white armbands standing at the back of the tent, "will be resurrected after twelve hours. Just try not to make it a habit."

There was a ripple of laughter around the tent.

"The enemy are being played by two Force Groups from the Rangers, and I have been told by the umpires we can expect attempts at infiltration to start immediately. I want everyone warned, and every Troop responsible for the security of their own area. Anyone wandering into an area that they shouldn't be in is to be stopped, and held for questioning. Group Leader Longman, I'll get you to send scouts out to try and locate the guerrillas' base."

Longman commanded the Group made up of reservists from the north side of the lake and, to Donald, their knowledge of the local terrain made them the obvious choice.

"You'll need to liaise with Captain D'Avril who commands the autogiros," Conrad continued, with a nod towards the Captain in the deep blue of an aviators' uniform standing by the entrance. "I want the scouts out straightaway. The rest of us will spend today fortifying the camp and laying out the airstrip. Tomorrow we begin refresher training for Troop formation, the day after that we move up Force level, and the day after that with the full Groups. By then we should have something back from the scouts and be able to move off. Any questions so far?"

There weren't and the briefing continued.

***

Now Donald couldn't help wishing he was still back at the briefing, because as he looked at the map he had the sinking feeling that they were well and truly lost. Conrad's prophesy about loosing a Troop seemed to coming true with a vengeance, except Donald seemed to have managed to lose three of them, all at once.

"Leader."

Donald looked up at his signaler. "Yes."

"From Headquarters. The Rangers managed to infiltrate the base and destroy all three autogiros. The Group Leader needs our present position."

Donald cursed softly. "Tell him to wait out."

He looked at the map again. All three Groups were still at least half a day's march from where the scouts had put the enemy's main camp and without airborne surveillance he doubted they'd be able to implement the pincer movement his brother had planned. Especially as it now looked like his own Force might have opened up a sizable gap in the line.

The umpire that had been traveling with them pulled his horse in next to him. "Problem?" he asked.

Donald shook his head. His finger traced the route he thought they'd been following which should have bought them out onto the upper bank of the Lovett River over two hours ago. He looked around hopefully, but nothing had changed. There was still no sign of water, and the thick stands of white cedar that surrounded them made the identification of any sort of landmark almost impossible.

"Troop Leader," he called to Bearclaw.

As the Troop Leader rode up the column to see what he wanted Donald kneed his horse away from the umpire. This was going to be embarrassing enough without witnesses.

"Yes?" Bearclaw asked.

"Any idea where we are?" Donald asked quietly, handing her the map.

Bearclaw looked up quickly to see if he was joking.

"I know where we should be," Donald said, indicating the point on the map. "Unfortunately we're not there."

Bearclaw studied the map for a moment, then looked around. "I'd say we're probably a bit south of there. We probably got turned round when we crossed the Strand."

"So what do you think, we're about here?" Donald indicated a point about ten miles south of where they were supposed to be. She nodded.

"Damn." That meant they'd somehow moved across in front of Force Leader Tumeric's division, opening up a gap of about twenty miles on their right flank. He scrutinized the map, trying to work out how they could confirm the position. The map showed a hill just to their north, but the trees hid any sign of it behind their canopy.

A single shot broke the stillness. Both leaders looked up, startled, trying to work out where it had come from. Another shot followed, then a moment later the rapid patter of automatic fire signaled the outbreak of hostilities proper.

"Force Leader," the signaler said interrupting, "Leader Wentworth reports contact with the enemy."

"How many?" Wentworth's Troop was at the end of the column.

"All of them, sir." Donald heard the excitement in Wentworth's voice even over the radio.

Donald rolled his eyes. "Bugler signal 'to arms'," he called. "You better take your Troop back and reinforce the line," he told Bearclaw as the bugle sounded its clarion over the escalating sound of battle. "I'd appreciate a slightly better estimate of their numbers if you can give it to me."

"Certainly Leader," and then Bearclaw was gone, spurring her mount back along the column to get her Troop into position.

"Take a message for the Group Leader," Donald told the signaler. "Have contacted the enemy at Grid Ref 0457 9134. Possible main body."

The signaler held up his hand as his radio crackled to life. The message was heavily distorted and he had to lift it to his ear to understand. "Leader Hanow confirms the enemy is at least Force strength."

"Right, include that in the message," Donald said, taking off after Bearclaw. He found her sheltering in the shadow of a giant pine as her Troop took up firing positions around her.

"How are we going?" Donald asked, dismounting to join her.

"Looks like a bloody shemozzle."

"Shemozzle or not, we have to keep them pinned down until Tumeric's Force can close up."

"How long?"

"At least an hour if we're where we thought we were."

Bearclaw nodded her understanding. "We'll need to extend the line, otherwise they'll just flank us."

"If we thin our line against odds of two to one, they'll just go straight through us." Donald tried to picture the terrain on the map he had been studying just before all this started. "We've got the hill behind us, so if we can pull back slowly enough they won't have time to flank us."

"Timing's going to be difficult."

"But not impossible. I'll go and warn Wentworth and Hanow, you keep your troops ready, and make sure the horses get pulled back as well; I don't want to leave mounts for the Rangers."

She waved her assent, but Donald was already gone, running bent over, along the firing line.

Hanow simply nodded when Donald explained the situation to him, and Donald moved on to find Wentworth.

The situation with Wentworth's Troop was chaotic, and it took him several minutes to locate the Troop Leader in the center of the battle, enthusiastically blazing away with the rest of his troops.

"Wentworth! What do you think you're doing?"

"Leader?" Wentworth said, obviously surprised by Donald's sudden appearance.

"You're a leader, not a grunt. Who's in command of your Troop?"

"Um, I am."

"Well it doesn't look like it. Start thinking instead of reacting. I need you to start pulling your Troop back, slowly, so the Rangers can't outflank us. Think you can do that?"

Wentworth nodded, subdued.

"Good, Tumeric's Force should get here in about an hour. We've got to hold them until then."

"Leader."

"Get to it then."

"Tendoy," Wentworth called. A Squad Leader popped a head up. "Pull your squad back twenty yards and get ready to cover us."

The Squad Leader acknowledged the order with a wave, and a moment later five Territorials sprinted back to take up fresh positions behind them.

"I'll leave you to it," Donald said, confident his orders would now be implemented.

Working his way back to Bearclaw along the line Donald felt a surge of pride at the way the Territorials were handling the situation.

"Everything under control?" Bearclaw asked, as Donald threw himself down next to her.

"Looks like it."

"Leader . . ." An umpire touched his shoulder lightly.

"Yes?"

"My apologies sir but you've been shot. Twice. Sniper fire. You're out of the battle."

"Damn!"

Bearclaw raised an eyebrow as the umpire pulled back.

"I was just starting to enjoy myself," Donald explained. "All right, you're in charge. Keep pulling the lines back, and make sure you keep your head down!"

"You're awfully talkative for a dead man," she told him with a smile. "You heard the umpire, you're out of the battle."

Donald let out a theatrical groan, and collapsed backward into a soft pile of leaf litter. "Better?"

"Much."

It wasn't long before Bearclaw pulled the line back again, and Donald watched as the Rangers pushed up, trying to break through before Tumeric's Force arrived to reinforce the line, or Conrad's main strength caught them in the rear. They were good troops, their green flecked camouflaged uniforms merging into the dappled undergrowth of the forest as they flitted from tree to tree, firing and moving, firing and moving. Their onslaught was relentless, and Donald wondered how his Force could hope to match them. But match them they did, and by the time Tumeric's Force arrived had almost fought them to a standstill.

Tumeric's arrival made that explicit, and Donald watched with interested as the Rangers started to pull back to regroup. He thought he caught sight of Raincloud at that stage, but if it was it was only for a moment. The Territorials kept the pressure on, however, and the Rangers had to hold where they were or risk being run down. It was still evenly matched an hour before dusk when bugles sounded from the south, and the two Groups that had been chasing the Rangers finally arrived to complete their encirclement. An hour later, as night fell, the exercise was declared over and the three Groups set up camp for the night.

***

Donald nursed a beer as he stared into the campfire later that night. Listening to a harmonica in the distance, he felt his fingers itching for the strings of his fiddle back at his flat on the Mainline, when he felt a hand on his shoulder.

"Hi stranger, where can a girl get a drink around here?"

"Wentworth," Donald called, without looking up. "A beer for my sister. So where's Jon?" he asked as Wentworth almost tripped over his own feet in his eagerness to get the beer.

"In the hospital."

"He's not injured is he?" Donald quite liked the young Force Leader, although perhaps not in the same way his sister seemed to.

"No, just checking on a couple of his troops. Someone managed to get bitten by a snake, and one of his scouts managed to break an arm."

"How did they do that?"

"It's a long story."

Donald patted the empty place on the log next to him. "Take a seat then."

"Thanks."

"Here you are, Force Leader." It was Wentworth. He held the bottle at arms-length, as though frightened Ivy would bite. Ivy rewarded the young Troop Leader with a smile, and Donald hid a grin as Wentworth backed away, almost falling over the log as he did so.

"Congratulations," Ivy said. "I heard it was your Force that pinned the Rangers down."

"Thanks." He decided not admit to being lost at the time.

"Hello Ivy, trust you to be here." It was Conrad, two bottles of small beer in his hand.

She raised the bottle. "Conrad."

"Pull up another log," Donald told him.

Conrad took a seat on the far side of the fire. "I just dropped by to tell you I've arranged for an autogiro to pick you up at six tomorrow to take you back to Leolie."

"Thanks. I was becoming a little worried about how I'd get back to Uni before term starts."

"No problem. So where's Jon?"

"Apparently in the hospital," Donald said.

"Anything serious?"

"Nah, he's just checking on two of his troops."

"So what happened?"

Both brothers looked expectantly at their sister.

She shrugged. "One of the scouts was up a tree when the branch he was standing on broke and he came down faster than he went up. Broke his arm in two places."

"Messy."

"And the snake?" Donald asked.

"Someone forgot to check their sleeping bag last night before they got into it."

"Any idea what it was?"

"Jon says it was a copperhead."

"So not life threatening?"

Ivy rocked a hand.

The fire crackled, and a trail of embers shot across the glade. As they died away Donald raised his bottle in a toast. "Clemhorn victorious."

Ivy and Donald clinked bottles while Conrad, on the other side of the fire, lifted his own in reply.

"Any idea on your next posting?" Donald asked his sister.

"I'm hoping the northern Alps. Get some combat experience."

"Then what? Staff College in three years?" Conrad asked.

"Maybe. Let's see what happens first though."

"And what about you?" Conrad asked his brother. "What do you want?"

"Tenure."

The other two laughed.

"No, seriously," Conrad said.

"I'm not quite sure," Donald admitted, after he'd considered the question for a while. "I've been thinking about writing a book about Traek's conquest of the Mainline. Something to celebrate the 100th anniversary."

"Isn't that what you were talking about doing last time I dropped by at the university?" Conrad said.

"Sort of. I still think there's a story in Traek's relationship with Iapura."

"Who was Iapura?" Ivy said.

"Leader Iapura was in command of the party that invaded the Mainline. Traek was merely the group's commissar. Their relationship was. . . difficult. It was only when Iapura was killed by the Tsar's bodyguard that Traek rose to command."

"A 'commissar'? How come I didn't know any this?" Ivy demanded.

"It's not exactly public knowledge," Donald said. "In fact Traek's diary is still on the proscribed list."

"Why?" Ivy said.

"Hey, don't bite the messenger. I don't set policy. Anyway, the whole reason for writing the book is to let people know what happened."

"It's not leaving you much time if you're aiming to have it out for the 100th," Conrad said.

"Yeh, but I like a challenge."

"The Nayarit Line must have been a hell of a place," Ivy said. "Biological plagues, radiation, total war for over eighty years. You can see why they thought the Mainline was paradise."

"Paradise or not, it was bloody amazing to conquer an entire line with fewer than 100 people in just six months," Conrad said, as he opened his second bottle.

"Do you think people will ever talk about us like that?" Ivy said wistfully.

"God, I hope not," Donald told her. "They almost succeeded in wiping themselves out."

"What a pleasant subject for a book," Ivy said, taking another swallow.

"But you see they didn't. That's what makes it so remarkable. And look at what he left us."

"Scientific stagnation and a level of technology that's actually regressed over the last seventy years?"

Donald grinned to hear his own words parroted back to him. "I think that's more the result of those that followed Treik than Treik himself. But what about Mexico?" he asked Conrad.

"Once the railway's through to Tumbez, what's your next goal?"

"Probably a canal through the isthmus."

Their conversation continued throughout the night and sky was lightening when Donald checked his watch, surprised to find it was after five. "I better get my stuff together if the giro's picking me up at six," he said regretfully.

"What's the time?" Conrad asked.

"About five thirty."

Conrad pulled a face and stood up. "I better head back myself, so I'll say good-bye now."

Donald held out his hand. "Best of luck in Mexico."

"Thanks, it's still going to be a couple of weeks till I head back though."

"If you've got time, why don't you drop by on the Mainline and see me?"

"I might do that."

"Good." Donald looked down at his sister. They'd just been playing soldiers for the last week, but she was going to be doing it for real. "Take care," he told her.

"Always."

He bent down to kiss her cheek, but she stood up and hugged him. She was so small. You always forgot that. Tears pricked at his eyes and he blinked them away.

"Look after yourself," she told him, as she released him.

"I'll try." He looked at Conrad. "See you soon."

Conrad nodded.

CHAPTER SIX

Leolie - Etu Line
September 1979 (95AE)

Conrad checked his watch. It was going to be close. He'd been hoping to be able to spend some more time with his sister before they had to take off for their respective corners of the world, and now the old man had well and truly stuffed that idea. He hoped she was around the house somewhere; if she wasn't he'd have to leave without even saying goodbye.

Luckily he found her with Jon, stretched out on the grass next to the pool at the foot of the waterfall, working on a tan.

"Conrad," Jon said, starting to get up.

Conrad shook his head. "Stay there, I've just come to say goodbye."

"Where are you off to?" Ivy said, rolling over to look at him.

"Mainline, Charleston first off, then Naisre. Papa needs me to run some messages."

"Is the First Leader worse?" Ivy asked.

"Not sure. Papa did say the situation in the Council is getting a bit sticky though."

"When are you leaving?" she asked.

Conrad checked his watch. "In just under an hour."

"That doesn't leave you much time?"

"That's why I'm here; I'm wondering if Jon could do me a favor."

Ivy pouted. "You didn't just come to say goodbye to me?"

No, his sister wasn't going to make it easy for him. "I'm wondering if you could pass my apologies to Force Leader Lola, Jon. I was supposed to be taking her to a game this afternoon but . . ."

"You couldn't just write her a note?" Ivy said. "Called away on urgent business or something."

"That wouldn't be polite."

"And getting your sister's boyfriend to pass on your apology is?" Ivy asked.

Conrad noticed Jon struggling to contain a smile and shook his head, acknowledging the situation. "Just tell her I'll write when I've got time," he told Jon.

"I'll tell her," he said.

"So what are you seeing Donald about?" Ivy asked.

Jon looked blank.

"Donald's studying at Charleston University," Ivy explained.

"Actually it's not Donald I'm seeing, it's Kaito, his flatmate," Conrad said.

"But you'll be seeing Donald?"

"Of course."

"Give him my best."

"I'll do that." He bent down to kiss Ivy's cheek. "Take care, make sure you write."

"You too, Conrad."

"Good luck, Jon." He shook the Force Leader's hand. As he turned back to the house he noticed Ivy rest a hand possessively on Jon's shoulder. Interesting, he thought, though he had more than enough trouble sorting out his own love life to worry about Ivy's.

***

It was late afternoon as Conrad climbed the flight of steps to Donald's flat. As a postgraduate student and tutor, Donald was entitled to a room in one of the new blocks on the other side of the river, but instead he'd selected a flat in the oldest part of the city. Donald argued it was more convenient and closer to the University, but Conrad thought it was simply that he was an incurable romantic.

The door was opened by Kaito. Conrad blinked at the heavy, dark green silk kimono Kaito wore over t-shirt and jeans.

"Conrad!" Donald's flatmate said, surprised. "Come in. Donald should be back in a couple of minutes. He's just got a tutorial."

"Actually, I'm here to see you."

"Me? What about?"

"Can I come in?"

"Of course."

Conrad dumped his bag just inside the door. "I'm not interrupting anything am I?" he asked, noticing the piles of papers spread across most of the dining room floor.

"No, just doing some sorting. I'm off to Constantinople in a week. Did you want a beer?"

"Thanks. Nice kimono," Conrad followed Kaito into the kitchen. "Where did you get it?" The kimono's thick silk glinted in the light.

"It was a Christmas present from my mother."

"She's Japanese? For some reason I thought she was Malaysian."

"No, Japanese, from Honshū. My parents met in Malaysia though. Dad was a diplomat there."

"Ah, now I remember," Conrad said. Kaito's father was a senior Croatian diplomat, while his mother's family were in tea. Kaito's joint parentage was quite visible in the shape and cast of his face, particularly his eyes.

"So what do you want to see me about?" Kaito asked as he handed Conrad a bottle of beer from the fridge.

"I was on my way to Naisre so Papa asked me to drop by and find out how your work's going." Kaito's interests lay in the hardware associated with the gates. Conrad often wondered how Kaito and Donald had met, given that his brother's interests lay more in what was on the other side of the gate than the hardware that got one there.

"Good. The latest tests on the new crystal substrate look very promising.'

"Which means?" Conrad asked as he took a seat at the kitchen table.

"That if the bond holds, we should be able to power-down a gate without it shattering into a million pieces."

Conrad's eyes widened as he considered the consequences. A gate was expensive to create, and once energized had to remain powered, otherwise it simply disintegrated into a spectacular, and very expensive, shower of splinters when the power was cut. "So when do you get to try it?" he asked.

"In about a month; that's why I'm off to Constantinople. Donald's contacts can only stretch so far, and with most of the funding now coming from the University there, they want to be involved in the final tests."

"If everything goes well, how long before you get it into production?"

"It will probably be a year or so before we can run a full-scale test. After that, maybe another year?"

Conrad nodded. Well at least he had the answer Papa was after.

There was a rattle of keys in the lock and Donald opened the door. "Conrad, when did you arrive?" he said, surprised to see his brother.

"A couple of minutes ago. I was hoping you could put me up for the night. I'm off to Naisre tomorrow."

"Yeah, of course, you can use the couch. When did you eat last?"

Conrad checked his watch. "Six hours ago."

"I'll get something started then. Kaito, you know Professor Maras?"

"Professor in theoretical chronology, joined the university a couple of months ago. Sure."

"Well, he was at the facility soiree this afternoon, and his daughter was there."

"I didn't know he had a daughter," Kaito said.

"Neither did I," Donald admitted.

"Who's Professor Maras?" Conrad asked.

"The person who developed the unified theory of time," Kaito said.

"At twenty," Donald chimed in.

"So what's she like?" Conrad asked.

"Matija?" Donald considered the question for a moment. "Obviously bright. I was only able to talk with her for a couple of minutes. Asked me a couple of tough questions about my PhD."

"I meant, what does she look like?"

Donald laughed. "It may surprise you, Conrad, to know that it's not all about appearance."

Conrad raised an eyebrow at Kaito, who shook his head sadly.

"So what does she look like?" Conrad said.

"Short, about five foot. Nice cheek bones. Gray eyes. Quite pretty."

"Sounds like she made an impression," Conrad said.

"As I said, bright."

Conrad raised his bottle. "Touché," he said, before taking a deep swallow. "Not bad," he added, checking the label.

Ah, Three Kings, that would explain it. They were one of his favorite Mainline brewers of pale ale.

***

That hadn't been the last beer he'd had, and as the party didn't break up until well after midnight, he was feeling a little under the weather when he was shown to his seat on board the airship for the early morning flight to Naisre. As a result he didn't pay much attention to his traveling companion until he'd finished doing up his seatbelt. When he did, however, his eyes immediately widened in appreciation. She was probably about twenty-five, with green dyed hair, bobbed short, and flawless olive skin. Most of the skin was on open display thanks to her short, sleeveless tunic, barely within the bounds of Mainline modesty. She had piercing green eyes that matched the color of her hair, and a small dagger tucked into the top of her knee-high boots that looked extremely functional.

"Good morning," he said brightly.

Uncertainly, she smiled a reply.

"Conrad Clemhorn." He put out his hand.

"Defella Haratan."

Her hand felt warm in his. "You have business in Naisre?"

"Business, yes. I am to become an aide to the World Leader."

"Which one?"

"Dynand. My grandmother is Continental Leader."

"Really," Conrad said interestedly. "The Dynand Line's near the edge of the Empire isn't it? Split off from the Mainline about 50,000 years ago."

She nodded, giving him an uncertain smile.

"So, is this your first trip to the Mainline?"

She nodded again.

"And what do you think of it so far?"

"Well I wasn't expecting so many men." Her eyes widened in surprise. "My grandmother warned me, but . . ."

Conrad caught himself admiring the way her tunic tightened distractingly over her breasts and quickly shifted his gaze back to her face. "So what else is different?" he asked, as the airship slowly lifted away from its mast.

***

Twenty-five hours later, as the airship came in slowly over the mountain peaks that surrounded Naisre, Defella watched eagerly through the full-length windows in the lounge for her first sight of the capital.

"There," Conrad said, pointing to the gray concrete shield below them, arching its protective mass over the valley below.

"It's enormous," she breathed.

"Damn near bankrupted the line when it was built, but that's what First Leader Traek wanted. A new fortress to mark his conquest of the line."

"Is it true that's where the portal came through?"

"Yes, there's even a museum dedicated to it, on the original site. I'll take you there if you like."

"Please."

Defella continued to watch their approach to the city while Conrad, who had seen it many times before, found himself watching Defella and the swift darting movement of her eyes as she tried to gather everything in.

"What?" she demanded, catching sight of his reflection in the window.

"Nothing," he said, and started to point out the airship port on the very apex of the shield.

***

"Is there anyone waiting for you?" Conrad asked Defella, eyeing the queues at security. He was still trying to work out which one was the shortest when he felt a hand on his shoulder and turned to find his godfather beaming down on him. A tall sparse man, his godfather's height, combined with the gray and maroon uniform of a Commander in Imperial Security, served to create a small barrier of space around them.

"Conrad, it's been too long," his godfather said.

"Uncle Lawrence," Conrad said pulling him into a hug. "What are you doing here?"

"Your grandfather asked if I could facilitate your arrival. I'm presently acting as his liaison with ImpSec. And when are you going to introduce me to this lovely lady?" he asked, smiling at Defella who still stood next to Conrad.

"Defella, this is my godfather Lawrence McArthur," Conrad said, suddenly remembering his companion. "He's not nearly as scary as the uniform makes him look. Uncle, this is Defella Haratan."

"Oh gods no. Not at all scary," Lawrence said with a broad smile.

"Defella is an aide to the World Leader of Dynand," Conrad explained.

Defella smiled shyly, then her face lit up as she recognized someone at the back of the crowd waving excitedly to her on the other side of the queues. "I must go," she said, reaching up to give Conrad a quick peck on the cheek. "I will see you again."

Both watched her as she disappeared into the crowd.

"Where did you meet her?" Lawrence asked.

"On the airship. Her grandmother's a Continental Leader on Dynand."

"Nice. You're looking well," Lawrence said, turning his attention back to his godchild.

"Thanks. And how is my grandfather?"

"The World Leader of Notway is in the very best of health, and looking forward to seeing you again. Speaking of which, do you have any luggage?"

"Another two cases. I've arranged for them to be directed through to the family suite though. Papa sends you his best wishes."

"And how is the old man?" Lawrence asked as he guided them past the queues.

"In the best of health. And the First Leader?"

Lawrence shook his head. "Unfortunately his condition's deteriorated again."

"Do they know what's wrong yet?"

Lawrence lowered his voice. "The medics think it's Sinclair's Syndrome."

"How long has he got?" The reaction against the Kelsor Virus was rare, but inevitably fatal.

"If it is Sinclair's, a couple of months, perhaps."

"Has he named his successor yet?"

"No. Ever since Treik's death he's refused to consider the matter."

"It was a pity about Treik, I went to the Academy with him here for ten years."

"Well, your grandfather's got more than enough work for you to do, even with the Council in virtual recess."

Conrad gave a small sigh, and his godfather laughed.

CHAPTER SEVEN

Charleston — Mainline
September 1979 (95AE)

Dew glistened on the grass as Donald jogged along the bike track, enjoying the early morning solitude. Beside him, placid and muted between its high brick embankments, the Ashley River flowed towards its junction with the Cooperley, and the ocean. An early morning rower was out on the river and Donald raised his hand in greeting.

The old stone town wall was in sight now, tall and gray, and he increased his pace. Reaching the massive tower that marked the end of the path he turned into the stairwell that wound its way up inside the wall. Taking the steps two at a time he emerged at the top, breathing heavily, and paused for a moment to look back over the town and the University's limestone buildings, stained and darkened by age, that dominated the skyline.

Another runner was taking a breather at the top of the stairs, stretching against the wall, and he cast an admiring glance over her figure before doing a double take. "Matija."

Matija looked round, surprised, then smiled when she recognized him. "Good morning Donald." She wore a loose t-shirt, shorts and pink running shoes. Her raven black hair was pulled back into a ponytail from her face, which glowed from her run.

"I didn't know you ran," Donald said. God, talk about being smooth.

"Whenever I can," she responded. "And it is so beautiful this early in the morning."

"You mean, before it gets spoiled with people?" Donald said, beginning a series of careful stretches himself.

She gave him a quick grin. "Something like that. Charleston is a very beautiful city, very English."

"You've been to England?'

"I grew up in England with my mother," she explained.

"Oh," Donald said, feeling he had somehow strayed into a minefield.

"My parents separated when I was very young. After my mother died when I was twelve I went to live with my father in Italy."

"I'm sorry."

"It was a while ago," she said with small sideways nod of her head.

"I had wondered about your accent," Donald admitted.

"You mean I don't sound Slavic enough?" she said, putting on a broad accent.

"Something like that," he agreed with a grin. "So what do you think of Charleston, apart from it being like England?"

"It is very quiet. In Rome we went out many nights a week, but here I stay at home with nothing to do."

"It's not that quiet," Donald said defensively. "Are you doing anything tomorrow night?"

She raised an eyebrow. "Why?"

"I wondered whether you'd like to come out to a concert with me at the Bowl. They're doing a series on classical music."

"Thank you, I would like that."

"I'll pick you up about seven then?"

"Do you need my address?"

"That would help," he admitted.

She gave him her address, which turned out to be in the newer part of the city, on the other side of the river.

"I'll see you at seven then," he said, still surprised she'd actually said yes.

"Seven," she said with a smile.

***

Dead on seven, Donald knocked on the Maras's front door. Matija opened it, smiling to see him. She had on a white silk blouse and black skirt, her hair tied back with a single, large white bow.

"Ready?" Pleased he'd decided to wear his uniform for the occasion. It had taken him ages to decide what to wear, and it had finally come down to the fact that the rest of his clothes were just sort of. . . blahh. He just wished the uniform's high collar wasn't so uncomfortable.

She nodded, smiling shyly.

"I thought we'd walk, if that's all right with you? It's a beautiful night, and it's not far."

"Of course." She took up a coat from its hook on the wall, and closed the door behind her.

"Your father not at home?" Donald asked. He'd been worried about having to meet him, but now he felt. . . cheated.

"No, he's in London. He had a presentation to make."

"Does he travel a lot?"

"Not as much as he used to. That was part of the reason my parents broke up."

"Ah."

"So you like British classical music?" Matija asked as they turned the corner into the main avenue. On their left the fountain that marked the entrance to the local park cascaded noisily into its basin. Behind it, the park merged into the shadows, dark and deserted.

"Not as much as Kaito, my flatmate, does. How about you?"

"I adore it. Hoyts particularly."

"Let's hope he's on the program for tonight then."

"He is," she said confidently, smiling up at him.

"You checked?"

She nodded, some of the stiffness leaving her.

It was a beautiful night and the weather provided a perfect backdrop for the Bowl, the large semi-covered theater near the edge of the river often used for public concerts. The music surpassed expectations, and as they headed out of the concert Donald had the feeling that if Matija hadn't been holding his arm she'd have been floating.

"Coffee?" Donald asked as they exited the stadium.

"Please."

"You seemed to enjoy the concert," Donald said, as he seated her at the table.

"You didn't?"

"Oh I did, just not as much as you. As I said, Kaito is the fanatic. My own taste runs more towards folk music."

"You mean like Ann Fitzpatrick?"

He nodded at the mention of the English folk singer who had toured America the previous year.

"I saw her in Rome a couple of years ago," Matija said. "Her voice is amazing."

"I missed her last tour. I was in Leolie and couldn't get away. I saw the tour before last though."

"Where's Leolie?"

"On Etu."

She frowned as a thought occurred to her. "Clemhorn? Any relation to the World Leader?"

"My father."

There was a sudden, uneasy silence.

"So what are you doing during the semester break?" Donald asked.

"Not much."

"There must be something?"

"There's a Tapestry Expo coming up I want to go to."

"That's right," he said remembering their conversation at the soiree, "you said you'd studied at the Rome Institute of Fine Arts."

She nodded. "Textile design."

"So are you doing much at the moment."

"Some research for a new tapestry I'm developing, and I'm also doing some postgraduate work at the local Industrial College."

"I didn't know we had an Industrial College," Donald admitted.

"The world isn't all about academia, as I keep telling Papa. But the College has some really good studios, and the only way I can get access to them is as a student. I don't suppose you'd like to come with me to the Expo?" she asked with a small, hesitant smile.

"I wish I could. Unfortunately I've promised to visit my cousins so I'll be away for the entire break. How long have you been interested in textiles?"

"About fifteen years. My mother was an artist and got me interested. I actually won a prize last year."

"Congratulations."

She colored prettily, and sipped her coffee. "So tell me about your family," she said.

"There's four of us, plus my parents. Conrad and Arnold, and Ivy, my sister."

"Are you close?"

"We used to be. Or at least Conrad, Ivy and I used to be. Arnold was always a bit of loner. Conrad's a Continental Leader in Mexico at the moment, and Ivy's busy forging a career for herself in the army, so we don't actually get to see each other much anymore. Last break was the first time I'd seen Ivy in three years."

"And what does Arnold do?"

"Pretty much whatever he wants. He's the black sheep of the family. He's working in an artistic commune in New York at the moment, so he's sort of in the same line of business as you." She looked up at him, surprised. "Really?"

"Really. And what about you? How many cousins do you have?"

"Twenty or so. My father comes from a big family."

"But you're an only child?"

She nodded. "And your cousins?"

"Are on Dontfrey, on the Mississippi."

She frowned thoughtfully. "That's going to be a long trip isn't it. Isn't Dontfrey's portal at Foochow?"

"Dontfrey's actually got three portals: Louisville, Constantinople, and Foochow."

"That's unusual."

"Tell me about it. According to my father maintaining one portal is ruinous enough."

"So how long will you be there for?"

"About two weeks. Would you like another coffee?" he asked, noticing that she'd finished hers.

"No, I better get back. I've got an appointment first thing tomorrow."

"On a Saturday?"

"At the hairdresser," she said with a smile.

"Are you doing anything tomorrow night then? We could check out the Folk Club."

"I'd like that."

"Shall we say seven thirty then?" he asked, helping her up.

"Sure. You might want to leave the uniform at home though."

"You don't like it?" Damn, he thought, he knew he shouldn't have worn it.

"No," she hurriedly rushed to reassure him. "It suits you. You look quite good in it." She blushed. "It's just it . . ."

"Doesn't suit the folk scene," he said, finishing it for her.

She nodded.

"No uniform," he promised with a grin.

CHAPTER EIGHT

New York — Mainline
September 1979 (95AE)

As Arnold listened to the sound of his own breath he felt his muscles start to relax and the tension of the day ease out of his body. Outside, New York seethed in the tumult of a business day, but inside the white draped meditation room the only sound to be heard was the muffled ticking of the clock.

He was disturbed by a knock on the door.

"What?"

Nedo poked his head round the corner of the door. "Can I come in?"

"Why not," Arnold said with a sigh. "You're already here."

Nedo pulled the door closed behind him and looked around, surprised. "Nice. I can see why you like it here."

"Thank you. I'm going to have to do something about the clock though."

Nedo frowned. "What clock?"

"You can't hear it?" Its steady ticking was quite noticeable.

Nedo listened carefully before shaking his head. "Sorry, can't hear a thing."

Arnold shrugged. . . strange, he thought. "What did you want to see me about?"

Nedo displayed the envelope he was holding. "My mother wants to see us."

"What about?"

"She doesn't say. Apparently your brother is visiting in a couple of weeks though and she thought it might be nice to see us at the same time."

"What's Conrad doing there?"

"It's actually Donald. Margaret invited him."

Arnold closed his eyes, trying to let go of the tension brought on by the mention of Conrad's name.

"Why do you let Conrad always get to you?" Nedo asked with interest.

"I do not," Arnold said opening his eyes.

"Bullshit."

Arnold shrugged. It seemed pointless to argue the point

with Nedo who knew him too well. "I'm not sure," he admitted.

"You're going to have to do something about it."

"I am," Arnold said with a half smile, indicating the room.

"It doesn't seem to be working,"

"Give it time."

Nedo stood there watching him and Arnold raised an eyebrow. "What?"

"Are we going?"

"Let me think about it. I was hoping to finish that sculpture."

"That abstract thing?"

"Square in a circle, yeah." He nodded. He was beginning to think it was the best he'd ever done.

"OK, let me know what you decide."

Arnold tilted his head enquiringly when Nedo still showed no sign of leaving. "Something else?"

"I was wondering whether you might want to join me at the squat tomorrow? There's been a rumor the Mayor has asked the police to finally take action."

Arnold sighed. Nedo had been involved with Active Resistance for over a year now and his interest still showed no sign of waning. Arnold himself supported their aims; with the number of vacant buildings in New York it only made sense to release some of them to the homeless, but . . . "You're aware it's not really going to achieve anything if you don't have the force to back it up," he pointed out.

"Which is why we need you," Nedo said with a grin.

Arnold shook his head. He still thought most of Active Resistance's members were dangerously naïve, believing that the world would change simply because they told it to, but it was Nedo who was asking so. . .

"It's the department store in Church Street?"

"Yep," Nedo said, his grin getting broader.

Active Resistance had occupied the derelict department store in Church Street for nearly six months now, and Arnold had been following the increasing agitation of City Hall through the newspapers with fascination. It was obvious the Mayor had been taking the squat as a personal slight, possibly because of its proximity to City Hall, and it appeared things were finally coming to a head.

"All right," Arnold sighed, accepting the inevitable. "After breakfast."

***

He was less enthusiastic the next morning, however, when he opened the door and saw the weather. A thick drizzle hid the top of the buildings on the other side of the street, and the stink of coal smoke gave the air a bitter, gritty texture. Unfortunately Nedo wasn't going to let him get out of going.

The house was still quiet, the rest of the commune at East 77th Street still in bed as Nedo pulled the door closed behind them. Most of those sharing the building tended to work late, and rise even later. It was a pity he wasn't being allowed to, Arnold thought regretfully.

The heavy thud of a steam shovel caused him to pause. They were extending the subway, pushing a line past the end of the street and under Central Park to link up with the Madison Avenue line. A tram rattled by at the end of the road, the overhead pickup sparking as it passed. He pulled his cap down, trying to keep the drizzle out of his eyes, glad he'd decided to wear coveralls. Admittedly they were Jimmy Choo, but so long as it didn't rain too heavily the heavy cotton fabric should keep him dry.

"Walk or take a cab?" he asked.

"Cab," Nedo said, opening his umbrella after a quick glance at the sky.

The closest rank was on 5th Avenue, fronting onto Central Park, and they made it just as the heavens opened up, and the city disappeared behind a heavy wall of rain.

Nedo snickered as Arnold pulled the cab door shut behind them.

"What?" Arnold demanded, as he settled himself more comfortably.

"You're wearing pumps?"

"So?"

"They don't really go with coveralls."

Arnold admired his patent leather pumps. "They're comfortable."

"Oh no, don't tell me. They're the Armani?"

"Is there any other type?"

Nedo rolled his eyes. "Well don't blame me if they get wrecked today."

"I'm going to have to blame someone if my 250 pound Armanis get wrecked," Arnold said comfortably, settling back into his seat.

The rain had eased off by the time the cab dropped them off in front of the squat, although they still had to dash across the road to reach the shelter of the portico over the main doors.

"Do you really think the police are going to do anything today?" Arnold said disbelievingly, leaning against the wall as he poured water out of his left shoe. He'd stepped into a puddle just before they'd reached shelter.

Nedo gave him a grin. "We can but hope."

As they entered the building Arnold noted the barricades ready to be pushed up against the main doors. At least someone had been doing some planning, he thought. Unfortunately that just left the plate glass windows that lined the entire bottom floor exposed. He shook his head in exasperation.

The store's dark-stained wooden floor was scuffed and sanded, but neatly swept, and there was someone mopping up the puddles of water that had been tracked in through the doors. With all its counters removed the store's interior space echoed cavernously. A massive jarrah staircase in the center in the store led from the basement to the fourth floor, winding its way up through the center of the space. A group of activists stood by the foot of the stair.

"Nedo!" A young woman with red hair, her slight figure hidden under an oversized flannelette shirt that looked suspiciously like one of Nedo's, waved happily to see them.

"You got here," she said, coming across to greet them, her eyes barely acknowledging Arnold's presence. There was a large smudge of dirt on one cheek.

"I said I would, Annette," Nedo said, leaning forward and wiping the dirt off her cheek with his thumb.

Arnold grinned at the flush that suddenly suffused her face. "Hi Annette."

Annette gave Arnold a distracted smile before turning her attention back to Nedo. "We've had quite an influx of volunteers today. I was wondering if you could take charge of one of the groups working on the fourth floor."

"Sure."

"Mikhail's already up there; he can tell you what the priorities are."

"You going to be here all day?"

She nodded.

"I'll see you at lunch then. Come on, Arnold."

"Bye Annette," Arnold said brightly.

Annette gave him a suspicious look.

Arnold's pumps squelched as they made their way across to the stairs, and looking down he suppressed a sigh.

Mikhail put Nedo in charge of a team dismantling the counters that still covered half the floor. Any timber that could be re-used was to be stacked neatly against one of the walls, while the remaining timber would be used to feed the steam heaters in the basement.

They'd been working for a couple of hours and were just taking a break, sitting against the wall, sipping on the coffees that had been handed out when Arnold heard what sounded like drums in the distance. Puzzled, he looked up, and saw a couple of others had also noticed. He hoisted himself to his feet and crossed to the window to see what it was. The rain had temporarily stopped again and he swore at the sight of the massed blue ranks of police marching down the road. There must have been close to two hundred of them, all carrying long rattan canes and plywood shields. Their large, distinctive NYPD silver badge on the front of their white custodian helmets gleamed in the weak light of the emerging sun.

"What?" Nedo said, joining him at the window. One glance was all that was needed, however, and Nedo was running for the stairs, yelling for the others to follow.

Arnold wondered whether to join them, but decided to stay where he was for the moment. As the front rank of police reached the intersection a solid block of fifty rushed the front doors, even as the rest spread out to block the intersection. There was the sound of breaking glass and then screaming and shouting from downstairs.

It had all happened so quickly there had been no time for the chanting and posing that normally accompanied these types of events. With a sigh Arnold reached under his shirt and removed his pistol from its concealed holster. He checked the clip, reloaded and cocked it, then made sure the pistol's safety was on before he replaced it in its holster. Only then did he cautiously head downstairs.

He heard the sound of fighting below even as he reached the first floor landing, and pulled back into the shadows, scanning the melee below looking for Nedo.

Glass littered the ground near the front of the store where the glass doors had shattered under the assault. A number of protestors lay curled up on the ground, trying to protect themselves from the rattan canes New York's finest wielded with enthusiasm. Outnumbered and under-prepared, the remaining protestors were already being pushed back towards the interior of the building.

There! Arnold finally caught sight of Nedo, whose group was making a stand about thirty feet away from the foot of the stairs. As most of those with Nedo had picked up lengths of wood before heading downstairs, they were one of the few groups armed with anything that matched the length of the police batons. Despite that, however, it was quite clear they were losing as well.

It was just as obvious the squat had come to an end, but extricating himself and his cousin looked almost impossible. Nedo had mentioned there was a link to the subway system via the basement, but to reach it he'd have to go through the chaos downstairs.

Suddenly his attention was caught by a policeman at the foot of the stairs raising his cane to strike at a protestor lying on the ground. The protestor's face was covered with blood, but with her distinctive red hair it couldn't be anyone other than Annette.

Annette didn't even flinch as the policeman had brought his cane down across her face and without thinking Arnold launched himself down the stairs as the policeman raised his arm for another blow. They both hit the ground hard, but Arnold came to his feet first, grabbed the officer's cane and brought it down on his face leaving a thick welt. The officer moaned and Arnold kicked him, hard, twice. He was just raising his foot to bring it down on the officer's face when Nedo grabbed him.

"Arnold, stop," his cousin said.

"He was hitting Annette," Arnold said.

Nedo glanced down and blanched. Bending down he quickly checked Annette's pulse, the three others with him unconsciously taking up a position around them.

"How is she?" Arnold asked, not taking his eyes off the fighting, which seemed to be temporarily moving away from them.

"Breathing," Nedo said, looking up at him. "We need to take her with us."

Arnold nodded, not trusting the police either. He looked at the three standing behind Nedo. All three clutched improvised weapons, and from their expressions seemed willing to use them. He spared a glance back towards the main entrance where a second wave of police was already starting to force their way through the doors. A couple of them carried shotguns.

"Subway?" Arnold asked

Nedo nodded.

"Are you going to be all right with Annette?" Arnold asked. She didn't look much of a weight.

"I'll help him," one of the three said.

"Let's go then." Arnold thought about kicking the officer again, for the way he'd been laying into the unconscious Annette just didn't seem fair, but a shout from the direction of the front door convinced him they didn't have the time.

They headed down the stairs and had just reached the mid-landing when there was a yell from behind them and he looked up to see an officer pointing a shotgun down at them.

"Go," he yelled, urging them faster.

Even as he turned to follow them he heard the dull report of the shotgun and a spark of fire stitched a line across his shoulders. Startled, he caromed into the rail, almost falling over the banister. Somehow he kept to his feet. "Keep going," he shouted, lurching into motion after them, even as Nedo reached the fire doors at the foot of the stairs.

They burst through without stopping, and as his cousin and the three others with him pounded their way across the deserted basement Arnold turned to slam the doors shut behind them, forcing the rattan cane he was still carrying into the handles to hold them closed. Then without waiting to see how effective it was going to be he started after the others. He caught up with them at the entrance to the subway.

"There's a problem," Nedo said.

"I can see that," Arnold said shortly, as the others clustered around the padlocked double door. "How's Annette?"

Nedo shrugged, looking worried.

Arnold looked around for something to use as a ram but the area around the door was clear of anything they could use.

"We could try charging the door," one of the protestors suggested.

Not exactly rocket science, Arnold thought, but he couldn't think of anything else.

The group backed up three steps then, wrapping their arms round each other, charged the door. Arnold winced as he felt his shoulder hit the door. The door bulged but failed to break.

"Again," Arnold said.

They backed up five steps this time, but even as they braced themselves to charge there was a sudden blast of a shotgun from behind them and the fire doors blocking the foot of the stairs slammed open.

"Go!" Arnold yelled.

This time as they hit the doors the left door collapsed, pulling out of its hinges. For a moment it seemed that they would all lose their balance, but then Arnold managed to grab the edge of the other door, narrowly avoiding collapsing the whole group.

"Nedo, get Annette!" Arnold said, crouching in the shelter of the door and drawing his pistol.

Even as Nedo started to lift Annette into his arms Arnold saw the first of the pursuing police burst through the remains of the fire doors. Carefully aiming high he squeezed the trigger, sending a bullet ricocheting off the concrete ceiling, and causing the officer to drop flat, even as the bullet he'd fired whirled off into the darkness.

"Arnold?" Nedo said, pausing uncertainly just inside the door.

"Go, I'll be there in a moment."

As Arnold watched his cousin disappear into the passage on the other side of the door he felt a flash of fear at the possibility that he might not see him again, and suddenly the taste of buttered copper flooded his mouth. He spat, trying to clear his mouth. He knew the fear was irrational, but he didn't know what he'd do if something happened to Nedo. At times it felt as though he was the only thing that could keep him grounded.

He transferred his attention back to the police just as they appeared to be preparing to rush him. Squeezing the trigger he fired again, off the floor this time, the bullet creating sparks as it caused the first officer to flinch back. OK, perhaps a bit too close; he didn't actually want to hit them.

He risked a glance behind him. Nedo had almost reached the cover of the first corner, and one of the others had already come back to help him with Annette. Quickly turning his attention back to the police he fired three quick rounds off the ceiling before wriggling back behind the shelter of the doorway and scrambling to his feet to sprint after the others.

The corridor, dimly lit by emergency lighting, was lined with white and blue tiles. A thin layer of red dust covered its floor. On reaching the end of the corridor he turned the corner and found himself on the platform of a deserted station. Nedo was bent over Annette who lay on one of the benches running down the center of the platform while the others clustered around a map laid out in the mural on the station's wall.

"Are you OK?" Nedo asked looking up.

"I'm fine," Arnold said, trying to ignore the pain from his shoulder and the fire across his upper back. "Which way?"

"North," the tallest of the three studying the map said, looking round. "We can get out at Odeon."

Arnold took a glance at the three rails. "Is it safe?"

"It should be fine so long as we don't touch the live rail."

"Which is?" Arnold asked.

"The far one. . . I think."

Arnold rolled his eyes, but holstering his pistol he jumped down onto the ballast-covered sleepers. "Here, pass me Annette," he said, reaching up to take her limp body. As he did so, however, she stirred and feebly tried to push him away.

"Hush," he said, "we need to get you to hospital." He felt happier as she went limp again although, he thought, he'd probably feel even happier if she'd been able to walk for herself. She wasn't exactly a light weight, and he wondered how Nedo had been managing. "Let's go," he said, looking nervously behind them.

The biggest problem turned out to be having to feel their way along the wall in the dark over the uneven ballast without turning an ankle but they reached Odeon station without disaster, and paused just out of the reach of the station's lights.

"Now what?" Nedo asked as they looked up the tunnel towards safety.

"Annette needs to get to hospital," Arnold said.

"No, no hospital," she whispered. "Put me down, I can walk now."

Arnold lowered her carefully to the ground. She balanced unsteadily, using the wall for support.

"Are you sure?" he asked.

"Positive, no hospital. They'll have the police there." She was white with strain, but returned his look defiantly.

"We'll get you to my doctor then," he said. And he could get something done about getting the shotgun pellets removed from his back. The earlier stinging had changed to a burning sensation that was really starting to hurt.

"And you three are going to have to disappear for a while," he told the other three protestors.

"Why?" one of them asked.

Arnold looked unbelievingly at them for a moment. "Excuse me — gun," he said, patting it under his shirt.

"But we didn't do anything."

"And do you think the police will care about that." He smiled at the sudden look of shock on their faces. "If it's any consolation I doubt they got a good look at you. Now me, that might be a different." He didn't think he'd been recognized though. He was still wearing his cap, and the coveralls were fairly nondescript. He might need do something about his hair.

"You three got somewhere to go?" Nedo asked.

The three looked at each other, then nodded.

"We'll go first," Arnold said. "Annette, you going to be all right?"

She started to nod, then closed her eyes and winced. "Yes," she said quietly.

With Arnold and Nedo on either side of her she cautiously climbed the five steps to the platform. As they entered the well-lit area of the platform Arnold caught sight of his shoes and grimaced. The once perfectly polished pumps, already soaked by the rain earlier in the day, were now scuffed beyond repair by the walk through the tunnel. Well that would teach him to wear pumps to a squat in future, not that there should be a next time.

As Annette settled herself onto the bench at the end of the platform with a shaky sigh Nedo suddenly frowned. "You're bleeding," he told his cousin, noticing the stains in the back of Arnold's coveralls as he straightened up.

"It doesn't matter."

"Let me see," Nedo said.

Later," Arnold said. They couldn't risk drawing any attention to themselves.

Nedo subsided, sparing a glance up the platform, but what few passengers there were appeared to be studiously avoiding them. "How bad is it?" he said, not willing to let it go directly.

Arnold shook his head, not wanting to talk about it, or at least not until the doctor had had the chance to see it. Talking about it was reminding him of how painful it was. Fortunately, Nedo subsided.

There was a hum from the rails and the squeal of wheels from the tunnel they'd just emerged from announcing their train.

"Maybe we should take your mother up on her invitation to visit," Arnold said, helping Annette to her feet.

Nedo looked at him, puzzled for a moment, before nodding, looking pleased.

Ah, if only it was that easy to make his own father pleased with his middle son, Arnold thought. He winced as the muscles pulled at his back but it looked as if they were going to get out this. Once they were back at the commune they could get the doctor to look at Annette and then he could some attention, and then off to Dontfrey. The sculpture could wait till he got back, and there were some ceramic techniques he'd wanted to check out on Dontfrey for some time. He started to smile; this might actually end up working out quite well.

CHAPTER NINE

Naisre — Mainline
September 1979 (95AE)

Conrad paused to survey the ballroom floor from the top of the stairs. The floor was crowded, the noise of multiple conversations almost drowning out the small chamber orchestra playing a waltz in the corner. Tonight's black and white theme was certainly a change from the normal gaud the room hosted. Adjusting his black silk cravat Conrad started down the stairs - gods he'd missed these.

"A drink, Leader?" The waiter at the bottom of the stairs politely offered the tray he was carrying.

Conrad eyed the tray doubtfully. It didn't look very hopeful. "Have you got any beer?"

"We have Kolosin or Three Kings."

"Kolosin thanks." He'd acquired a taste for the dark ale during his time at the Academy.

"I'll just get it for you, sir."

Conrad watched the waiter disappear into the crowd, then turned and snagged the last sausage roll from a passing tray. The servitor gave him a startled smile before continuing on her way. Conrad watched the gentle swing of her hips as she made her way back to the servery until a hand dropped on his shoulder and he flinched guiltily.

He turned to find Hayden McArthur, a classmate from the Academy, smiling up at him. Hayden, already starting to go bald, was a short, dapper, dandy of a man with the steel-trap mind of a banker.

"Hayden," Conrad said, pleased to see him. "I thought you were still on Clyde."

"Mary wanted to catch up with some of her friends at Court, so here we are."

"Where is Mary?" Conrad asked, scanning the ballroom for the tall blond. He'd known Mary almost as long as he'd known Hayden, she being the younger sister of a mutual friend.

"Just powdering her nose."

"How is she? I haven't seen her since the christening."

"She's good. I take it you're still single?"

"Afraid so."

"Leader." It was the waiter with the glass of beer on his tray.

Conrad took the beer.

"And I see your tastes haven't changed," Hayden said.

Conrad raised the glass in salute. "Of course, you wouldn't know — I've opened my own brewery."

"You still in Etu Mexico?"

Conrad nodded. "And you're still assisting your father?" Hayden's father, the World Leader of Clyde, was aligned with the Progressives.

Hayden shook his head. "Mark's resumed the role. I'm the Continental Leader of Australia at the moment."

Mark was Hayden's elder brother, and the designated heir, but Australia?

Hayden laughed. "If you could have seen your face. You're thinking Mainline Australia. Clyde had major migration of Chinese during the second Khanate, about 1,500 years ago. Ended up settling most of the Pacific basin, including Australia. It had a population close to six million before the Decimation hit."

"I was trying to be polite."

"Which I appreciate."

"Hello, Conrad."

It was Mary. Conrad did a double take. A very pregnant Mary! He glared at Hayden who hadn't warned him, then bowed and kissed her hand. "Mary. Pregnancy suits you; you look ravishing."

"Now take note, Hayden, how a lady should be treated."

"Oh, I already know that."

"Then why can't you do it?"

"Because if people saw me doing it they'd think I was madly in love with my wife. I'd never live it down." The fond smile on his face belied his words.

"And this isn't enough of a signal?" she replied with a matching smile, patting the bulge of her stomach.

Conrad found the open display of familial love a little unsettling. "When's it due to pop?" he asked.

"Seven weeks."

"And how's Felicity?" Conrad asked.

"Our daughter was more than happy to stay at home with

the new pony we got her for her birthday. In fact, it would probably have been difficult to have pried her away from it. However, as godfather you might want to consider actually visiting once in a while."

"Of course. It's just I've been a little busy."

"For the last five years?"

"Oh bugger," Hayden said. "Who let him in?"

"Who?" Conrad started to say, then stopped. There was no mistaking the person approaching. Petro Raputa, only son and heir to Miro, World Leader of Dontfrey. Petro's puffed doublet and tight trousers could be only loosely described as black; in reality they were more like a very dark green, with the Raputa jaguar picked out in silver thread on his breast. Trust Petro not to follow the rules, Conrad thought. His normal shoulder length white-blond hair had been pulled back into a short ponytail.

"Good afternoon gentlemen," Petro said. "Mary, delightful to see you again."

Mary simply stared down her nose at him.

Conrad frowned. He was obviously missing something, Mary was polite to everyone.

"Conrad, please pass my congratulations to your sister on her promotion," Petro said.

Oh, smooth. Just a little hint that their spies were keeping them informed. Conrad smiled, showing his teeth, and didn't say anything.

"You have the gall." Hayden stepped forward.

Mary tried to pull him back. "Hayden, it's not worth it."

And then Hayden swung at him, Petro didn't even see it coming. The blow was as solid as it was unexpected and Petro landed flat on his bum, a waiter narrowly avoiding getting knocked down with him.

Petro bounced to his feet, spitting, eyes flaming, but this time Conrad was there - his bulk providing an immovable barrier between the two adversaries.

"Calm down, or do you want your nose broken again?" Conrad warned him, reminding him of the time several years before when he'd broken the little snot's nose.

Petro felt his lip, which was bleeding freely, and spat on the floor. "You'll keep, Conrad, you and your whole damn family. Just wait until you see what we've got planned for you."

"You better go and clean up," Conrad said evenly.

Petro suddenly tensed as his gaze focused at something over Conrad's shoulder. Conrad stiffened, only to relax when he heard his god-father's voice.

"Good evening, Leaders."

Conrad turned his head to see both his godfather and grandfather standing there. "Uncle Lawrence, Grandfather."

"Is there a problem?" his grandfather asked. The World Leader of Notway, a tall, lean man, with thinning white hair, normally possessed the slightly distracted air of a scholar — not at the moment though. His attention was firmly fixed on the three of them.

Conrad looked back at Petro, who shook his head.

"No problem," Conrad said.

"Then perhaps you should go and see to your face, Petro," the World Leader suggested.

Petro looked at Hayden for a moment, then turned and pushed through the small crowd that had gathered to watch.

"Mary, perhaps you better take Hayden to the buffet," Conrad's godfather suggested.

"Thank you," Mary said, smiling. "Come on you idiot," she said affectionately to her husband, taking his arm.

"I'll catch up with you later," Conrad promised.

Hayden nodded, obviously still too angry to talk.

"I'll see you later Conrad," his grandfather said before, with a nod, continuing his passage around the room, the small crowd that had gathered dispersing in his wake.

"Come on Conrad," his godfather said, guiding him out onto the nearest terrace. The terrace overlooked a Nayarit meditation garden, it's neatly raked gravel patterns gleaming silver in the light of the full moon.

"So what was that all about?" Lawrence asked.

"Petro being his normal obnoxious self."

"It doesn't always end up with Petro sporting a blood lip."

"He might learn some manners if it did," Conrad said tartly. Lawrence refused to be drawn and Conrad sighed. "I had hoped you could tell me. I'm not really sure what happened. Hayden was upset about something, then when Petro congratulated me on Ivy's promotion Hayden just let go. I don't even know what triggered it."

"Ah, of course, you weren't here for the last season."

"What did I miss?"

"Mary came to the season with her sister. Petro was here as well and he and Nyree spent a little bit more time together than was wise."

Conrad wracked his brains, trying to remember Nyree. He had a dim memory of her from Felicity's christening. Shorter then Mary, blond he thought. "What did her husband say about it?"

"She's not married, so at least we avoided that particular difficulty. Unfortunately she managed to get herself pregnant and when she named Petro as the father he denied all responsibility."

"That sounds like Petro."

"Unfortunately, it got even messier when she tried to commit suicide and lost the baby."

"And no one called Petro out?" he said, surprised. At least now he knew why Mary had treated him the way she had.

"His father sent him home the next day, so there was no time."

"Well he's here now," Conrad said.

"No," Lawrence said sternly. "You are not to call Petro out. And I would appreciate it if you could prevail on Hayden not to issue a challenge either. Things are at rather a delicate stage at the moment in the Council."

Conrad sighed, admitting the sense of it. "I won't back away from a challenge, especially from Petro, but I won't go looking for fight either. And I'll speak to Mary. Petro's a mean fighter, Hayden wouldn't stand a chance."

"Thanks."

"There is one thing I think you should know though. When he was fronting me Petro made rather an interesting threat."

"Oh? What did he say?"

"It was something along the lines of: you'll keep, you and your family. Just wait and see what we've got planned for you."

"That doesn't sound very specific."

"No, but it was the way he acted when he saw Grandfather. As though worried he'd just blabbed something he shouldn't have."

Lawrence frowned. "The First Leader is barely conscious at the moment. I can't see how he could make any sort of declaration."

"That bad?"

Lawrence nodded.

"Could Daneka be arranging something?" The First Leader's wife was Petro's sister.

Lawrence considered the question. "I've had some people keeping her under observation, but perhaps I should increase the level. I have been working on the basis she wasn't an active player."

"Maybe, but there's always the chance her father could persuade her to take a more active role."

"I'll see what I can do. Perhaps you better get back to the party. It looks like I've got some work to do before I can join you and it wouldn't be a good idea if people got the idea we were plotting a coup."

"Are we?"

His godfather smiled grimly. "My loyalty is to, and remains with, the First Leader." He slapped Conrad's shoulder. "Now get back in there and circulate. And make sure Mary and Haydon are all right."

Conrad clicked his heels.

CHAPTER TEN

Neu Stuttgart — Etu Line
November 1979 (95AE)

Once again Ivy checked that Jon's last letter was secure in her breast pocket. It rustled reassuringly when she patted it. Around her swirled the light conversation of the party being held in her honor.

"Leader." It was the Military Governor of Neu Stuttgart, the party's host. A small, squat man, he had impressed Ivy with his air of being an officious toad. A native of Central America, he had lived in Europe for the last ten years.

"Governor," she replied, unconsciously straightening her spine.

"I'd like to introduce you to my wife," he said, turning to the woman on his arm. She was a large, comfortable looking woman with blond hair and startlingly blue eyes, who towered over her husband.

"I'm pleased to meet you, Leader Clemhorn."

"Ivy, please," Ivy responded politely.

"I'm sorry I wasn't here to greet you when you arrived but Henrietta finally decided to give birth."

"I hope everything went well?" Ivy asked.

"Oh excellently. Another six children."

Ivy raised an eyebrow.

"My wife breeds whippets," the Governor explained.

"Of course," Ivy said smoothly, trying to hide her smile. Dogs, what next?

"As everyone's here perhaps we'll go in for dinner," the Governor said, looking around. Ivy didn't catch the signal, but a moment later the major-domo started to move everyone into the dining room.

Not unexpectedly, Ivy found herself seated with the Governor and his wife. With two Group Leaders, a Battlegroup Leader, and their partners, Ivy was the lowest ranked officer in the group. At least she was no longer a simple a Troop Leader, she thought; now that had been embarrassing.

"So where was your last posting?" a Group Leader asked politely, her tabs indicating she was in intelligence.

"Italy, near Perugia. I was with the 96th Mounted Infantry, 72nd Battle Group. Mainly policing duties."

"And where will you be stationed this time?" the Group Leader's partner asked, leaning across the table towards her.

"Fort Larsa. It's a small fort on the Danube, near Mainline Vienna."

"Your first independent command?"

"Yes."

"Congratulations," he said, raising his glass to her.

"Thank you."

"I've arranged for her to travel south to Fort Knot with a relief Troop tomorrow," the Governor said.

"Well, rather you than me," the second Group Leader said. "It's not the easiest of postings. Thank the gods I'm mustering out in a month."

"Oh?"

"Those around here are relatively happy with us. They'd never really developed much beyond the village level, and just sort of got assimilated into the system. But there's been quite a sophisticated confederacy in the Alps for a couple of hundred years now, and they've been causing us a lot of grief recently."

"Apparently they've got a new war leader. Aris, or someone or other," the Governor's wife said.

"Aris," the Intelligence officer confirmed. "Unfortunately we don't know much about him. Our intelligence is, shall we say, rather lacking when it comes to the mountain tribes."

She lowered her voice. "We lost a whole Troop last month, near Salzburg. Out on patrol and they just disappeared without a trace."

"Deserted?"

"No, we use a lot of native troops for garrison duty. Don't really have a choice, but never closer than 500 miles to their home. These were American Regulars though."

"I'm sure shop talk can wait until after dinner," the Governor said, breaking in. "Perhaps the Leader could bring us up to date on the last Festival,"

"Of course," Ivy said politely.

***

Now, as the horses of the Troop picked their way gingerly down the center of the road, trying to avoid the worst of its deep, rain filled ruts, she wished she'd taken the opportunity to pick the brains of the Intelligence officer for more information on the local situation. The briefing she'd received from the Governor the next morning had been concise to the point of uselessness.

Another gust of wind whirled around her as the rain lifted an extra notch and she pulled the cover of the poncho tighter around her face. It had been wet ever since they'd left Neu Stuttgart, alternating between a fine mist and a constant drizzle the entire way. The road was a morass, mud splattering their horses' legs up to their withers. Ivy's hands were frozen on the reins, and all she could think about was a hot bath and a dry set of clothes.

"How much farther to the transit station do you think, Sergeant?" she said, leaning across to the burly non-com with the ginger hair riding next to her. Sergeant Horsing was in charge of the squad accompanying her to Fort Larsa and, quiet to the point of curtness, hadn't said more than a couple of words to her during the entire trip.

It was obvious he wasn't going to change now as he simply shrugged and adjusted his poncho as the track dipped down again through the bare trees. Five minutes later, however, they finally broke out onto a low hill overlooking the Rhine and the small fort from which they were to catch their boat.

Ivy grimaced at the sight that greeted her. "Doesn't look very promising."

"No," Sergeant Horsing said laconically.

The fort was little more than a wooden stockade across the throat of a small peninsula with two machinegun towers on either end of the main palisade to provide cover for those defending the stockade wall. There was a warehouse near the landing, and a long wooden building running down one side of the peninsula for the barracks. It was obvious the facilities would be pretty basic.

Fortunately their transport, a stern-wheeler, was already berthed at the pier, a thin stream of smoke struggling to escape from the smokestack that rose high above the three levels of its superstructure. Although they were waved straight through the gate by the sentry it was another hour before they were all on board, and their mounts been brushed down and settled for the night. The delay did give the captain time to build up steam, however, and by the time they'd finished there was enough hot water for Ivy to soak away her aches in a hot bath.

When she woke the next day to the rhythmic splash of the paddle wheeler underway she was pleased to discover the weather had finally decided to make a change for the better, and while the bare trees that lined the river still glistened from yesterday's rain, the mill-smooth surface of the river reflected a gloriously cloudless sky.

Leaning out of the window of her cabin she caught sight of a small, flat-bottomed paddle-steamer tied up at the quay on the far bank, smoke rising gently from its funnel to merge imperceptibly with that from the charcoal burners further up the hill. Mist drifting off the high hills on either side of the river gave everything an eerie sense of unreality. Gods it was beautiful, she thought — the only thing she could have done without was the smell from the stables at the rear of the boat.

She was working her way around the boat later that afternoon when she caught sight of a flash of ginger hair, a moment before she recognized Sergeant Horsing dangling a fishing line over the side.

"Any luck?" she asked as she approached.

He had been staring out over the river, his eyes fixed on a tug, its three barges following like ducklings behind their mother, forging its way through the river towards them, and it was a moment before her words seemed to register. "Leader?"

"Just asked if you were having any luck."

He shook his head. "Not with a bare hook," he said with a slow smile.

She raised an eyebrow enquiringly.

"I like fishing," he explained. "It gives me an opportunity to sit doing nothing. But I'm not hungry so . . ." He shrugged.

She nodded, understanding. "You mind if I sit down?"

"Go ahead."

"You're from Iberia aren't you Sergeant?" she said, settling herself beside him.

"On the west coast," he said nodding. "Near Mainline Lisbon."

"This your first posting here?"

He shook his head. "My third, and last. My fifteen years comes up next year."

Ivy tried to hide her surprise. He didn't look thirty-five, but perhaps he'd enlisted at fifteen; she knew some did.

"So what are you going to do next year?" she asked. "Take your land grant here, or back home?"

"Back home. My brother and I want to use our grants to establish a ranch."

"Horses?"

"Either horses or cattle. Probably aurochs. The army is a big market for dried meat."

She nodded. One of her jobs on her last posting had involved assisting the fort's supply officer, and the sheer amount of supplies required to keep the unit fed and supplied on a weekly basis had stunned her.

"So where's your brother stationed?" she asked.

"Further down the Rhine. Maybe four, five hundred miles from here."

"From darkened forest in the Rhine's mirrored waters beauty stands revealed," she quoted.

She couldn't help a smile at his expression of blank incomprehension. "It's a haiku," she explained. "That one was written by Christos, a Mainline poet. My parents gave me a book of them when I was young and that was one of my favorites."

"A haiku?"

"It's a form of Japanese poetry, not a style that appeals to everyone," she said.

"I can see why."

She gave a sigh of mock exasperation. "The world is full of philistines."

He shrugged, unconcerned. Suddenly his attention focused on the far bank. "Raiders!"

"Where?"

"There." He pointed at the bank. It was obvious the captain had also sighted them as the boat started to edge towards the center of the river.

"How many?" Ivy asked, unable to spot anything.

"Just the four. They were moving parallel to us down the river."

The rail was now crowded with soldiers trying to catch a sight of the raiders.

"Do you think we're at risk?"

"I doubt it, not with the cargo we're carrying," he said, indicating the soldiers lining the side of the boat. He paused. " . . . unless they're after the mounts, and there are easier ways of getting them."

She nodded. "We better double the guard though, just in case."

"I'll see to it."

There were no other sightings, and Ivy went to bed that night confident it had been a false alarm.

***

It had seemed she'd barely fallen asleep when she was jolted awake by an explosion. Sitting up, she'd swung her feet over the edge of the bed and was trying to locate her boots by feel when there was a knock on the door.

"Leader?" It was Sergeant Horsing.

"Hold on," she called. It was pitch-black in the cabin, even though she'd tied the curtains over the window back out the way. The boat seemed to settle, and as she felt the floor tilt away from underneath her she scrambled to her feet, giving up on trying to find her boots. She'd reached the door when she heard someone yell, "Abandon ship!" and frantically scrabbled to unlock it. There was the sound of rushing water and the door suddenly slammed open in her face, hurling her back against the wall and into darkness.

Dragging herself back to consciousness she found she was shivering with cold. Her clothes were soaked, and as her fingers dug into the ground beneath her she discovered she was lying on what felt like leaf mold. Opening her eyes she couldn't see anything, and instinctively her hand reached up to feel the side of her face, which ached from the force of the blow it had taken.

"Careful." It was Sergeant Horsing.

"I can't see," she whispered.

"It's dark; just give your eyes a moment to adjust."

She pulled herself up onto an elbow, and was reassured to be able to make out the darker silhouette of a tree against the fractionally lighter sky. "What happened?"

"Not sure, it was probably a mine from the sound of the explosion. Whatever it was though, it didn't take long for the boat to sink. I was lucky to get you out."

"Any others get away?"

"Don't know. If they did they're probably scattered up and down both sides of the river."

"Raiders?"

"Probably."

There was a moment of silence as each considered the situation.

Ivy shivered, thankful that because of the cold she had at least worn her shirt and trousers to bed, and considered her bare feet. "I don't suppose you brought my boots with you?"

"I'm afraid not. I sleep in mine when I'm traveling."

"Remind me to do the same in future. Weapons?"

"Nothing. Everything went to shit when we went under and there wasn't enough time to go looking."

Damn, Ivy suddenly remembered Jon's letter was in the pocket of her jacket, a jacket that was now presumably under several feet of water. Right, now she was really pissed.

The Sergeant touched her shoulder and she nodded, getting to her knees. She'd heard it as well. There was someone moving through the undergrowth at the edge of the river.

"I'll take them, back me up," Ivy whispered softly.

She heard the Sergeant's short grunt of agreement even as she started forward, trying to match her own movements to those of the other. Whoever it was, they were doing their best to move as quietly as possible. Reaching the bank Ivy paused, and then as they came within reach, she launched herself, trying to judge the angle so they'd land with the minimum of noise.

They landed heavily, and noisily, in what felt like a small shrub. "Stop struggling!" she hissed.

The female under her immediately lay still.

"What unit are you with?" Ivy demanded, not releasing her in case the raiders were now using females.

"The Sixth, Leader."

"Pecos?" the Sergeant said, suddenly beside them.

"That's right, Sergeant."

"Anyone with you?"

"No, Sergeant. Just me."

Ivy helped Pecos to her feet. "We better move," she said, worried about the noise they'd made. "Any suggestions?"

There was a moment of uneasy silence. Obviously this was where she was expected to start earning her money, Ivy thought sourly. "All right, we'll move away from the river a little, then head upstream. In the morning we'll try and make our way back, and wait for the next boat."

"It might be a while," the Sergeant said.

"Not that long," Ivy said confidently. In fact when Continental Command found out she was missing she anticipated some rather sharp orders being sent out to find them. Being the World Leader's daughter had to come with some benefits. "When we don't make our next port they'll radio in and come looking for us. All we have to do is remain out of trouble for a day or so."

"Right," the Sergeant said. "A day. With a possible war band looking for our scalps."

OK, maybe it was going to be a little bit more difficult than she thought.

Moving out in patrol formation, the Sergeant in the lead, they'd been traveling for less than ten minutes when Ivy called a halt.

"I need to do something about my feet," she said. "Anyone got a knife?"

Wordlessly Pecos handed her one. Ivy slipped off her top and hacked off its sleeves, noticing with amusement the speed with which the Sergeant started to check the surrounding bush as soon as he saw she wasn't wearing anything underneath. She was lucky the shirt was thick calico and would offer some protection for her feet. Putting the now sleeveless shirt back on she slid its sleeves over her feet and tied them on as best she could.

"Let's go," she said, handing the knife back to Pecos.

They made slow progress, inching their way inland through the dense forest. They'd been traveling for about an hour when finally, shivering with cold, Ivy called a halt. They made camp in a small hollow, shaded by bushes and thick trees. Unable to light a fire for fear of being seen they huddled together for warmth, and waited for morning.

The night seemed endless, but at last the faint glow of sunlight penetrated the bare branches of the trees overhead, bringing them to their feet. In the weak dawn Ivy was able to get her first look at Pecos. She was a tough-looking Greek, short, heavily muscled, wearing an undershirt and trousers. A knife-sheath was strapped to her arm.

"Let's move," Ivy said, noticing with some amusement the way Sergeant Horsing was trying to avoid looking at her. After last night she'd have thought he'd have got over any embarrassment, but it appeared to have returned with the light of day.

Bruises stiffening, they struck out through the forest, still moving parallel to the river in case of raiders. They'd been traveling for about two hours when the Sergeant suddenly halted, and held up his hand. Ivy and Pecos moved forward cautiously to find him looking down on a rough track that wound its way through the trees, its banks shrouded in ivy. It was raining again, a light drizzle that cut visibility to twenty yards or so. With the cold and the rain Ivy's teeth were chattering.

"What's wrong?" Ivy asked, noticing the Sergeant's frown.

"I'm worried we haven't met anyone else from the boat."

Ivy nodded as Peco nervously cast a look behind them. "I think it's time we had a look at the river," she said.

The Sergeant frowned. "If it was raiders they might still be looking for survivors."

"If they are we've probably moved far enough upstream to be out of their immediate area of operation and can risk having a look," Ivy said, rubbing her arms and wishing the drizzle would stop. She craned her head round the trunk of the gigantic oak that was providing them with their cover to have another look. "All right, we'll follow the track back, but we'll keep about fifty yards in. Sergeant, you keep point. Pecos, take the rear."

They moved cautiously, taking advantage of every bit of cover, and traveling so slowly that in the next hour they had covered less than five hundred yards. Ivy was concentrating on where to put her next foot when Horsing suddenly squatted down. The other two immediately followed his example and a moment later a party of twenty raiders appeared through the trees on the track, moving away from the river. They wore heavy, sleeveless leather jackets and tanned hide trousers, and were armed with a combination of bows and long-handled throwing axes. They were jogging, moving at a pace that would eat up the miles.

As soon as they were out of sight again Ivy waved the other two in to join her.

"Think that's all of them?" Ivy asked the Sergeant.

"Probably, although they could have left a couple behind to pick up any stragglers. It's a favorite trick of theirs."

"So, if I was to head in by myself there might still be a couple around who'd try to count coup?"

The Sergeant nodded slowly as he realized she was suggesting a trap with herself as bait. "It's possible. Dangerous though."

"They were carrying trophies," Pecos said, referring to the habit of the raiders to take the ear of those they'd killed as a token.

"Then it's worth the risk. We better move quickly though," Ivy said, "otherwise we'll get people arriving to look for us, and won't get a chance at them."

***

As she weaved her way down the track, cradling her left arm carefully to avoid jolting, it was obvious she was in pain. She staggered, pausing a moment to rest, holding her splinted arm against her chest, then pushed on again, limping exhaustedly. The splint was make-do, a flattened branch held in place with a dirty piece of cloth, and did little to protect her arm.

Ivy thought she might be overdoing it a bit, but it was the only way she could move slowly enough to allow Horsing and Pecos to keep up with her without being seen. She felt exposed, and very vulnerable, and wondered what Jon would say if he could see her now. It was a thought she quickly buried, to concentrate on the role she was playing.

For fifteen minutes she staggered down the track, all the time wondering when the blow would fall, and whether she would know when it did or whether it would simply come as an arrow in the back. Finally the track burst out onto the river, and as she leant tiredly against a tree, she was grabbed, and jerked back into the shelter of the forest.

Ivy managed a shriek of simulated pain from her broken arm before a hand was roughly slapped across her mouth. The shriek was the signal previously agreed with the others. So far so good; now all she had to do was avoid getting killed.

A shove sent her sprawling to the ground and she looked up to see her captor for the first time. He was a small swarthy man, about five foot tall, with a dark, uneven complexion, wearing buckskins that had been cut and sewn into the shape of a regular army jacket. For a moment her attention focused on the jacket's bone buttons. She'd never seen anything like them before; they even had the double-headed Clemhorn eagle curved into their surface.

Her captor grinned evilly when he saw her face, and said something to a person behind her. Ivy tried to scramble away, no longer acting, as his companion appeared, but the splint on her arm made it difficult. The newcomer was taller than his companion, and was carrying two bows in his right hand, a hatchet loosely in his left hand.

The smaller of the two crouched to pull her trousers off. Close to, the smell of the bear grease was overpowering. She brought her knees up and angrily he struck her across the face. The blow disorientated her for a moment, and when she was aware of what was going on again she discovered her trousers were down around her knees and he was unfastening his own leggings.

That wasn't part of the plan, she was a god-damn Clemhorn, not some poor foot-slogger! Where the hell were Horsing and Pecos? The raider grinned down at her and snarling her anger she punched up, aiming for his throat. The end of the splint caught him under the chin, penetrating and throwing him back with a solid 'thwack'. Swinging her legs up she brought them back down to propel him across the clearing. When she looked up to find what had happened to the second one she found Pecos holding a knife to his throat.

"You took your time," she said, getting to her feet. She swore when she discovered she'd lost the buttons to her trousers. "Bastards!"

"Remind me never to get you angry at me," the Sergeant said, looking up from the sprawled body of the raider on the other side of the clearing.

"Dead?" No need to ask how, the end of the splint was covered in blood.

"As a gate nail."

"Door nail Sergeant," she said automatically as she bent over to see for herself. He was probably about twenty. Well there was someone who was never going to see twenty-five.

The Sergeant unstrung one of the raider's bows and moved across to secure Pecos' prisoner. The bow-string was thin and there was a good chance of gangrene if it wasn't released soon, but Ivy didn't feel much in the mood for kindness. There were two ears, the blood still fresh on them, hanging from his belt.

By the time Horsing had finished securing their prisoner she'd managed to fix her trousers.

"Here," the Sergeant said, passing her one of the hatchets.

She swung it experimentally. "Nice. So what happens to him?" she asked, jerking her head at the prisoner.

"He'll be questioned, then hanged. We can't afford to keep them as prisoners, and you can't trust them about changing sides. We've lost too many people who trusted these vermin."

She nodded, then paused. "What's that?" she asked at the unfamiliar noise coming from downstream.

The Sergeant tilted his head on his side, listening. A slow smile appeared on his face. "That would be our rescue party," he said, giving their prisoner a kick, as Ivy finally made out the putt-putt-putt of a small outboard motor.

It was the Fort's commander himself who worriedly stepped ashore from the first launch, concerned at what he'd find.

"Force Leader Clemhorn, thank the gods you're all right," he said, audible relief in his voice as he recognized her. "What happened?"

Ivy bit back a bitter retort. It wasn't his fault she was who she was, but it would have been nice if he'd even pretended to have had a bit of concern for the others on the boat. "We were attacked by raiders." She gestured at their single prisoner. "This one might be able to give you more information, but the first thing we need to do is find out if there are any other survivors."

He nodded. "Of course. My troops will conduct a preliminary search. I understand that detachments from Fort Hui and Fort McGovern will be here within an hour to assist with at least two autogiros. In the meantime I'd like to get you and the other two back to the fort."

She shook her head. "We'll stay until you've completed your sweep." She could feel Horsing and Pecos nodding their agreement behind her.

He opened his mouth to argue, then simply gave a short nod. "Very well. I'll arrange for my medic to check you over."

“Of course. Let us know as soon as you find anyone else.”

He nodded, and calling for his communications officer headed off to organize the search.

Unfortunately in the end fewer than five survivors were located, although sixteen bodies were recovered, and it was a somber party that headed back to the fort that night.

CHAPTER ELEVEN

Louisville — Dontfrey
October 1979 (95AE)

Arnold cautiously stepped down from the train and had to stand for a moment to regain his balance as the platform whirled uneasily under him. In the distance, at the throat of the station, the massive portal shimmered in the light that struggled to penetrate the thick, armored glass skylights lining the roof of the building. He looked around, surprised at how close it felt, and realized the windows and enormous doors, normally open to allow the air to circulate, were shut. With the windows closed the huge ceiling fans, powered by waterwheels from the nearby river, struggled to lift the oppressive humidity from the engines steaming gently at their platforms.

The sound of the bells tolling in the distance, which he had noticed as soon as he stepped off the train, was starting to fade, and he straightened carefully, trying not to trigger a fresh surge of vertigo.

"Are you all right?" Nedo asked worriedly.

"I think so. The portal must have shaken me up more than usual. What's with the bells though? I don't remember any last time I was here."

"Bells?" Nedo put his head on his side to listen before shaking his head. "No, I don't think we've got any."

"Oh." Arnold concentrated but all he could hear now was the steady ticking of the clock that seemed to have become his constant companion. "Well whatever it was it's gone now."

"Did you want to sit down?"

"No, I'm OK." Arnold adjusted his duffle bag over his shoulder and took a careful step to demonstrate.

Nedo gave him an uneasy glance, but nodded. "Let's get outside; at least there might be a breeze."

"So what's with the lockdown?"

Nedo looked around, puzzled, then shrugged. "No idea," he admitted as led them past security and the series of concrete bunkers built into the walls of the station. Once outside Nedo looked around sourly. "Ah, home. Welcome to the arse end of the Empire."

"It's not that bad," Arnold told him, although the humidity seemed just as bad as it had been inside. Low, heavy clouds weren't helping, and he nodded to the four soldiers sweltering in their thick, black woolen uniforms as they stood guard at the entrance to the station.

"Flies, sand, and squalor. I can't imagine anywhere worse," Nedo retorted.

"Compared to Etu, it's almost paradise."

"Oh come on," Nedo protested. "Etu hasn't got any flies."

"Only because the midges and mosquitoes ate them all."

"I still don't think it's as bad as you make out."

Arnold conceded the point with shrug. "Perhaps not. But this place isn't as bad as you make out either."

Nedo blew a raspberry. "Compared to the Mainline it's the pits."

"Ah yes, civilisation. Telephones, running water, restaurants . . ."

"Shoe shops," Nedo offered.

Arnold considered his now badly scuffed Armani pumps. "Shoe shops," he agreed looking back up and giving his cousin a smile. "So, how are we going to get to the Palace?"

"Walk?" Nedo suggested.

Arnold glanced up at the high limestone wall enclosing the top of the steep hill on the far side of the river. "Well, I'm game."

"Me and my big mouth." Nedo sighed.

"If you'd wanted a pedicab you should have said," Arnold said, hoisting his duffle bag higher onto his shoulder. "But when we're back you owe me a new pair of shoes."

"Perhaps, we should take a pedicab," Nedo said looking hopefully at the rank on the far side of the empty plaza.

"Too late." Arnold laughed, starting down the road.

When the building housing the portal had been built thirty years ago it had been well outside the city's limits. Over time, the city had spread out to engulf it and the station was now surrounded on all sides by a low sprawl of red brick warehouses and shops. The streets were broad and treeless, and Arnold could feel the sweat soaking into his shirt well before they reached the river.

At the foot of the broad marble steps that led up onto the main bridge across the river, Arnold paused to look back up the road.

"It's a bit quiet," he remarked. Last time he visited the streets had been thronged with people. Now they were almost deserted except for the small groups of youths loitering on each corner. The youths suspiciously watched the two cousins as they made their way down the street. "Is anything on?"

He gave a wave to the nearest group of youths in their white cotton shifts and trousers stained yellow with sweat and the coal smoke that seemed to bathe the city in a perpetual haze. The group pointedly ignored the gesture.

"Not that I know about," Nedo said.

At the top of the steps Arnold paused to catch his breath. Luckily the main bridge was lined with shops, and once they'd stepped into the shade of the first building he immediately started to feel more comfortable. He wasn't looking forward to the walk up to the palace though. And there was no chance of catching a pedicab from here.

While not exactly crowded, the bridge didn't look as deserted as the rest of the city. Hardly surprising, Arnold thought, given that it was one of only two bridges to cross the river — unless you wanted to take the ferry, or one of the small scurry boats available for hire.

Threading their way through the shoppers, Nedo paused at the entrance to a small bar they had frequented a couple of times on their last visit. "Drink?" he asked hopefully.

"Good idea," Arnold said, dumping his duffle bag on the ground and settling himself on a stool near the window. "I'll have a small beer, thanks."

Nedo made a face but went to get their orders.

At the sound of Arnold's voice one of the men nursing a drink at the bar turned round, and seeing Arnold frowned and leaned across to mutter something to his neighbor. Arnold raised an eyebrow as his neighbor in turn drew their arrival to the attention of his neighbor. He watched the news travel down the bar away from him.

"So what's going on?" Arnold asked, when Nedo had returned with their drinks.

Nedo shrugged. "I haven't the foggiest. Mama didn't mention anything in her letter."

Arnold held a pound coin up between his fingers and waved the server over with it. "Rietta, isn't it?" he asked the young waitress.

"Yes, sir," she said doubtfully at being recognized. "Can I do anything for you?"

"I hope so," Arnold said. "Is today a holiday of some sort?"

"No sir," she said, surprised.

"It just it seemed very quiet on the way over here from the portal."

She looked around uncomfortably, and lowered her voice. "It's the Charterists. They've announced a ban against allowing any goods through the Portal."

"Oh? Is there a reason?"

"It's the increase in taxes."

Arnold looked at Nedo. "Taxes?"

Nedo shook his head and shrugged.

"And how much have taxes gone up?" Arnold asked the waitress.

"Twenty-three percent."

"Well I can understand why they would be unhappy then," he said with a smile, and placed a couple of coins on her tray. "Please put this on the bar."

"Of course, sir."

"Come on, Nedo," Arnold said, downing his beer.

Nedo gave him a cold look, but swallowed his beer and followed him outside. "What was that about?" he demanded.

"I just thought it might stir things up a bit."

"And just how did you remember that waitress's name . . . Riella wasn't it?"

"Rietta. I just think it's important to know the name of pretty women."

"Arnold, you can be such a tosser sometimes," Nedo told him with a laugh as they headed off the bridge and up the hill.

"Really," Arnold said surprised. "Well there you are. That's why I need you around. I need someone to tell me when I'm being a tosser."

Nedo rolled his eyes and paused for a moment. "Are you sure you don't want a pedicab?" he asked, eyeing the steep climb still in front of them.

"And where are we going to find one of those?" Arnold asked. "Come on, we're just out of shape. By the end of the week we'll be running up and down here without raising a sweat."

"Speak for yourself," Nedo said reluctantly straightening his shoulders.

CHAPTER TWELVE

Louisville — Dontfrey
October 1979 (95AE)

"Anything wrong?" Donald asked, as Rajko waved away the waiting customs officer and led him past security and outside to where two troopers were waiting for them, their horses fidgeting in the cool.

"Why do you ask?" Rajko said.

"The uniform." Rajko was wearing Dontfrey's black field uniform with its silver facings. "And there was a one hour delay on the other side of the portal while we were waiting for some military supplies to get moved through ahead of us."

"Nothing to worry about," Rajko said, helping Donald to hitch his bag behind his saddle. "There's some minor unrest in the city and we're just taking precautions."

Donald nodded at the sentries in full combat gear standing guard at the entrance. "More precautions?"

Rajko gave a wry smile. "I'll explain everything once we get to the Palace."

The streets leading down to the river seemed unusually quiet. Groups of shirtless youth in long baggy cotton pants eyed them sullenly from the far side of the street as Rajko turned down towards the bridge that led to the Palace, but made no effort to interfere with their progress.

Once across the bridge it was a stiff climb up the hill to the high limestone wall that enclosed the Palace and the main barracks, as well as the several acres of parkland behind it that covered the top of the hill. Despite the hour the main gates to the Palace were closed, and they had to wait for them to be opened before they could enter.

Precautions indeed, Donald thought as the gates closed behind them with a heavy thud.

Dismounting in front of the Palace, a sprawling affair of red, yellow, and black marble, Donald was surprised to see Arnold coming down the steps. He looked as if he'd gone native with his long, gray tunic and off-white baggy cotton pants.

"Arnold," Donald called, attracting his attention.

"Hi Donald. Rajko."

Rajko acknowledged his cousin with a curt nod.

"What's with the clothes?" Donald asked.

"Just trying to fit in. You might have noticed the natives seem a little restless, and we're not exactly the most popular people around here."

"So what are you doing here? I wasn't expecting to see you for a while."

"We. . . ran into a little difficulty in New York. Nedo wanted to come home for a visit anyway, so he persuaded me to come with him. There's a method of glazing the natives use. I wanted to check it out."

"How's the commune going?"

"Good," Arnold's face suddenly animated. "The shop's made a couple of sales. We might even make a profit next quarter."

"I bet that will disappoint you."

"Of course," Arnold said with a smile.

"Donald!" it was Margaret. She was wearing the jeans, blouse, and embroidered leather vest she normally wore at home, her long, red hair pulled back into a single braid.

"Hi Margaret," he said, giving her a kiss. "I got here."

"So I see."

"I've got to take him up to see Papa, sis," Rajko said.

"I'll see you when you're out."

"I'll catch you later, Arnold," Donald said.

"Sure."

"So what's this about?" Donald asked Rajko as he was led upstairs to his uncle's office.

"Nothing. Papa just wanted to see you when you got here."

Stranger and stranger, Donald thought. This was definitely not the holiday he had expected.

His uncle's office was a large, airy room with windows that overlooked the red brick city and river below. "How's the family?" his uncle asked, waving them to towards the conference table in the corner. The Continental Leader was also in uniform, which was highly unusual; he normally preferred civilian garb.

"Good. I saw Conrad a couple of weeks ago and he said everyone was all right. Arnold might know more than me."

"Ah, yes, Arnold," his uncle said, his voice indicating how little he thought of his nephew. There was a pause. "Rajko told you about the trouble we're having?"

"A little. I certainly didn't notice many smiles when we were riding up here."

Rajko echoed the statement with a tight grin.

"The Charterists have been stirring up the people with talk of self-determination. Self-determination!" his uncle snorted. "When we arrived they were a bunch of peasants scratching a living from the Mississippi; now look at them, rulers of an entire continent."

"Are these Charterists dangerous?"

"Yes," Rajko said.

"No," his uncle said at the same time.

Rajko shifted uneasily in his seat.

"They know what would happen to them if there was trouble," his uncle continued.

"I'm not sure they care," Rajko said. "This issue with taxes has really stirred them up."

"Taxes?" Donald asked.

"We had to raise the tax on property and salt again," Rajko said.

His father frowned. "And what else could I do? It was a direct order from the World Leader."

"If he didn't waste so much he wouldn't need to raise so much," Rajko said sourly. "I've got no idea where he's spending it; none of it's coming back here."

"Rajko," his father said warningly.

Rajko glowered. "It doesn't really matter does it? He's created a problem and we have to solve it. Assuming we can't rely on the militia, we've got less than two thousand troops to try and hold down a population of several million."

"Two thousand, so what — two Battlegroups?" Donald said. "That should be enough to hold the capital."

Rajko shook his head. "That's for the whole continent. There's only about six hundred stationed here."

Donald winced. "And what's wrong with the militia?"

His uncle frowned. "We had to cut their pay last year. And some of the officers we've been getting from Foochow seem . . ."

"Culturally insensitive," Rajko offered.

His father acknowledged the suggestion with a nod.

"Six hundred is definitely not enough for any sort of trouble," Donald said. "You're going to have to ask for more troops."

"That's just what I've been saying," Rajko pointed out.

"I know and I've tried," his father said. "But all I get back from Miro is a lecture on how much it costs to hire Mainline troops."

"A revolt is going to be even more expensive," Rajko pointed out. "He'll miss out on the tax we raise for a couple of years, he'd have to explain to the Council what happened, and he'd still have to pay for the Mainline troops to put it down."

His father sighed. "I'll talk to his envoy again. We might be able to save some money if he transfers in some of his own household troops, though they'd probably take too long to get here if he has to move them from Foochow. A couple of months at least, and everything will be over by then, one way or another."

"Did you want to pack the two girls off to Etu?" Donald asked, referring to the youngest of his cousins. "I'm sure my parents would be happy to see them again."

His uncle shook his head. "Thanks for the offer, but they're safe here for the moment. This Palace could hold off a full Battlegroup for a couple of days, so I'm not worried about an unarmed rabble. I will try again with the World Leader though."

***

The next day, with the news that Miro had finally agreed to supply two additional Battlegroups, Margaret decided to take Donald out to her farm.

The farm was a good hour's ride north of the city, following the river, so with their escort of two troopers keeping a discreet distance behind them they left early in the morning.

"So what's so important you've got to drag me all the way out here to show me?" Donald asked, looking out over the river as he settled into the early morning ride.

The river, broad and shallow at this point in its travel to join the Mississippi, and running low because of the late summer, was covered with lilies, their heavy fragrance scenting the air even as far as the road. A shoal of herring disturbed the surface of the water in the center of the river. Suddenly the shadow of a large catfish, weaving its way through the lilies, attracted Donald's attention and he wondered if he'd be able to borrow a rod from Rajko.

"Beets."

"Beets?" Donald said, his attention abruptly yanked back to his cousin.

"You know, fodder beet, beetroot, sugar beet, I've even got some chard in as well. They're looking quite promising at the moment."

"Sounds riveting," he said, and grinned.

"Well if I can persuade the local farmers to take them up, we'll be able to increase the productivity of local farms by at least fifty percent," Margaret said without umbrage.

"Not bad," Donald admitted.

"Is it all right if I ask a question?"

"Of course."

"You've been awfully quiet since you arrived, is anything wrong?"

"No, nothing."

She looked at him quizzically for a moment. "So who is she?"

He raised an eyebrow. "What makes you think it's anyone at all?"

"Come on, give," Margaret said, refusing to be diverted. "Who is she?"

Donald smiled, accepting the inevitable. "Her name's Matija. She's the daughter of one of the professors at the university."

"Pretty?"

"Very."

"So tell. How did you meet her?"

The rest of the trip was spent with Margaret grilling Donald about Matija, and it wasn't until they reached the farm, and there was no one to meet them, that Donald finally paid any notice to how quiet the road had been.

As they turned in through the gate Margaret let out a very unladylike "merde" and slid out of her saddle.

"What?" Donald demanded, following her over to where she stared angrily at the field.

"It hasn't been watered," she said, gesturing at the wilting crop. "Where is everyone?"

Donald looked around, and as he did he felt the hairs on the back of his neck start to rise as he realized the farm was totally deserted. Behind them he noticed their two escorts loosening the tops of their rifle holsters.

"We better head back," Donald said.

"Not till we've watered the crops," Margaret said.

"Margaret."

Margaret stared at him defiantly.

"How long will it take?" Donald asked finally.

"Half an hour."

Donald had an idea it might take longer than that, but it was obvious Margaret had no intention of leaving without watering the crops, and he couldn't see how they could force her. "All right."

"It will be faster with four," Margaret said.

Donald looked back at their escort. "Three," he said.

"Fine," Margaret said, starting for the first sluice gate.

"Trooper, you're with us," Donald said to the closer of the two, before following Margaret to where she was struggling to lift the first sluice gate. "What do we need to do?" he asked.

"Just lift these, and once the water has filled the furrows to the end you drop them back."

"Sounds easy enough."

It might have sounded easy enough but it was hard work, and by the time they'd finished Donald was exhausted. Checking his watch he was not surprised to find two hours had passed. "We better head back now."

Margaret looked out over the plants, already reviving, and nodded her agreement.

They were about half way home when Margaret suddenly reined in and pointed at the cloud of dirty smoke rising up into the clear blue sky over the city. "What's that?"

"A fire?" Donald suggested.

"It's a bloody big fire then. It wasn't there a moment ago."

There was a dull thud from the direction of the city, quickly followed by another, and then a moment later what sounded like small firecrackers on the eighth of July. Donald's heart sank — that didn't sound good at all.

"That's shooting," Margaret said.

"It looks like it's coming from the armory," one of the escort offered.

Margaret glared at him, as though he'd been responsible.

"We better get back as quickly as we can," Donald said. "If they've tried to seize the armory we could be in a lot of trouble. Do either of you have a spare weapon?" he asked their two escorts.

Wordlessly one of the escort offered him a carbine.

"Margaret," Donald said, holding it out to her.

"No thanks Donald. I'm already armed," she said pulling a machine pistol with a drum magazine out of the roll behind her saddle.

"Fine, let's get a move on."

The smart canter they set quickly covered the distance back to the Palace. The roads remained deserted, but there was no break from the sound of small arms in the distance. By the time they reached the Palace dense plumes of black smoke were rising from the city in three locations.

The palace's central courtyard was a bedlam of noise and confusion as they rode in.

"What's going on?" Donald asked a Group Leader struggling to tighten the cinch on his horse. Behind him the rest of his Troop appeared to be preparing to ride out.

"There's been an attempt at the armory," he was told. The officer suddenly recognized him. "Leader Clemhorn?"

"Yes."

"Good, we were just going out to look for you. Troop Leader," he yelled to another officer. "The first group's just come back, but we still need the second one."

"The second one?" Margaret asked.

"Your brother and his cousin; we think they were in the town when everything started."

"Where's my father?" Margaret asked.

"In the Command Center."

"This way," Margaret told Donald, already starting up the steps.

They found her father studying a huge map set up over a table with two senior officers and Rajko. Rajko waved them in. "Have Nedo and Arnold returned yet?" he asked.

"Not yet," Margaret said. "It looked like the first party was going out just as we were coming in. What's happened?"

"The shit's hit the fan," Rajko said pointing to a large map of North America on the wall covered in red and blue pins. "There have been attacks all over the continent. The red pins are units presently under attack. The blue are units which are quiet at the moment." Even as he spoke one of those working on the maps removed a blue pin and replaced it with a red.

"And here?" Donald asked.

"They attacked the armory and managed to ransack it before we could mount a counterattack. We've still got the portal, and we're holding both bridges so the Palace is safe, but we've lost most of the city. Father has already requested aid from the Mainline. All we have to do now is hold on until help arrives."

"How long?" Margaret asked.

"Thirty-six, forty-eight hours? You better report to your unit," he told her. "I'll make sure you know when there's word on Nedo."

She nodded and left them.

He looked at Donald. "Father's declared martial law, so I'm afraid you're being called up. I don't suppose you brought a uniform?"

Donald shook his head.

"I'll try and find you one then, and in the meantime you better stick close to me. I just wish I knew where Arnold and Nedo were."

***

By eight that night the earlier intensity of most of the fighting had died down, except for around the portal where the insurgents seemed to be concentrating their efforts. Donald, now wearing one of Rajko's old uniforms, was putting the final touches to a SitRep for the Continental Leader, when one of the patrols finally returned with the news they'd been waiting for.

"Donald."

Donald looked up from the report to see Rajko. "What?" The high collar of the loaned uniform he was wearing was even more uncomfortable than the Clemhorn version.

"One of the patrols found Uijam. He was with Arnold and Nedo when they disappeared. He's in the hospital."

"Let me just get rid of this report," Donald said.

Uijam was lying in a bunk being attended to by a doctor when Rajko and Donald arrived. He looked a mess, both his lip and eyebrow were split, and thick bruises covered his torso and face. His hair had been roughly hacked off and his scalp painted purple to mark him as a collaborator. Despite his injuries he struggled to rise as Rajko appeared.

"Don't get up," Rajko told him. "What happened?"

"We were looking for vases, in the Shevs district, near the Temple. There were about ten of them, armed with knives. There wasn't anything we could do." He winced as the doctor prodded his abdomen. "They put us in separate rooms. Roughed me up pretty bad, called me a traitor. Bastards." He spat over the side of the bed.

"And my brother?"

"I don't know, Leader. I didn't see them after we were taken into the house. I could hear them, but . . . it sounded bad."

"How did you get away?" Donald asked.

"When they finished with me they just threw me out on the street. Said it was a warning. I think they were expecting me to be strung up by the street gangs. I managed to make it down to the river. That's where the patrol found me."

"Can you get us back to the house?"

Uijam nodded weakly.

"You're not well enough," the doctor started to protest.

"Uijam?" Rajko asked.

"I can manage."

"I need to speak to my father," Rajko announced.

Donald followed him out of the room. "It could be a trap," he warned.

Rajko shrugged. "What choice do we have? I'll be back in a moment."

Donald waited uncomfortably until his cousin returned, trying to stay out of the way of the doctors frantically trying to cope with the stream of wounded returning from the battle across the river.

"Well?" he demanded when Rajko finally reappeared.

"Papa's given us the Kommandos. There's only a Troop, but they'll be waiting for us down at the jetty."

***

The collar of his uniform pinched Donald's neck as he tried to concentrate on keeping his strokes quiet, and in time to the others in the boat. This was hardly the holiday he was expecting, he thought. A thick layer of mist had descended over the river, muffling the sound of gunfire from the direction of the portal. They'd been lucky the insurgents hadn't managed to seize any of the artillery, and he winced at the thought of what that would have meant.

"Rest oars," came the hushed order.

The muffled sound of oars stilled as the boat glided on over the river's millpond surface. On either side the two other boats of the Kommandos threw up patches of phosphorous from their bows, black uniforms disappearing into the mist. The stink of dead fish seemed stronger now. Suddenly Donald felt the grate of shingle under the keel, and the boat jerked to a stop. Immediately the Kommandos were over the side and racing up the small beach to take shelter behind the low bank.

Donald, clutching his carbine, dashed up the beach after Rajko. Reaching the low bank he found himself next to Rajko, Uijam and the Kommandos' Troop Leader.

"Do you know where the house is from here?" the Troop Leader asked.

Uijam pointed. "About two blocks that way."

"You're sure?" Rajko asked.

"Yes, Leader."

"Right, Gornda, keep your squad here to keep an eye on the boats. We may need them in a hurry," the Troop Leader said. "Deskae, you've got the flank. Let's move." With a minimum of noise the Kommandos moved cautiously up the road.

Donald sensed Rajko's impatience with the pace the Force Leader set, and he would have preferred to move quicker as well, but there was no point in rushing into what could still be a trap. Luckily, they reached the corner of the block the house was on without being discovered, their advance covered by the strengthening fog.

Donald peered round the corner at the three-story house, two down from them, with purple curtains in its windows. There was a single guard sitting on the stoop, cleaning his fingernails with a stiletto. Donald's stomach was a tight ball, but when he looked down at his hand he was relieved to see no tremor to betray him.

A muffled shot from a sniper's silenced rifle jerked his attention back to the sentry, who collapsed slowly into the street, a dark stain on the wall behind where he'd been sitting. Two Kommandos dashed forward to take up position next to the door, carbines at the ready. At a nod from one the other went in through the door. A moment later he reappeared and waved the rest of the squad in. With Deskae's squad forming a defensive cordon around the house, Rajko and Donald followed the Force Leader into the building.

The entrance hall was lined with heavy velvet tapestries which showed pornographic scenes in explicit detail that left nothing to the imagination. Most, Donald was shocked to see, showed men in various positions of buggery. The Kommandos moved quietly, but efficiently, from room to room, three men covering each other at all times, but finding no one.

The ground floor clear, they met at the foot of the staircase.

"Upstairs?" the Force Leader asked.

Rajko nodded.

The first floor passage also appeared deserted, but as they arrived on the landing Donald heard voices from the floor above. He pointed upstairs with one finger. The Force Leader nodded, and signaled for one of the Kommandos to stay. He led the rest cautiously up the stairs. Three rooms led off the corridor, which was once again deserted. The sound of loud laughter from the front room, however, indicated that at least one of them was occupied.

"Remember, no shooting unless you have to," Rajko warned them quietly.

The Kommandos nodded, and Donald pulled back to allow them to move down the corridor. Three troopers took up position on each door while Donald, his mouth dry with anxiety, moved closer to Rajko.

"Now!" Rajko whispered.

The trooper closest to each door slammed out with the butt of his carbine, and as the door swung open jumped aside, allowing the one behind him to move into the room, carbine up ready to fire. As he moved forward he was followed by the third, who took up position by the side of the door. Those inside appeared completely taken by surprise, but as Donald followed Rajko into the front room there was an explosion of fire from the room next to them. A moment later Donald heard the sound of someone moaning.

"Cleared," a voice shouted.

Donald turned his attention back to the three men sitting at a small coffee table in front of him. There were glasses and empty bottles on the table, and the room was thick with cigarette smoke. A large bed took up the center of the room. Arnold was tied face down on it, naked, his back covered in cigarette burns, and a hatch-mark pattern of shallow cuts that oozed blood. Deeper cuts marked his arms, and blood had pooled between his legs. Beneath the blood, deep, purple bruises covered his skin.

"Against the wall, now!" Rajko commanded, his carbine emphasizing the order. The table fell against the floor as the three jumped to obey.

One of the Kommandos had started to cut the bonds that held Arnold to the bed and Donald went around the bed to help him.

"Arnold?" he said anxiously, but his brother's eyes were worryingly blank.

"Leader." It was a Kommando from one of the other rooms.

"Yes?" Rajko said.

"Your brother, Leader."

"I'll look after Arnold," Donald told him. "Go."

"Someone get this scum downstairs," Rajko ordered, as he left to see to his brother.

Arnold let out a soft moan. "It's all right," Donald said, patting his shoulder. He had never felt so powerless in his life. Where was the medic?

Arnold tried to say something, but even when Donald put his ear closer to his mouth he couldn't understand.

"Everything's going to be all right," Donald said reassuringly. He looked round for his brother's clothes, but there was no sign of them in the room.

"Help me get this round him," he said to the Kommando who was still standing there, watching, as he pulled the sheet free.

There were some shots from outside and Donald froze. Had they been discovered? When nothing else happened he returned to wrapping the sheet round Arnold. They had just got him to his feet when the Force Leader appeared.

"Can you get him downstairs?" he asked. "We need to leave."

They were at the bottom of the stairs when Rajko clattered down behind them. "How's Arnold?" he asked.

Donald looked at the blood staining the sheet where it touched his brother's skin and shrugged. "Nedo?" he asked.

"Dead." Rajko's voice was flat, his face emotionless

The medic appeared behind Rajko and took over from Donald, allowing him to follow Rajko as he moved to inspect the three prisoners they'd captured.

One of them spat at him, and was rewarded by a backhanded slap from a Kommando.

"Dog!" the prisoner said, holding his face. The trooper moved to slap him again but Rajko shook his head, stopping him.

"Shoot them," he said simply.

The Kommando looked stunned.

"Rajko," Donald started.

"My brother's dead. We can't take them with us. Do it!"

The Kommando raised his carbine, and three quick shots immediately followed each other. The Force Leader ran into the room, carbine at the ready. "What happened?" he demanded.

"I just had the prisoners shot. My brother will be ready to transport in a moment."

The Force Leader looked for a moment as though he would say something, but finally just nodded. "We need to hurry."

Rajko nodded and went back upstairs to help bring his brother down.

The medic was still strapping Arnold into his stretcher. "How is he?" Donald asked, squatting down to take Arnold's hand.

"He's lost a lot of blood," the medic said, as he pulled the last strap tight. "I'll be happier when I can rig up an IV, but he'll make it."

There was the noise of boots on the stairs and Rajko and the rest of the Kommandos appeared, Nedo strapped into a stretcher, a sheet over his face.

"Let's go," Rajko said.

They started back to the boats at a trot, Deskae's squad holding a loose skirmish line behind them. The fog had continued to thicken while they were inside, and visibility was down to a couple of yards by the time they reached the river. There was an anxious five minutes as they waited for a couple of stragglers but finally they were climbing onto the boats and pushing off for the opposite bank.

Back at the Palace, Donald just had time to make see Arnold admitted into the hospital before he was called into a staff meeting. He was one of the last to arrive, and nodded apologetically to his uncle as he took a seat at the back of the room. His uncle looked several years older than he that morning, and Donald wondered how he was coping.

"Leaders," the Continental Leader uncle said, calling the meeting to order. As the quiet buzz of conversation died away his uncle rubbed his forehead tiredly. Then straightening his shoulders he faced those crowded into the small meeting room. "Unfortunately the latest news we have just received word from Gaagii is that the garrison there has surrendered. It would appear the rebels were able to capture the artillery barracks without resistance."

Donald's heart sank. Gaagii was only thirty miles away, and with artillery they could simply blow the portal apart. If they lost the portal it could be weeks, perhaps months before the Mainline could reestablish a new one large enough for the reinforcements they needed to restore control.

"How long before they get the guns here?" It was the Battlegroup Leader in charge of the defense at the portal. His uniform was stained with sweat and a heavy five o'clock shadow emphasized his exhaustion.

"Six, maybe eight hours? I've asked Force Leader Wattan to summarize the situation for us."

Force Leader Wattan cleared her throat uneasily as she took the podium, and gestured at the two maps behind her. One showed the North American continent, while the other was a large scale map of the capital.

"As you are all undoubtedly aware, the rebels launched simultaneous attacks on most of our garrisons across the continent. At Gaagii, Taren, and Tapco they were successful, capturing both the city and the garrison. At Sewati and Broken Arrow the attack was shattered and the rebel groups destroyed. The situation is not as clear-cut at most other locations, with garrisons tending to retreat into their forts, leaving the surrounding city in the hands of the rebels, much as what happened here. Most of the militia appear to have opted to wait things out."

"Thank the gods," Rajko muttered under his breath.

Donald nodded; at least they weren't actively helping the rebels — yet.

"The situation here, however, is made more complex by the location of the portal in the city, separated from both the armory and the main garrison here at the Palace." She indicated both on the map. "We continue to hold both bridges and the portal itself, but no longer have any effective control in the city. It would appear that the rebels' goal has been either to control, or to destroy the portal and they have launched almost continuous attacks since capturing the armory. Their losses have been high, however, with over 500 estimated killed or wounded."

"And our losses?" someone asked.

"76 dead, 195 wounded."

That was almost a third of their strength. Donald could feel a headache starting at the back of his head.

"The situation at the portal is precarious to say the least. We have been pushed back into the portal building itself, and if the rebels bring in artillery it won't last longer than five minutes. The building was never built to withstand artillery fire."

"If we survive that's something we'll undoubtedly look into remedying," Donald's uncle said dryly. "What's the latest ETA on the first Mainline Battlegroup?"

"Thirteen hours," Force Leader Wattan replied.

"Can we delay the arrival of the rebels from Gaagii? We only need five hours."

The Force Leader shook her head. "Our scouts report they have close to 2,000 troops, most with militia training. Even if we stripped the Palace they'd still outnumber us twenty to one."

A Battlegroup Leader at the back of the room raised his arm to be recognized. At a nod from Donald's uncle he rose to his feet. The Leader's black uniform was immaculate, and his peaked hat was tucked neatly under his arm. Donald recognized him as the World Leader Miro's envoy at the Palace. "Leaders, I must inform you that the World Leader has authorized the use of nerve gas."

Several stared at him, horrified.

"And civilian deaths?" demanded Rajko.

"Will be restricted to the area of the bombardment."

"Unless the wind shifts," someone muttered under their breath.

Madness, Donald thought. "You can't do that," he whispered to Rajko, appalled.

"Father, we can't," Rajko said. "We only have enough antidote for the regular troops. It would be murder."

"Perhaps I phrased that badly," the liaison officer said. "The World Leader has ordered the use of gas! May I point out that without the gas we cannot prevent the rebels being reinforced, and we will lose the portal. If we lose that we will lose control of the continent. It will take us years to recover, and the cost would be enormous. If we use the gas we will be able to hold until reinforcements arrive. The World Leader was quite definite."

"What you're proposing is both ethically, and legally, wrong. To use nerve gas you need the approval of the First Leader," Donald protested, coming to his feet.

"Ah yes, Leader Clemhorn, isn't it?"

Donald nodded.

"Well, Leader, you're a long way from your own line and we do things differently on Dontfrey. No fussing around native sensitivities. However, I will point out that article 4-8 of the C-TE Charter specifically authorizes the use of all and any necessary means to restore order at a time of insurrection."

Donald bridled but Rajko's hand on his arm was hauling him back down.

"I must emphasize that the World Leader is not proposing a wholesale bombardment of the city," he continued. "Only of those areas presently exhibiting resistance."

Donald looked at his uncle. For a minute the Continental Leader simply stared out over the room, his face ashen, before giving a short, abrupt shrug. "We have our orders then." He glanced towards Donald and Rajko, then looked down at his papers. "Force Leader Wattan, perhaps you could bring us up to date with regard to the Palace's gas stocks."

***

In the cold, bleak light of a new day Donald looked down on the city from the Palace parapets. Laid out before him, the city appeared deceptively peaceful. The air smelled fresh and clean, and only the occasional sound of gunfire, like small firecrackers in the distance, could be heard from the direction of the portal.

Turning around to head downstairs to join the unit he'd been seconded to he noticed a smudge of what might be dust on the horizon. One of the sentries had also noticed it, and a short time later a group of officers clattered up the stairs to look. That would be the rebels from Gaagii, Donald thought.

Just then the first of the howitzers on the terrace below opened up, and a moment later the fall of the first shell was marked by a plume of thick yellow smoke near the portal. Nerve gas was both colorless and odorless, but it had long been combined with smoke to indicate its fall. Donald felt almost physically sick at the thought of what it was already doing to those in the city below.

Without waiting for the next howitzer to fire, Donald headed downstairs. He found his unit assembling in the courtyard, and quietly reported to the Troop Leader he'd been assigned to. She set him to double-checking the fit of the gas masks and hazard suits everyone had been issued with. The courtyard was eerily quiet, with no hint of the nervous conversation that normally presaged battle. Outside the continuous firing of the howitzers continued to sound the city's death knell. Finally, however, the dull thud of howitzers fell silent and the gate was opened.

Across the bridge the thick lenses of Donald's mask cast the city into a swirling fog of yellow murk. A place where people died, not gently, but in jerking, spasmodic convulsions. Where masked men loomed out of the fog like ancient devils, killing all who faced them, though more often out of mercy than in hate.

Of course there was resistance. The gas had not fallen evenly and where they could the rebels fought back, but resistance was limited and death followed quickly in the gas's swirling path. Soon enough, as resistance petered out to its dismal end; the city had become a charnal house for its dead.

They were retracing their steps to the Palace when Donald stumbled across a woman crouching by the side of the road. She was cradling her six-month-old baby in her arms. Vomit stained the front of the woman's blouse. Wordlessly the woman held the baby up to him, her eyes pleading for help. Donald's legs seemed powerless to take him away from her, and all he could do was stare at her. Abruptly he was shouldered aside by the Troop Leader.

"Keep moving," she ordered gruffly. He had taken fewer than five steps when two single shots rang out in quick succession. Startled he swung back. A trooper stood over the dead body of the young mother, now sprawled haphazardly in the ditch next to her child. Donald's guts heaved, and ripping his mask off he retched up what little remained in his stomach.

He felt a hand on his shoulder. It was the Troop Leader. "Put your mask on."

Donald wiped his mouth against the back of his hand and complied. The Troop Leader looked at the trooper who had performed the execution and shrugged.

"What else can we do?" she asked.

"It shouldn't have been done in the first place," Donald said.

Suddenly he felt a tightness in his chest and his eyes blurred. He was hot, sweating, and frantically he tried to find the antidote in its auto-injector but it was already too late. His arms jerked, and as his legs collapsed under him he could hear the Leader calling frantically for the medic. He tried to pull his mask off but there was someone there, restraining him as he heaved again, and again. Then he felt the prick of the needle and a moment later lost consciousness.

CHAPTER THIRTEEN

Naisre — Mainline
October 1979 (95AE)

Arnold spasmed with remembered pain. His breathing was fast and irregular as he started to panic, hearing the laughter of those who captured them. There had been five of them, wrapping their sadism in the meager rag of their leader's call to arms. Arnold had begged for their lives, for Nedo's life, offering himself up in his place, but they had simply laughed, telling him there would be more than enough time for both of them. When they'd taken Nedo into the other room he'd had to listen to his cousin's screams until all that was left were the broken sobs and gasps coming from a throat ripped raw of any conscious thought. Then, in the end, there was only final, blessed silence.

For a time he hoped they had forgotten him, and he had rubbed his wrists raw, trying to pull loose of the ropes but then, finally they'd returned and it had been his turn. He had tried to be strong, but had still flinched at the first gentle, almost loving touch of a hand as it ran down his back, caressing his skin. He had screamed with shock at the sudden, agonizing pain of the lighted cigarette on his skin, then someone had laughed as the neck of a bottle was slowly run down his back until it reached his buttocks. With shame he remembered the abrupt thrust of the bottle against his anus, ripping his skin and shredding his resolve as he sobbed his powerlessness against the pain, and those who had captured him. And then the light had come, taking him, and for a time he had been safe.

As he slowly found himself drifting back to reality he heard someone calling his name. He thought he recognized the voice, but really he wasn't sure, and the effort was well beyond anything reasonable. For the first time in his life he seemed free to simply - be.

"How is he?" the voice asked.

The steady ticking of the clock filled the background, and Arnold wondered why they simply didn't take it away and let him sleep.

"Still comatose," a second voice replied. He didn't like that voice; too bossy, and he turned his mind from the talking, focusing on the steady beat of the clock, adjusting his breathing in time, in-out, in-out, until he drifted off to sleep.

It was the sound of the steady ticking of the clock that woke him, and for the first time he realized it was beating in time to his heart. Tick-tock, tick-tock. Something was happening. He concentrated, and felt the air thickening around him. As each beat pulsated through him, the pressure built until it felt as though he would implode. Abruptly the pressure eased and for a moment he was floating, weightless, before he felt the ground settle under his feet and his weight slowly return.

He was standing in a darkness so dense his eyes ached. Putting his hands out, he took a cautious step.

"I wouldn't do that if I were you," said a voice. It seemed to come from all around him, pulsating in time to the beating of his heart. "There might be a hole or something you could fall into."

"And is there?" He was surprised at how calm he sounded.

Silence answered him, the absence of any reply pressing down on him.

"Where am I?" Arnold asked finally. It seemed a safe question, non-threatening. But why would that worry him? he wondered. Instinctively though he realized that wherever he was it was unsafe — and that 'safe' was very important.

"You are here."

"That's not very helpful," Arnold pointed out.

"It's not supposed to be."

For a time he simply let the calm regularity of the clock's ticking absorb him, then finally he roused.

"Am I dead?" he asked.

"Not precisely. Or perhaps I should have said, that is still being decided. Did you want to be?"

"Is Nedo?"

"Dead? An interesting question. Not one I was expecting given your present . . . state. But to answer your question — yes. He is."

Arnold wasn't surprised, but in considering whether he now wanted to live, he didn't think he could. He had begun to consider that perhaps he wasn't exactly 'normal', according to society's standards. Too calm, too separated. Aware of society's norms, but not bound by them. But Nedo had grounded him, had helped him fit in, and without his cousin's calming presence he knew he would continue to drift further away from society's concept of normal.

"Without Nedo, no. I would prefer not to live."

"Then be thankful that the choice is not up to you."

Once again Arnold's attention became absorbed by the steady sound of the clock, the other patiently waiting until his concentration returned to his surroundings.

"Why am I here?" he asked after considering the question. It did seem strange, to say the least.

"That isn't the question you need to ask." The air throbbed in time with each syllable the voice pronounced.

Arnold considered the answer carefully. He had an idea that he wasn't here to ask a hundred questions and if he took too long, or asked too many questions this . . . whatever this might be, could come to an abrupt end, and in a way that wouldn't be to his benefit.

"What do you want of me?" he asked finally.

"That is the question." The air around him started to glow with a soft, golden light and he looked around him with interest, but there was no sign of the speaker.

"So what do you want of me?" he asked when the speaker seemed to have no intention of further explaining.

"Your life."

"And what do I get in exchange?" In the circumstances that seemed a perfectly logical question.

"The chance to be part of something larger. To be accepted for what you are."

This was really all he had been searching for all of his life; what Nedo had given him, until his death had ripped that anchor away.

"So what do I have to do?"

"Firstly you must find me. When you have done that the rest will be clear."

"And I find you — where?"

"In the quiet spaces between the cracks of time."

Oh that was so not useful, Arnold thought. But the light was increasing in intensity, indicating his time for questions might be coming to an end.

"But how do I recognize you?" he asked plaintively.

"You will know me by my deeds."

The voice stroked his mind, just the once in a soft caress, then between one breath and the next it was gone. As the light started to fade he realized he was, perhaps for the first time in his life, truly alone. And with that knowledge the memory Nedo's death came crashing down upon him, leaving him racked with sobs. Then as despair threatened to crush him completely, just for a moment he felt the merest hint of the other, and heard the soft whisper of a remembered promise.

CHAPTER FOURTEEN

Charleston — Mainline
October 1979 (95AE)

Donald paused at the top of the steps to catch his breath, the short walk from the airship's forward cabin already having exhausted him.

"Are you all right sir?" the steward asked, concerned.

Donald nodded, not trusting his voice. The doctors had assured him there would be no long-term consequences from the gas, although they had warned him that for the next month or so any sort of physical activity would exhaust him. He hadn't realized the exhaustion would be quite so — tiring.

Holding firmly to the handrail for support he started down the steps. He could feel the steward's eyes on his back but he was damned if he was going to ask for a wheelchair. By the time he got to the bottom, however, he was regretting the gesture.

The bus waited at the foot of the stairs to take them the short distance to the terminal. It was already full but someone immediately stood up and offered him a seat and he fell into it with a grateful nod, too exhausted to even look up to see who'd stood up for him.

His father was waiting for him inside the terminal. "You look terrible," the World Leader said with a worried frown. "How do you feel?"

"Terrible."

"Are you all right?"

"Just exhausted," Donald said, trying to sound reassuring. "The doctors said it might take another couple of weeks to fully recover."

"That's what we were told. Here, come and sit down. James, can you locate Donald's luggage?" his father asked his aide-de-camp.

"It's the green duffel bag," Donald said, as he allowed himself to be seated.

James nodded and headed off to see to his task.

"You're sure you're all right?" his father asked, lightly resting his hand on Donald's shoulder.

"Positive."

His father took the seat next to Donald. "Your mother sends her apologies. She didn't think she could leave Arnold at the moment."

"How is he?"

"A little better. It's going to take him a couple of months to recover physically. Psychologically though . . ." His father shrugged uncertainly.

"Did you get to Nedo's funeral?"

"Conrad did. He was the only one who could get there in time."

How was it?"

"How are any funerals?"

There was silence for a moment.

"Can I get you something to drink?" his father asked.

"A coffee please."

His father hoisted himself out of his seat. "White, no sugar?"

Donald nodded.

When his father came back the conversation drifted by mutual consent to Nedo, and the memory of when he'd been alive. Finally, however, as his father stared into his empty cup, the conversation trailed to a close.

"I suppose we'd better get you back to your flat," his father said finally.

Donald nodded, too exhausted to say anything.

The gas lamps were already lit, and dusk was fast approaching as the car drew up outside the entrance to Donald's flat. "Are you sure you don't need me to stay?" his father asked.

"I'll be fine," Donald said, trying to sound more reassuring than he felt. "The doctors gave me some tablets. I'll go straight to bed."

"I'll drop by tomorrow before I leave."

"Leave?" Donald said, surprised. "Where to?" He'd been hoping his father would be able to stay at least for a couple of days.

"I have to return to Naisre. It's the First Leader again."

"How is he?"

His father shook his head hopelessly. "It's only the transfusions that are keeping him alive."

"Thanks for meeting me," Donald said, as James opened the car door for him. "I'll see you tomorrow then."

"Take care, Donald."

James carried his bag up to the flat for him before, with a nod, heading back downstairs to the car.

The flat was cold and seemed very deserted without Kaito, and dropping his case next to the door, Donald turned the heating on before filling the kettle for a cup of tea. As the kettle boiled, however, he remembered there wasn't any milk, and cursed as he added a couple of extra spoonfuls of sugar to the cup. Taking the cup back into the living room he collapsed onto the chair next to the telephone.

Suddenly remembering that he hadn't told Matija he was back, he checked the clock on the mantel. Seven o'clock. Picking the phone up he dialed Matija's number.

Matija answered. "Maras residence."

"Matija, it's Donald." He could already feel himself starting to relax at the sound of her voice.

"Donald. Where are you? I heard about the fighting. I've been so worried."

She'd been worried; at least something good had come of it! "At the flat. I just got out of hospital."

"Hospital. What happened?"

"I got gassed. I'm fine now, but I couldn't phone you."

"Well, stay there, I'll be right over." There was a moment's pause. "What's your address?"

He told her, and she hung up before he could say anything.

Sipping his tea, he stretched out on the couch. He woke up with a jerk a quarter of an hour later, still holding the mug of now cold tea. He put it on the end table and sighed. He'd have to contact the university tomorrow, he thought glumly. Term had started four days ago but he didn't think he'd be up for classes for at least another week. The gods would know what the Dean would say. His father had told him he'd made sure they knew what was going on, but even so. . .

The doorbell rang and he hoisted himself out of the chair, muscles aching.

"What's wrong?" Matija demanded, seeing him leaning against the doorframe.

"Just tired," he said, allowing himself to be led back to the couch.

"Can I get you anything?"

"A cup of tea if you want to make it. Unfortunately there's no milk."

She draped her jacket over the back of a seat, and headed off to put the kettle on.

"So what happened?" she asked when she reappeared with two mugs. "I was worried sick when the news came in about what was happening on Dontfrey."

"I'm sorry, I'd have phoned if I could."

"How bad was it?"

For some reason those four simple words served as a key to unlock memories that Donald had tried to forget. He thought of the baby crying in its mother's arms, unable to understand what was happening as its skin blistered and boiled . . . its mother unable to help, vainly trying to protect it, and then the sharp crack of a bullet and the explosion of flesh. He found himself crying, unable to stop as the memories he'd suppressed came welling back. Somehow Nedo was all tangled up with it, and he just couldn't stop.

He couldn't remember how he got there, but Matija was rocking him gently in her arms when his sobs began to subside into hiccups. Embarrassed, he started to pull away but she tightened her arms, holding him there for a moment before releasing him.

"I won't ask again," she promised.

"Ask. I'll tell you one day, but not yet, it's all too fresh."

They looked at each other, uncertain where to go next, until she leaned forward and kissed him.

"What was that for?" he asked.

"I wanted to."

"I missed you, you know," he said, leaning forward to return the kiss.

He felt her hands on his chest. "Not tonight," she said. "You look like a feather would knock you over."

"Will you stay?" he asked, unable to argue her statement.

She studied his face, then nodded. "Come on, let's get you to bed," she said, offering him her hand to help him up.

***

The doorbell rang, dragging Donald from sleep. He opened his eyes to find Matija sleeping next to him, her hair spread over the pillow. She'd taken her shirt and skirt off last night before coming to bed, and her chemise clung to her skin. Sunlight spilled into the room, and Matija stirred at the sound of the doorbell, muttering to herself. He smiled as she opened her eyes to see him.

"Morning sleepyhead," he said.

She smiled back at him, the smile lighting up her entire face, and if the doorbell hadn't rung again he'd have taken advantage of the invitation in that smile. Unfortunately the real world was waiting to be let in.

"Matija," he said carefully. "I think it's my father."

Her eyes flew open in shock as she realized where she was.

"Can you get dressed while I hold him off?" he asked.

She nodded, and leaning forward he kissed her gently on the forehead.

Putting on his dressing gown he went to answer the door, stopping in the living room to pick up her jacket and return it to the bedroom. Matija was just getting out of bed and froze like a startled rabbit when he opened the door. He smiled reassuringly. "Your jacket," he said, holding it up to show her.

On returning to the front door he opened it to find James, his father's aide-de-camp, there.

"Leader," James said. "Your father's apologizes but he had to leave for the capital earlier than anticipated. He said he'd phone you tonight." A smart salute, and then spinning on his heel he was gone.

So what was that all about, Donald thought, closing the door after the aide. Oh well, he'd probably find out when his father called. "You don't have to worry," he told Matija, opening the bedroom door. "That was just a message from my father that he had to leave for Naisre."

Matija had already finished dressing, however, and was just slipping on her shoes. "I've got to go. I told my father I was staying at a friend's place and I should get home before he starts to worry."

“You didn’t say where you were staying here, did you?” he asked anxiously.

“No,” she said laughing at his tone. “A girlfriend’s.”

“When can I see you again?”

“Tonight,” she said. “Pick me up at seven.”

He followed her to the door, where she gave him a quick peck on the side of the cheek.

“Tonight,” she said with a laugh, evading his hands.

Donald leaned against the doorframe, watching her until she had disappeared down the stairs, before returning to bed. His sheets were filled with Matija’s perfume, and he fell asleep surrounded by her scent.

CHAPTER FIFTEEN

Fort Larsa — Etu Line
November 1979 (95AE)

As the paddle wheeler rounded the curve in the river Ivy leaned out over the edge of the rail to catch her first sight of the fort. Her fort. It had been a long trip, not least the two week stay at Fort Mungi as they waited for a boat, but it was almost over now.

She patted the breast top pocket of her new uniform, and the two letters from Jon, and the five from her mother, that had arrived with the boat. Her mother wrote every week. She had been embarrassed by them at the Academy, but had grown to appreciate them during her two long years at Fort Perusia as a link to happier times.

The new uniform felt stiff and uncomfortable, but at least Fort Mungi's tailor knew his stuff. She just wished it didn't look quite so . . . new. It was going to be bad enough taking over a new command without looking the complete newbie.

A raindrop stung her cheek, and worriedly she checked the sky. The forecast had been for rain today, but with luck it looked as though it might hold off for another hour or two.

The paddles slowed to a crawl as the steamer eased round the curve, and there was her new command.

The fort was situated on top of a small hill about five hundred yards from the river. The hill was covered by a billiard-smooth emerald lawn, cropped close by the sheep still grazing on it. At the foot of the hill, next to the river, sheltered a good-sized village of about twenty houses. She gave a low whistle of surprise at its size. The fort also looked more substantial than she had expected, with a stone-faced outer wall and deep ditch.

Gods, she hoped she was up to it.

The paddles reversed then stilled, and in the sudden silence the boat berthed with a gentle bump. Ivy felt someone standing behind her and turned to see Horsing, his uniform just as new as hers.

"Well, Sergeant. Looks like we finally got here."

He nodded silently.

A very young Squad Leader, about twelve or thirteen, was waiting on the pier, and as the gangplank was lowered stepped on board.

He looked around for a moment, then seeing her standing by the rail came over uncertainly. “Force Leader Clemhorn?” He seemed very serious and intent, as only the very young can be when entrusted with an adult task for the first time.

Ivy smiled reassuringly at him and nodded.

He snapped to attention and saluted. Ivy struggled to suppress a smile. She hadn’t seen a salute delivered with such. . . enthusiasm since she’d left the Academy.

“Acting Force Leader’s compliments. I am to escort you to the Fort.” He looked at the small bag at her feet. “Is that all your baggage?”

She nodded. “I lost the rest when the barge was attacked.”

“We heard of the attack. Was it bad?”

“Squad Leader!” the Sergeant barked.

The young Squad Leader snapped to attention.

“Thank you Sergeant,” Ivy said gently. She bent and picking up her bag handed it to the young officer. “Shall we go?”

They paused for a moment on the pier to allow Pecos to catch up with them, then followed the young Squad Leader along the graveled road that ran through the village and up the hill to the fort. The village, its houses all whitewashed wattle and daub, gave an overwhelming impression of Germanic neatness.

Pausing for a moment at the top of the hill to catch her breath, Ivy was caught by surprise at the beauty of the scene laid out below them, the river sweeping out into a broad curve around the headland. Behind them Ivy heard a bugle call parade and, turning back to the open gate, saw the Force forming up on the parade ground beyond.

Her Force, her fort! It raced in circles through her mind.

Suppressing the butterflies in her stomach she followed the Squad Leader through the gate and onto the parade ground where two of the fort’s three Troops waited for her. The Troops’ light blue uniforms formed a solid block of color in the center of the red, sawdust-pressed surface of the parade ground. Behind them a smaller block in the deeper blue of the aviators’ uniform marked out the fort’s three aircrew. Behind her she felt Sergeant Horsing and Pecos came to a halt.

The Troop Leader heading the parade, a slight woman with fair hair and piercing blue eyes, snapped to attention as Ivy came to a halt in front of her.

"Force Leader Clemhorn, welcome to Fort Larsa. I'm Troop Leader Daniels."

"Thank you Troop Leader," Ivy said, returning Daniels' salute. "I'm pleased to finally be here. A neat display," she said, indicating the parade, and wondering just how much practice it had taken to attain those very precise rows.

"Would the Force Leader like to inspect the troops?"

"Perhaps a quick inspection," Ivy said, glancing at the threatening clouds overhead.

Daniels gave her quick grin. "That might be best," she agreed. "First of all, may I introduce Troop Leader Yellow Elk." Ivy acknowledged the introduction to Daniel's tall companion with a short nod. "Troop Leader Marsha is presently out on patrol," Daniels explained.

Daniels guided her onto the front row, and Ivy stopped in front of front row's 'marker'. He towered over her, being at least six and a half feet tall with the mass to match. His shoulder length hair had been braided with beads and given his size she pitied the horse that had to carry him.

Leaning forward she read his tag. "Trooper Monahan."

"Leader." His eyes fixed in the distance over her head.

"Where are you from, Trooper?"

"England, Leader."

She cocked an eyebrow. "Druidic?" she asked, guessing at the hair beads.

"Yes, Leader."

"How long have you been here?"

"At Fort Larsa?"

"Yes, Monahan."

"Five years, Leader."

Not a conscript then. She nodded and moved onto the next, stopping to talk every now and then. Daniels had done a good job and there was nothing to draw an adverse comment. Finally she reached the small group of aviators.

"Lieutenant Williams of the Flying Wing," Daniels said in introduction.

"Lieutenant," Ivy said. "I take it we only have the one giro?" She nodded in the direction of the autogiro parked under its open shelter against the end of the barracks.

"That's correct, Leader."

"You have enough fuel for regular training?" She knew it was a common complaint among aviators that they were never provided with enough fuel for training.

"Certainly, Leader."

"Perhaps you could show me over your facilities tomorrow?"

"Of course, Leader. I will look forward to that."

With a nod to the other two mechanics she returned to the front of the parade. Standing there she felt a surge of pride. They were hers!

"Force Alpha, Second Mounted Infantry," she said, immediately wondering if it was too formal. She shrugged mentally, it was too late now and anyway she'd heard other Leaders start off that way.

"By now I am sure that you are as aware of my own record as I am." There was small answering chuckle. "But for the record I was commissioned as a Squad Leader in 92, and promoted to Troop Leader the same year. I've served three years in Italy, of which one year was spent chasing guerrillas in the southern Alps . To allow us to meet, and to get to know each other in less formal circumstances, I will be broaching a cask of wine tonight, and hope you will join me in consuming it."

She nodded to Daniels to dismiss them.

"Would you like to see your quarters now?" Daniels asked as the troopers broke back to their barracks and a fine drizzle started to fall.

"If you could detail someone to look after Sergeant Horsing and Trooper Pecos."

"Archos."

The young Squad Leader saluted.

"Archos is the son of a local chief," Daniels explained, leading Ivy towards the admin building, Yellow Elk accompanying them. "We're giving him some instruction before he heads off to officer training."

"That's a good idea. It's bad enough getting transferred to a new country without having to learn everything from scratch at the same time."

"I'm thankful you survived the ambush. But I'd have preferred it if the replacement squad could have got through as well. We just lost a squad on transfer to Spain, and there's another nine troopers coming up for discharge in a month."

"I did put in a request for an immediate relief squad to be sent," Ivy said. "But I don't know that we'll have any success. From what Sergeant Horsing was telling me on the way down we were lucky to get the squad in the first place."

Daniels nodded. "Everyone's stretched pretty thin at the moment, particularly with all the trouble we've been having with Aris and his war bands." She opened the door and waved Ivy in. "Your quarters."

While the four rooms were compact, they were larger than anything she'd possessed as Troop Leader. There was someone in the kitchen, and Daniels took her through.

"Force Leader, this is Ban," she said, introducing her to the small, wizened man in his mid-fifties with a compressed snub of a nose and red cheeks who was busy preparing dinner.

Ban waved a crumbed chicken leg at her. "Dinner's in half an hour. Don't be late." Although his accent was almost undecipherable, the meaning was quite clear.

"You'll have to forgive Ban," Yellow Elk said as Daniels ushered them out, closing the door behind them. "Unfortunately he's priceless, as you'll find out once you've tasted his cooking."

"I'll take your word for it, but as we seem to have half an hour, perhaps you could show me over the rest of the fort. Not a formal inspection; we'll do that tomorrow, just something to let me get an idea of where everything is."

"Of course," Daniels said.

While built of stone rather than the more usual wood, the fort still followed the standard model. Stables ran along the north side of the ground with the shelter for the autogiro at one end. The barracks and Ivy's rooms were on the east side while on the opposite side of the ground were the armory and mess hall. A small herb garden had been built next to the mess hall, bare in the approaching winter. Only the south side was free of buildings and two basketball hoops with backboards framed the main gate. The fort's solitary gun was in the center of the ground, its limber parked behind it.

At dinner Ivy quickly discovered what Daniels had been talking about when she had described Ban's cooking, and there was little conversation as she, Daniels, and Yellow Elk concentrated on giving the food their full attention. After dinner, however, she worked to draw the two Troop Leaders out, deciding after an hour that while Yellow Elk was a practical, though perhaps overly cautious Leader, Daniels seemed to offer all she might have wished for in a 2IC.

About eight she and other two Leaders joined the rest of the Force in the mess hall for the promised cask of wine. It was an exhausted Force Leader who made her excuses at ten that night, although the party she'd started continued until well after midnight.

CHAPTER SIXTEEN

Naisre — Mainline
October 1979 (95AE)

Conrad jerked awake at the sound of the front door opening. He blinked blearily, hoisting himself up from where he'd fallen asleep on the sofa. That should be Donald, he thought, and now maybe he could get to bed - he'd only stayed up to make sure there was someone to meet him.

"Hi Donald," he said as his brother appeared.

Donald simply grunted, and dumping his suitcase just inside the entrance to the suite headed straight for the kitchen, and the fridge.

"Rough flight?" Conrad said sympathetically, closing the door after him.

"You would not believe it," Donald said cracking the top off a beer. He took a long swallow.

"Yes, thank you for asking, I will have a beer."

Donald pulled a face at him and reached back into the fridge.

"Thanks," Conrad said, catching the bottle Donald tossed him.

"So what time's this funeral?" Donald asked.

"Three o'clock."

"You know I'd only been back in Charleston two weeks?"

"Yep, and I'm sure that if the First Leader could have put off dying for a couple of weeks for you, he would have."

"Ha, ha," Donald said, and took another swallow.

"So, did you have any difficulty getting time off from your university?"

"Hardly, I hadn't even started yet. It was more difficult to tell Matija. I'd only been back a fortnight and then I get dragged off again."

"Ah, yes, the girl you were telling me about last time I saw you. How's that going?"

Donald gave a slow smile at the memory of the previous night, and Conrad smirked. "That good eh?" He raised his bottle. "How's your health?"

"Good, recovering slowly. I still get exhausted, but so long as I don't try anything too energetic it's not too bad. I really miss not being able to run though."

"The flight should have given you the chance to rest up."

Donald snorted. "Hardly, twenty hours of unmitigated hell. All the best flights were already booked out because of the funeral so I had to take a red-eye. There was a strike of baggage handlers just before we left, which delayed departure by two hours. Then when we did leave we were battling crosswinds and turbulence all the way so they couldn't serve any refreshment. And let's not talk about when we hit the mountains." He shuddered dramatically, then frowned. "What are you still doing up anyway?"

"I had to read some papers for Grandfather so I thought I'd wait up for you. I've been helping him with his campaign. Wining, dining and canvassing. It's a hard life but someone's got to do it."

"So he's definitely standing?"

"When the only alternative is Miro, and that little snot of his son, of course he is."

"What did Petro do to upset you so much?" Donald asked, surprised.

"I attended the Academy with him. Broke his nose once. I have never met a more obnoxious, spoiled individual in my life. And did I say he cheated? He finally got caught in his last year and was going to be kept down when his father intervened. Turns out he hasn't changed all that much."

"Oh?"

"Just found out a couple of weeks ago. You know Mary, Hayden's wife?"

Donald nodded.

"Petro managed to get her sister pregnant last year, and then denied all responsibility. Unfortunately it got even messier when she tried to commit suicide and lost the baby."

Donald grimaced.

"Yes, so I don't like him. And his father's not much better. I had a run-in with him when I was in my graduating year when he tried to have one of my juniors expelled for standing up to his son. If he had his way he'd drag us back to the days of Traek and the Hraffor. You should know, you were on Dontfrey when he authorized the use of gas."

"Ordered."

Conrad made a placating gesture.

Donald glanced at his watch. "Another beer?"

"Why not."

Donald got up and claimed another two bottles from the fridge. "Are these some of yours?" he asked inspecting the label which showed a skull in a wig.

"Yes. I had a couple of cases shipped in last week."

"Still no one buying them?"

"I'll have yours if you don't want it," Conrad threatened.

"No, I'm fine. Are the Perics here yet?"

"They got here a couple of days ago."

"How are they?"

Conrad thought about it for a moment. "Subdued. Uncle Roland looks like he's aged about ten years, and Rajko hasn't said a thing."

"To Nedo," Donald said, raising his beer.

Conrad silently raised his bottle in reply.

"So, how's Arnold?" Donald asked.

"Still in hospital. I dropped in and saw him yesterday. Physically he's all right, but mentally . . ." he shrugged. "Mama said he blames himself for Nedo's death."

"That's ridiculous!"

"Well, perhaps you can tell him that while you're here."

There was another silence.

"Did you know Jon's here?" Conrad asked suddenly.

"Raincloud? No, I didn't. I thought he was going to Europe to join Ivy?"

"I think Papa is trying to cool the relationship a bit, because he brought Jon with him as a member of his staff."

"I wonder what Ivy had to say about that?"

"Probably a lot. She does have rather a colorful turn of phrase doesn't she?"

Donald laughed. "That's one way of putting it."

"Anyway, he turns out to be quite a decent poker player."

"Really?"

"I thought that would get your interest," Conrad said with a laugh.

Donald shrugged, too honest to deny it.

Conrad drained his beer and hoisted himself to his feet. "I'm off. I'll see you in the morning. You've got your normal room," and with that he headed off to bed.

***

"Good morning Conrad," his father said he arrived at the table for breakfast the next day. "Late night?"

"Yes," Conrad said shortly, hoping it wouldn't be much longer before the aspirin he'd taken kicked in.

"I hope you'll be well enough for the funeral this afternoon."

"So do I," Conrad said sincerely.

"Donald got in all right?"

"Late, but he's here."

"How is he?"

"He's fine," Donald said cheerfully, appearing.

Conrad considered his brother sourly.

"I'm sorry I had to pull you away just as you got back, Donald," his father said.

Donald shrugged. "S'right. I was wondering why you needed me though."

"The Council's going to have its first vote after the funeral, and I thought it best if the family presented a united front."

"Of course," Donald said. "What do you think Grandfather's chances are?"

His father shrugged. "Honestly? I haven't the foggiest. We need seventy-five percent of the vote and the Council is split right down the middle." He frowned into his coffee.

Conrad sighed; no, the odds didn't sound terribly good.

***

The funeral took place in the First Leader's sepulcher, an enormous, stone vaulted room cut deep into the city's bedrock. Its size always reminded Conrad of a cathedral, although it had apparently been modelled on a temple from Treik's own line.

Marble columns rose in soaring grandeur to a central dome 360 feet above them. Below the dome, oversized statues of demons stood guard in alcoves cut into the stones, faces carved into bestial parodies of the humans far below.

Conrad let his eyes follow the gentle curve of a column as it rose to the gallery that ran around the inside of the base of the dome, before turning his gaze back to those who surrounded him. Two and a half thousand people, in a rainbow of house colors, filled the simple wooden benches of the central nave to capacity.

Beyond the transcept, a wall of green polished marble lined the apse. Stainless steel hatches were embedded in the marble. Behind two of these, previous First Leaders lay in frozen, endless sleep, their doors coated in condensation. The third door was latched back, and from this a continuous stream of fog drifted down to the floor beneath.

At three o'clock precisely, Daneka, Manek's widow, took her place at the top of the nave. A trumpet's single clarion brought the audience to its feet as the First Leader's casket appeared, escorted by six of the First Leader's Guard in full dress uniforms, their dark green uniforms adding further sobriety to the ceremony. Slowly the casket made its way down the nave, its surface covered in a thin layer of frost. As it passed him Conrad felt a sudden drop in temperature.

Reaching the apse the six guardsmen braced themselves, then as one lifted the casket up and into its final resting place. As the guard came to attention, the door swung closed behind it and there was a dull thump as the chamber, now holding the casket, was flooded with liquid nitrogen. With a rustling of clothing the audience resumed their seats.

Conrad's father learned back in his seat. "Now it begins."

The Chairman of the Council of Leaders took his place in the center of the stage. He carried an ornately carved steel rod, a symbol of his authority, and wore a knee length frock coat and striped pants, a fashion popular among the ruling classes at the turn of the previous century. Conrad thought he looked ridiculous. Then again, his own uniform probably wasn't any less ridiculous, high collar, braiding, cuffs and all. Tradition was an important part of what bound the Empire together.

The Chairman banged his rod against the floor, then waited for silence.

"Manek, First Leader of the Empire, lies in Eternal Sleep. He died without a successor, and as authorized by the Council I call for nominations from those who would take his place."

Almost immediately Miro bounced to his feet, a short, squat man, with a red, fleshy face, whose black and silver uniform only served to emphasize his weight.

"I, Miro Raputa, Leader of Dontfrey, father-in-law to Manek, former First Leader, nominate myself for the position," he pronounced in his distinctive gravelly voice. He glared out at the audience, as though daring anyone to challenge his right to nominate.

There was a stir in the audience as his challenge was met with silence, and Conrad felt Donald shift uncomfortably next to him. Finally their grandfather stood up, and turned to face them. Thin and scholarly; he was the exact opposite of Miro's brazen aggressiveness. When he spoke his voice was clear, and low.

"I, Griffin Windsor, Leader of Notway, brother-in-law to Treac, father to Manek, nominate myself for the position of First Leader."

The Chairman waited for a moment, before banging his rod on the floor again — the metal rod ringing off the marble. "Two leaders have nominated for the post of First Leader. I call a meeting of the full Council tomorrow morning to decide between them." Nodding politely to the two nominees he stepped back into the shadows.

"So that's it," Conrad said.

"Looks like it," his father said. "It's going to be a long night." He looked at his wife. "I doubt you'll see much of me for a while." She smiled understandingly at him. "When do I ever?"

With a quick peck on her cheek he was off into the crowd, just as Margaret appeared.

"We've been looking everywhere for you," Margaret said. "The rest of the family's over there." She waved towards the back of the cavern. "Mama wanted to know if you were going to be in this afternoon?"

"I don't know about these two," his mother said, indicating her sons. "But I'll be in and would certainly appreciate the company."

Conrad shrugged and looked at Donald.

"I haven't got anything else to do," Donald said.

"Good, I'll tell Mama we'll see you, then," she said.

***

The small piazza in front of the Chamber of Leaders was so crowded with people that Conrad struggled to see over their heads to the Chamber's main doors on the far side of the square.

"I don't think we're going to be able to get in," he told his brother, as he surveyed the crowd.

"No," Donald grunted, his attention momentarily lifting from the small television screen he'd been watching in the nearby shop window. The two had been hoping to be able to get into the Chamber's public gallery to watch the vote but so, it appeared, had several hundred other people.

"So, what do you want to do?" Conrad asked.

"Let's just stay for a moment. It looks like the vote's being taken," Donald said, indicating the TV.

The two watched as the roll was taken. A progressive tally was projected as a running total below the picture.

When the count reached twenty-seven to twenty against their grandfather Conrad found himself holding his breath. As the next five went to their grandfather giving a final count of twenty-eight to twenty-five he started breathing again.

"That doesn't look good," Donald said.

"And unexpected," Conrad admitted. "I thought we'd at least be ahead on the first vote. And with Grandfather now needing another fifteen votes to win, and Miro's core of supporters being tighter . . . no, not good at all."

"Well let's hope the thought of the consequence if they can't select someone helps concentrate their minds. The Empire isn't going to be able operate for long without a head."

"What consequence?" Conrad asked, puzzled.

"War."

"Oh, it won't come to that," Conrad said with a laugh, before noticing that Donald hadn't smiled. "Could it?"

"I hope not. But this is the first change in dynasty the Empire's ever had. And wars have started over far lesser things than that."

What?" Conrad demanded as Donald's attention suddenly shifted to something over his shoulder. "Oh damn," Conrad said, turning and catching sight of the disturbance a short distance away, a flash of green hair at its center. "That looks like Defella."

"Who's Defella?" Donald started to demand even as Conrad forced his way through the crowd towards the disturbance.

It was Defella, and he reached her just in time to see the woman arguing with her swing a fist at her. Defella stumbled backward, to be brought up short by the press of people behind her. Defella was wearing the short, sleeveless tunic she'd worn on the airship, and although diverted by the sight of her tanned skin, Conrad still had enough presence of mind to notice that the woman who'd thrown the punch was wearing the light-green uniform and bonnet of a Dynand embassy guard.

"That's enough," he said, starting to move between them. Even as he did so, however, Defella had recovered her balance and stooped to pull out the small knife in the top of her right boot.

"Out of the way, Conrad," Defella snarled. Her eyes fixed on those of her opponent, her knife marking small circles between them. "I'm about to teach this motherless daughter a long overdue lesson."

Conrad catalogued the professional handling of the knife, even as the crowd tried to edge away. Unfortunately they were hemmed in and unable to move far.

"So kitten wants to play?" her opponent taunted, pulling her own knife from its belt sheath and moving into an answering crouch.

Defella lunged forward, trying to avoid Conrad who grabbed her arm and wrist as she moved past, swinging her up and over his hip to drop her on the ground. There was an explosion of breath, a grunt of pain and she dropped the knife with a yelp as he pressed his boot against her wrist. A sudden shout from Donald made him whirl, but his brother had already blocked the embassy guard's lunge, and had followed up with a short jab to the solar plexus that folded her over. A knee in the face and both brothers were staring at the guard lying on the ground before them. Bending over, Conrad picked up the two knives, then looked over to see Donald massaging his arm.

"You all right?" he asked.

"Sort of. That hurt though," Donald complained, still massaging his arm.

"Thanks, I didn't see her coming." Extending an arm, Conrad hauled Defella to her feet.

She scowled at him as she accepted the knife he held out to her.

"Come on, let's go," he said, not loosening his hold on her shoulder.

"Perhaps you could introduce us," Donald suggested, having to hurry to keep up.

"Donald, this is Defella Haratan," Conrad said not slowing down. The sooner they were away from there the better. "I met her on the airship coming into Naisre. Her mother's a Continental Leader on Dynand. Defella, this is my brother Donald."

Defella gave him an embarrassed smile.

"So what was all that about?" Conrad demanded, when they'd managed to force their way out of piazza and back into one of the thoroughfares.

"My World Leader had just announced his vote to Miro and I was expressing my feelings on the matter when that motherless daughter called your grandfather a useless fool. I suggested she might want to reconsider her choice of words, and things went downhill from there."

"And who is this motherless daughter when she's at home?" Conrad asked, hiding a smile at her choice of words.

"She's minor nobility. But her whole family's been putting on airs ever since her sister married the World Leader's second son a year ago."

"So you support our grandfather?" Donald said.

"Of course," Defella said, shocked he might have thought otherwise. "My mother said that if the Continental Leaders were given the vote your grandfather would get in on a landslide."

"Because most Continental Leaders are native?"

She nodded.

Donald looked at his brother. "Perhaps that's something we should mention to Grandfather?"

"Perhaps," Conrad conceded. "But given that I don't think we'll get into the Council today - can I buy you a drink?" he asked Defella. "And you can explain to me why your mother thinks my grandfather is the best choice for First Leader."

"We," Donald said. "Can we buy you a drink."

"Oh," she said, coloring prettily, obviously appreciating the attention of two males. "Thank you, I'd like that."

***

A couple of hours later, after dropping Defella back to her apartment, Conrad and Donald returned to their suite to find two

Notway troopers stationed outside the entrance.

"Good afternoon sirs, how can I help you?" the young Notway Squad Leader said, politely blocking their way.

Conrad raised an eyebrow. "We live here," he said.

The Squad Leader flushed, and quickly checked the clipboard. "My apologies Leaders, please go in."

The suite was filled with the heavy fug of tobacco smoke. Conrad and Donald followed the source through to the suite's conference room where their grandfather, godfather, father, and six other World Leaders were gathered around the main table. There was half a tray of sandwiches on the sideboard, and four overflowing ashtrays scattered around the room. Conrad wrinkled his nose in disgust.

"Donald," his grandfather, the World Leader of Notway, said, rising to greet them. His normally immaculate white hair was tousled and disheveled. "I haven't seen you for a while."

"About two and a half years," Donald agreed.

"Gentlemen," their grandfather said. "You know Conrad, and this is his brother Donald, presently at the University of Charleston."

The others nodded their greeting.

"Please take a seat." He indicated a couple of unoccupied chairs at the foot of the table. "This concerns you as well. Lawrence, please continue," he told the ImpSec Commander.

Conrad's godfather ran a hand through his hair. "As I was saying, there's no doubt that Dontfrey is moving to a war footing. Of course the blame is being put on the recent insurrection in North America, but even with that, measures now being taken seem quite excessive."

"And they are?" Brian said.

"Recall of all regulars to their barracks, accelerated commissioning of officers coming out of the Academy, requisitioning of supplies. There have also been a number of heavy bookings on commercial flights from Mainline Foochow, which as you know is Miro's main portal."

"So you think he's preparing to bypass the Council?"

"It's possible."

"And you suggest what?" Romanov asked. The World Leader of Neu-Moscow was a tall, thin individual with a strong resemblance to his cousin, the present Russian Emperor.

"Unfortunately, Leader, I can't suggest — merely report. To do otherwise could very well be construed as destroying the neutrality of Imperial Security."

"Griffin?" Romanov asked, turning his attention to Donald's grandfather.

"Similar mobilization of all our forces. In addition an approach should be made to the First Leader's Joint Chiefs of Staff to find out which way they would react if there were any trouble. My own belief is that they will remain neutral unless any of the arsenals are attacked, or the Council of Leaders finally make a decision."

Lawrence nodded at that suggestion.

"Should we try and bring in any of our own forces?" someone asked.

"Not at this stage. However, they'll need to be ready to move immediately if necessary." Of those gathered there, Etu was the only line with large numbers of troops on the American continent. If any immediate assistance were to be given it would have to be from them. " I will also be putting in a couple of Groups to hold the Mainline side of my portal, just in case."

"Is that acceptable, gentlemen?" the Notway World Leader asked. Everyone was looking unhappy at the results of discussion, but all nodded their agreement to it. "Then I think we should be out campaigning again. George, what's the score so far?"

A paunchy looking individual wearing an unbuttoned light green jacket cleared his throat. "Not good," he admitted. "The vote should have been in our favor this morning. I've got Harold out there now, trying to find out why some of those votes we'd been promised didn't deliver." He shrugged apologetically. "We're going to have to discuss what we can offer those Leaders on the list I gave you."

"I suppose if we have to."

Conrad thought from his grandfather's voice that he might have preferred to have taken a mouthful of acid.

"It is, Griffin," George said earnestly. "We've still got a chance, not a good one, but a chance. The thing is we're going to have to fight for it." He suddenly realized what he had said. "Figuratively speaking," he said with an uneasy smile.

Conrad winced, thinking of Defella.

"Well let's hope so," their grandfather said. He stood up and the rest of those there did the same.

"Grandfather," Donald said, grabbing Conrad to stop him disappearing. "I know you're busy, but there's an idea someone suggested you should hear about."

"Yes?"

"It's the Continental Leaders. As most of them would support you, is there any way we can get them to put pressure on their World Leaders for you?"

Their grandfather thought about it for a moment. "It's a good idea, but it might take a while, which we may not have. I'll get someone onto it though. So, are you two doing anything tonight, or can you join us for tea?"

"Conrad won't be here," Brian said, interrupting. "I'm afraid you have to get back to Etu to arrange the mobilization."

Well there went any chance of taking Defella out again in the near future, Conrad thought.

"If you come with me," his father continued, "I'll get the orders done up and we can work out what you're going to have to do."

"Can I take Raincloud?" Conrad asked. "I'll need an aide, and I'd rather it was someone I knew."

His father looked at him for a moment, then nodded. "Come on then."

CHAPTER SEVENTEEN

Naisre — Mainline
October 1979 (95AE)

"Margaret, we've been looking for them for half an hour, can't we take a break?" Donald asked plaintively.

They were standing in front of a diorama at the Imperial Museum. Behind the glass a robot-mannequin writhed in simulated pain on the torture table as nobles in long wigs and multilayered silk robes gathered round to gossip. The torturer, wearing a sleeveless red cotton surgical gown over his robes, was studying a half opened scroll of anatomical drawings held up for him by a slave. On the table, beside the sign which indicated that the scene was from the Meso-American civilization, Horwith Line, was a tray containing the torturer's collection of surgical bronze implements.

Donald smiled wryly at the artfully draped sheet that covered the victim's lower limbs. While torture and violence was apparently fine for an educational display, nudity just as obviously wasn't.

"I promised Mama I'd keep an eye on them," Margaret said. She scowled. "Just how difficult is — 'Don't wander off'?" she asked rhetorically.

Donald dragged his mind back to the question of his two missing cousins. He gestured helplessly, trying to indicate the magnitude of the task of finding the two girls among the miles of corridors and dozens of separate exhibitions that made up the museum.

"Obviously quite difficult for those two," Donald replied. "Look, we'll find them when it's time to go. We've hardly looked at the 'Growth of Civilizations' exhibit, and if you remember, you were the one who wanted to see it."

They were interrupted by a harassed-looking teacher entering the chamber, leading a small group of middle-school students, most of who were gossiping and seemed totally uninterested in the display.

Margaret fumed silently, then shook her head. "Come on, let's try down here," she said, pulling him down a passage lined with huge, gray stone statues that towered over those passing beneath.

After another half an hour of fruitless searching, however, Donald finally put his foot down. "I need a drink," he said.

She glared at him, before, with a shrug, allowing herself to be led over to the nearest café.

"So what's wrong?" he said, pulling the chair back from the table for her and waving a waitress over to take their order.

"Nothing. It's just those two . . ."

Donald raised an eyebrow. "Those two don't normally upset you as much as this. Besides, you've got a museum bulging with the accumulated loot of over a hundred lines and you haven't even glanced at the jewelry." From the expression on her face he knew, even as he had said it, that his attempt at humor had fallen flat.

"I just wish the Council would get on and elect a First Leader," Margaret said, staring into her coffee.

"It's only been a week. They'll make up their minds eventually."

"And what happens if they can't? Your line's already gone onto a war footing."

"So's yours," Donald pointed out.

Both of them fell silent.

"They'll make a choice; no-one wants a war," Donald said finally.

Let's hope so." But neither felt very confident.

***

Later that night Donald had just put the phone down after talking to Matija for an hour when it rang. "Yes," he said, picking it up.

"Donald." It was his father. "You better put your uniform on."

"What's wrong?" His father had arranged for his Clemhorn uniform to be delivered a couple of days ago. Donald was still embarrassed by the new Force Leader tabs his father had insisted on giving him.

"Someone's attacked the armory at St. Paul," his father said. "I've ordered Conrad to bring his troops through, and I want you to act as liaison officer. Conrad can't spare anyone, and we have to know what's happening."

"St. Paul?" Donald said, shocked. St. Paul was North America's major armory, one of the largest on the line, and if Miro got his hands on it there'd be hell to pay! "How do I get there?" he asked, realizing something more was expected of him.

"Lawrence is arranging transport. He said he'd contact you."

"I better change then."

"Take care."

Donald had just finished pulling his boots on when Lawrence knocked on the door.

"You ready?" he asked.

Donald finished pocketing his wallet and identification card. "Yep. So what happened?"

"Apparently some militia tried to gain access to the armory, and were refused entrance. Fighting broke out, and now there's a full-scale battle going on around the town. There's rumors of martial law being declared, but no one's really sure who's going to declare it."

"So how am I getting there?"

"I've arranged for a rocket and pilot to take you through to Columbus. It was difficult, all public flights have been grounded, but the Air Marshall owed me a favor."

"Some favor," Donald remarked. Rockets were hideously expensive, and notoriously unreliable. Unfortunately their tech had been easier to maintain than the jets the military had been trying to get funding to develop for the last couple of years.

Lawrence acknowledged that with a nod. "If anyone asks what you're doing, you're working for Imperial Security."

"In this?" Donald said dryly, indicating his light blue tunic, the Clemhorn double-headed eagle on his right arm.

"Let's hope no one asks then. Unfortunately I haven't got time to get you any papers so if there is a problem get them to phone me."

"Thanks. What happens when I get to Columbus?"

"Conrad's arranging transport. Just remember your job is to keep us informed, don't get involved in any fighting."

"Sure." As though that was going to be difficult.

Upstairs, they stepped out of the elevator into the middle of an early winter storm. Clouds hung heavily overhead while the wind whipped snow across the bare concrete and into their faces under the harsh illumination of the overhead lights. Two burly sergeants met them at the elevator, and after bidding goodbye to Lawrence, Donald followed them across the tarmac to where the rocket plane waited for them in its cradle, its streamlining marred by the solid booster strapped beneath each wing.

His pilot waited beside the plane, a helmet and spare pair of overalls in his arms.

"You'll need to put these on." He held the overalls out to Donald.

They were a trifle large, and as Donald finished zipping them up he couldn't help feeling about five years old again, dressing up in his father's old clothes.

"Have you flown in one of these before?" his pilot asked, jerking his head towards the plane as he handed Donald the helmet.

"No." Donald surreptitiously dried to dry his palms on the legs of his overalls. A sudden gust of wind brought with it the reek of fuel, and he wrinkled his nose at the acrid stink.

"Well there's nothing to be afraid of," his pilot reassured him as he helped Donald up the steps and into the cockpit. He plugged the cables from Donald's helmet into the panel beside him, checked he was comfortable, then swung himself up into his own seat just behind Donald's.

"This bird's flown the equivalent of eight times round the world, and never once given a hint of trouble." The pilot's voice was distorted through the earphones set into Donald's helmet.

Donald nodded, hardly reassured at the thought of the distance it had traveled. It would probably fall apart as soon as it launched.

The canopy swung forward with a hiss of compressed air. Donald swallowed, trying to release the pressure in his ears. Outside the steps were wheeled away as the external fuel lines were disconnected.

"Ready?" the pilot asked.

Donald nodded, before remembering the pilot couldn't see him. "Yes," he managed. This was even worse than having to go through a portal. He swallowed again, nervously, wondering where to put his hands.

Darkness surrounded them, the falling snow obscuring his view out of the canopy. When nothing happened Donald wondered if something had gone wrong.

"We're just waiting for clearance," the pilot said calmly, as though reading Donald's thoughts. "We're going to be pushing a couple of g's when we take off, so try not to forget to breathe.

"Hold on, here we go," the pilot said and a moment later there was a sudden explosion of sound from behind them as the boosters opened up. The pilot said something, but his voice was lost in the howl from the engines that filled Donald's ears, leaving no room for thought.

Gradually, over the noise, Donald became aware they were moving. Slowly at first, but quickly gaining speed, the plane clawed its way into the air on twin pillars of fire.

Donald struggled to breathe against the pressure that forced him back into his seat until suddenly the engine spluttered and stopped. Donald let out an unconscious murmur of protest as there was a solid thud that he felt through the base of his seat and the plane shivered. Below them the curve of the Earth seemed very far away.

"Just the boosters detaching," said the pilot cheerfully. "Nothing to worry about."

Great! Bits were falling off the plane and there was nothing to worry about.

Abruptly he was slammed back into his seat again as the main engine ignited and pounded by the noise, Donald closed his eyes, fighting against a rising surge of nausea as the plane levelled off, swinging north to follow the 46th parallel east towards the Great Lakes.

There was no effortless grace to this flight, the plane simply bludgeoned its way through the thin air on the edge of space. Below them the thunder of their passing rolled over the ground, rattling the windows of those few scattered homesteads below their path. Donald clenched his eyes tighter and waited for the flight to end.

Finally, the pilot throttled the main engine back and as it spluttered into silence Donald opened his eyes again and cautiously checked his watch in the dim light of the instrument panel. Just over an hour; well that wasn't too bad. The plane dipped and Donald swallowed his words as the pilot did a quick jig to line up with lights on the runway just ahead.

A moment later the wheels hit the ground and Donald was slammed forward against his harness as the parachute caught the air behind them. Outside, the ground was a blur of black, slowing as he watched it, until sooner than he had expected they had come to a complete stop and the only sound Donald could hear was the ringing in his ears.

"Flying Coffin Airways is happy to announce our safe landing in Columbus. Please remain seated until the cockpit latch is released," the pilot said cheerfully.

Donald grunted, simply happy to have survived the flight.

By the time the pilot finally released the cockpit cover, Donald had recovered enough to manage the climb down the steps by himself. This was about as much as he could manage however, and the pilot had to help him out of his overalls.

He was just starting to make his cautious way towards the terminal when he heard someone calling his name and looked round to see Raincloud bearing down on him.

"Donald. You made good time. I wasn't expecting you for another thirty minutes or so. How was the flight?"

"Brutal. What transport have you got?"

"An autogiro. It's just round the corner."

Behind them the plane that had brought Donald from Naisre was already being towed off the runway to where it could be refueled, and readied for its return.

"What's happening?" Donald asked.

"Conrad's got the Rangers through, and the Battlegroup should be well on its way to St Paul by now. But as to what's happening, well your guess is as good as mine."

"Typical." He eyed the giro's open cockpit with distaste, but at least it didn't look as though it was going to snow this side of the continent — the sky was a haze of stars. "I don't suppose you've got any aspirin."

"Headache?" Raincloud asked sympathetically, pulling out the small first-aid kit the giro contained.

Donald nodded.

"Have some water." Raincloud offered him his canteen.

"Thanks."

Leaning into the cockpit Raincloud produced a fur lined jacket and gloves. "You better put these on, it's going to get cold."

"How long do you think it will take to catch up with Conrad?" Donald asked, pulling the jacket on thankfully. Zipping it up he already started to feel warmer.

"Four, five hours," Raincloud offered. "He's got a good head start on us."

Donald grimaced. "Let's go then."

"I hope you brought a pack of cards," Raincloud said as he settled himself into the front seat.

"If you're hoping to get back some of the money you owe me you've got no chance."

"You can't keep winning."

"Against someone who plays poker as badly as you do I can't help it."

Raincloud raised a finger.

CHAPTER EIGHTEEN

St Paul — Mainline
November 1979 (95AE)

Conrad shifted uncomfortably. The seat was far too small to sleep in, especially for someone of his size. It was almost dawn, the sky just starting to lighten in the west. He tried moving the pillow into a more comfortable position against the window and closed his eyes again.

"Leader." It was one of the radio operators.

"Yes?" he said with a sigh as his small command group stirred into life around him.

"The rear coach reports an autogiro approaching from the east."

"Have you tried raising it?"

"Yes, Leader. There's no reply."

"It should be Raincloud with my brother. Inform the other coaches that it's friendly. I don't want any accidents."

In a minute Conrad heard the autogiro himself. It came in low, buzzed the convoy once, then accelerated away to find somewhere it could land and wait for them to catch up.

Five minutes later, as the sun appeared above of the horizon and color flooded back into world, Conrad's coach pulled onto the shoulder next to the landed autogiro.

"Want a lift?" Conrad asked, poking his head out of the window.

"Thanks," Donald said, as the second coach in the convoy thundered by, causing Conrad's bus to rock back on its springs. "I'll stick with the giro," Raincloud said. "Do you have a radio I can use though? This one hasn't got anything that uses military frequencies."

"Sergeant," Conrad called back into the bus as Donald mounted the steps and swung himself into an empty seat at the front. "Can we have a spare handheld for the Leader?"

A Sergeant brought a radio forward and handed it to Raincloud.

"See you in St. Paul," Conrad told Raincloud, as the coach started to pull away from the verge.

"How many coaches did you get?" Donald asked, looking around at the shambles they'd made of the interior. Most of the seats, except for a couple of rows at the front and the back, had been pulled out and replaced with tables and chairs. Map boards had been set up against one side of the bus and three radios on the other, only one of which was presently staffed by an operator.

"Thirteen."

"So who's paying for all this?"

"Grandfather," Conrad said with a grin. "I signed the chits myself. You know the Battlegroup Leader don't you?" he said, introducing him to the giant of a man sitting just behind them.

"Running Bear, yes, we met at a dinner at the house a year or so ago." Donald held out his hand.

Running Bear was a full-blood Choctaw, bronze skinned with a broad, impassive face that creased into an enormous smile as he shook Donald's hand. "Glad you could join us."

"Thanks. So what's the latest on St. Paul?" he asked, accepting a mug of coffee from someone.

"Apparently the garrison is still holding out. The latest estimate puts the attackers at about two or three hundred people, but they've got the garrison pinned down."

"I thought the armory would have been held by at least a Battlegroup? Why haven't they managed to chase them off?"

Conrad shrugged; it was something he'd worried about himself. "Perhaps they were caught by surprise."

"Any news from the capital?"

"Still quiet."

"Let's hope it stays that way."

"Amen to that."

"So who did you bring?" Donald asked, looking about him.

"Just the Rangers. But I've mobilized the militia; and made arrangements to recall some of the regulars from Europe, as well as strip the South American garrisons if we need them."

"You think it could be that serious?"

Conrad shrugged, privately worrying it could get even worse. Rummaging in the bag wedged under his seat he pulled out a bar of chocolate. "Want something to eat?"

"Thanks," Donald said. "How long before we get there?"

"Another couple of hours. Try and get some rest; there's nothing we can do till we get there."

Donald nodded, and leaning back in his chair, closed his eyes.

Conrad watched his brother for a moment, then sighed softly to himself. Now he had someone else to worry about.

***

"Leader?" It was the Battlegroup Leader.

"What?" Conrad blearily checked his watch. He'd been out for about an hour. He stifled a yawn, noticing Donald was already awake.

"We're just entering the outskirts of St. Paul," Running Bear said.

"Thanks." He stretched carefully, before moving over to refresh his memory of the maps.

Five minutes later, as they pulled off the road into a newly swept hotel car park, a muffled explosion in the distance caused him to jerk his head around. Through the side window of the bus he saw a dense column of smoke climbing into the air.

"What's happening?" Donald asked, joining him at the window.

"I don't know," Conrad admitted. "I'm hoping Raincloud can tell me. The armory is still about two miles away, but I want to get a report from him before we move in."

The rest of the convoy pulled into the parking area behind them, troops starting to disembark to stretch their legs. Suddenly there was a knock on the coach door.

"Yes?" Conrad said, leaning out to adress the tall gentleman in hotel livery who'd knocked.

"Are you in charge?"

"Why?"

"You'll need to move your coaches. This is private property."

Conrad considered him disbelievingly for a couple of seconds. They were going into combat in a couple of minutes, and this lackey was telling they couldn't park here! He was just opening his mouth to give him a piece of his mind when the radio operator handed him a message. Conrad glanced at it and swore. That's all he needed. "I'm afraid we'll have to discuss this later," he said turning his back on the concierge and leaving him with no choice but to retreat to the hotel's front porch.

"What does it say?" Donald asked.

Conrad handed him the message, which was from their father. "Suspect further movement of troops towards St. Paul. Imperative you restore order and secure control of the armory immediately."

"It doesn't say how long we've got," Donald said, passing the note to the Battlegroup Leader.

"Leader."

Conrad turned to see the second radio operator holding up a handpiece. "Leader Raincloud is reporting. He's over the armory."

"Put it on the speakers," Conrad ordered.

"They've managed to take the vehicle park," Raincloud announced.

Conrad found he had to concentrate to make out what Raincloud was saying over the heavy beat of rotors in the background.

"I can't see any sign of those armored cars we were told were there. There's fighting in the main park, mostly small arms and sniper fire at the moment. It looks as if they've managed to penetrate the main perimeter but haven't been able to consolidate anywhere."

"What about the fuel dump?" Running Bear, the Battlegroup Leader, asked.

"Nothing, sir. There are guards there, but they're just standing around at the moment. Hold on." There was a moment of silence during which all of them wondered what he had noticed. "There's a couple of armored cars moving in on the fuel dump now," he said when he came back on the air. "They must have got them from the vehicle park."

The Battlegroup Leader looked towards Conrad, who nodded.

"Stay up there Raincloud, but be careful," Running Bear ordered. "Group Leader Hayden, get your men sorted out and ready to go. You're responsible for sealing off the area. I don't want anyone else in, or out. Group Leader Drakikson, I want you to lead the main attack through here." He indicated one of the side entrances on the map of the armory hung up on the wall. "It's close enough to the fuel dump for you to secure it without disrupting the rest of your attack. Group Leader Nichols, you're in charge of the reserve. Your jumping off point will be the main car park. You all remember the briefing last night?"

There were nods all round.

"Remember to keep radio conversation to the absolute minimum, and if anyone contacts those armored cars pull back and let the Special Troop take over. Questions?"

Everyone shook their heads.

"All right, you've got your orders."

Five minutes later the first of the coaches pulled out of the parking lot as the three Groups left to take up their positions. As silence descended over the lot again Conrad joined Donald on the front step of the bus.

"Penny for your thoughts," Conrad said, settling beside him.

The sun had removed the hard chill from the morning air, and only a few clouds marred the perfect blue of the clear winter sky. Smoke, drifting across from the hotel's chimneys, carried with it the smell of spruce, and from a row of pines on the far side of the parking lot a lone raven cawed his welcome to the new day.

"It seems a shame to spoil such a beautiful day."

Conrad sighed; it was. "We're not the ones who started it."

"Leader." It was a radio operator again. "The Battlegroup's Leader's respects. Leader Drakikson's Group is in position."

Regretfully Conrad stood up, resting his hand for a moment on his brother's shoulder. "Looks like this is it."

Two minutes later Drakikson's troops ran into fierce resistance just inside the main gate, and the Battlegroup Leader was forced to commit his reserves. As Conrad listened to the developing battle over the radio he realized he had never felt so useless, nor so out of touch with what was really happening. With radio chatter restricted to the bare minimum it seemed there were times when all Conrad could do was watch the slow movement of the clock's minute hand around its face and hope.

His sense of powerlessness was not helped by the fact that it took almost ten minutes to move Hayden's reserves forward to assist Drakikson's troops, the delay allowing those attacking the armory to pull back some of their force to meet this new threat. Because of the delay the initial attack was less successful than initially hoped for, and progress was painfully slow.

Twenty minutes later Conrad had taken a break to stretch his back at the door to the coach when he was interrupted by Running Bear. "The Special Troop have contacted the armored cars," the Battlegroup Leader told him.

"There's still the six?"

"According to Raincloud's latest report."

"Well let's hope the rockets are effective."

"I can't see why they won't be," Donald said, getting to his feet. "They were originally used by the Nayarit as anti-tank weapons. We've just kept them on because of their effectiveness against bunkers."

"We'll see," Conrad replied, not feeling as confident as Donald.

Contact was reported shortly after, and for a few moments the flurry of combat in the far corner of the armory dominated the battle.

Luckily Donald's estimate about the effectiveness of the rockets was borne out by the total destruction of the six armored cars, although at the cost of over half the Special Troop either killed or wounded.

Raincloud's status reports on the progress of the battle had been a useful adjunct to the radio's irregular messages, but once the armored cars had been destroyed his ability to spot large movements was lost. He offered to come in lower but Conrad ordered him to maintain his height, not wanting to have to face Ivy if he allowed Raincloud to get himself killed.

The battle went slowly, with the Groups responsible for entering the armory making slow progress. Gradually, however, the rebels were pushed back from the entrance, and as they did so Hayden, responsible for maintaining the outer perimeter, moved his Group within its walls to tighten the noose.

Slowly they continued to fight their way into the armory. Progress continued to be sluggish for the first thirty minutes, but then came the first jubilant report of prisoners, and ten minutes later the whole thing was over as the rebels started to run out of ammunition.

"You better let Papa know," Conrad said, standing up and straightening his back tiredly. It was still too early to relax, but he had to admit that things had gone a lot better than they might have.

Donald nodded. "And what now?" he asked.

"Now I have to tell the armory's commander that their problems are not quite over yet."

The commander met Conrad at the main gate. "Battlegroup Leader Solderez," she said, introducing herself. A compact, stocky woman, about forty or forty-five, wearing a sweat stained gray uniform, her eyes were bleary and red rimmed from the smoke of the battle.

"Continental Leader Conrad Clemhorn," Conrad said, introducing himself. "My brother Donald, and our Battlegroup Leader, Running Bear."

She acknowledged the introductions with a nod. "Obviously we're pleased to see you, but . . ."

"You'd like to know what we're going to do now?"

"Exactly."

Conrad tried a reassuring smile. He wasn't sure how successful he was. "For the moment my orders are simply to prevent another attack. You will retain control of the armory, although I'd appreciate it if any decisions relating to placement and movement of troops were cleared by either the Battlegroup Leader or myself. We'd also like to borrow a couple of rooms to question the prisoners. The Council is eager to learn what has been going on."

"Of course," Solderez said with a tired smile. "I would also be interested in finding out what you learn."

"I'll make sure you're told. My brother will act as our liaison officer. I'm sure if you've got any problems he can sort them out." He smiled at Donald's grimace.

"With your permission then I'll see to my troops."

"Of course." Conrad watched her return to her jeep, wondering if she was presently unattached, before turning back to see to his own troops. The biggest problem he faced was how to distribute their casualties among St. Paul's six hospitals without overloading any particular one.

Immersed in the task he didn't realize how much time had passed until someone put a cup of tea in front of him and he checked his watch. Three hours! Even the battle hadn't taken that long. He stretched, suddenly realizing how sore his back was. At least the effort had been worth it, he thought gratefully. They'd finished securing the outer perimeter of the arsenal, and all their casualties had been transferred to hospital.

"Any word from Naisre?" he asked Running Bear, who had just come up.

The Battlegroup Leader nodded. "This came in a moment ago."

Conrad read the slip and sighed. "I guess we better see Battlegroup Leader Solderez."

The drive along the armory's main road provided ample testimony to the violence of the battle. Here and there gutted buildings still smoldered, while the stark, blackened remains of an armored car blocked one of the side streets, waiting for someone to remove it.

He found Donald sitting on the outside step of a two-story building, his head resting against a verandah post, eyes closed.

"Donald," he said gently, hand resting on his shoulder.

His brother opened his eyes. "It's all right, I wasn't asleep." In fact he'd been thinking of Matija.

"How's it going here?" Conrad asked.

Donald stretched, joints cracking as he did so. "Good. I don't think Solderez is actually on our side, but she certainly appreciates being left alone to run her own business."

"Oh," said Conrad doubtfully.

"Something wrong?"

"I'll tell you inside."

"Leaders," Solderez said, standing up as they entered.

The Battlegroup Leader's office was large, but sparsely furnished. The blinds on both windows had been fully opened, and dust motes danced in the light. A bookcase occupied the alcove next to the left hand window, procedural manuals filling its shelves, while an ancient three-drawer filing cabinet stood sentry on the opposite side. Old linoleum covered the floor, its pattern almost worn away by age.

"You've finished questioning the prisoners?" Solderez asked, as Conrad and Donald took their seats.

"Yes," Conrad said. "It turns out they were Mainline militia, loyal to the conservative faction though not directly under Miro's control."

"So he can evade responsibility for what happened?" Donald said.

"To an extent," Conrad said. "Interestingly, my grandfather appears to have found evidence of a wider conspiracy. Leader, had you received any new orders recently?"

Solderez nodded, embarrassed. "Two days ago I received orders from National Headquarters to surrender the armory to the local militia."

"Why didn't you?" Conrad asked.

"No one asked me to."

Donald laughed and Conrad glared at him. "Would you be prepared to testify to that in front of the Council?" he asked. Such testimony might bring the army's high command around to their side. At the very least it would allow their grandfather to identify those members of the armed forces loyal to Miro.

Solderez nodded.

Conrad pulled out the latest message from his father and tapped it nervously with his thumb. "I'm afraid I've got some bad news for you. I've just received orders to place the armory directly under our control. I hope we will continue to receive your assistance."

"Of course," Solderez said dryly.

Conrad gave her a smile. "Thanks. One of my aides will give you a list of our requirements. Donald, if I can see you outside."

"Well?" Donald asked, as soon as they had stepped onto the verandah.

"Grandfather wants to see you back at the capital straightaway. He's setting up an appearance for you before the full Council."

"You'll be all right here?"

"With Battlegroup Leader Solderez's assistance. You better tell Papa we need reinforcements though, and quickly."

"I'll do that," Donald promised. "How do I get back?"

"The same way you got here. There's a rocket standing by for you at Columbus." He couldn't hide a grin at the way his brother's face fell at the news. "Raincloud will give you a ride there once he's refueled. We shouldn't aim to keep the Council waiting."

CHAPTER NINETEEN

Naisre — Mainline
November 1979 (95AE)

As Donald climbed tiredly down from the plane at Naisre he wondered how much longer he could keep going. He hadn't slept properly for over thirty-six hours, his muscles were so tired they ached, and his headache had come back.

"There's an elevator over there," the pilot said, accepting Donald's helmet. "It connects with the A-line."

"Thanks," Donald said, peering through the drifting snow in the direction the pilot had indicated. The early dusk that masked the surrounding mountains, as well as the thick layer of snow that now covered the city's concrete dome, disorientated him. Finally spotting some lights in the distance Donald nodded to the pilot and headed for the entrance. It turned out to be closer than it had looked and as he stepped inside the heat of the city engulfed him, bringing with it a sudden surge of weakness. Leaning back against the wall, Donald closed his eyes.

"Are you all right, Leader?"

Donald became aware that the inside doors of the lift had opened and an aide was peering in at him. "Just tired," he said, pushing himself away from the wall, as the distinctive, slightly stale, blend of smells that was uniquely Naisre filled his nostrils. A change in air pressure signaled a train pulling into the station behind the aide.

"Force Leader Clemhorn?" the aide asked, refusing to budge. Donald managed to focus enough to make out the dark green uniform with its red facings, and finally to recognize one of his grandfather's aides.

"That's me," Donald said.

"My apologies sir. The World Leader of Notway would like to see you at once."

"Can we pick up some food on the way?"

"The World Leader did say at once."

"It won't slow us down," Donald assured him.

The sandwiches in their sealed container that they picked up on the way were well past their use-by date, but by the time they reached their destination he'd finished the lot and was feeling slightly more prepared for what was to come. His grandfather had taken over a couple of rooms at the Imperial University, and Donald was shown straight into the lecture theater where the meeting was being held. Despite the hour, the small auditorium was filled to capacity with World Leaders and their aides. Three tables had been set up at the foot of the chamber, facing the rows of desks that rose to the ceiling at the back of the room. The World Leader of Notway occupied the central chair; Donald's father the seat beside him. A map of St. Paul was projected on the front screen, and Lawrence had just sat down after explaining something about it.

Donald's father smiled wearily at him as his son was ushered in and leaned across to say something to his father-in-law. The World Leader of Notway looked up from the report he was scanning and, seeing Donald, stood up.

"Leaders!" The buzz of conversation quickly died. "This is Force Leader Clemhorn who has just returned from St. Paul. Do you want to come round here Donald," he suggested, indicating the spare seat next to him. "There may be some questions for you."

Donald, who had been wondering where he was to sit, took the offer thankfully.

"You've all received the briefing on what happened. Are there any questions you want to put?" his grandfather asked.

A woman on the front row put up her hand. "We were told the troops used in the assault were from Etu. I assume they haven't been used off that line before. How did they cope with the transfer to the Mainline?"

His grandfather nodded to Donald to take the question.

"Without difficulty, World Leader." Donald instinctively pitched his voice to carry to the back of the auditorium.

"I would have thought the real question was how troops used to facing bows and arrows would stand up to cannon and machine gun fire," Donald's father broke in.

"That wasn't a problem," Donald said. "Just remember Dontfrey's troops are in exactly the same situation."

There were a couple more questions then, as a lull appeared in the meeting, his grandfather called it to an end.

"Donald, if you could stay for a moment," his grandfather said, as people started to file out of the theatre.

"What's happening?" Donald asked his father quietly as they waited for the room to clear.

"We're mobilizing," his father told him, a note of weary resignation in his voice.

"Why?" Donald said, surprised.

"Because we hold the armory."

"Couldn't we hand it back to the army?" Donald asked. He could see how their control of the armory would worry the Conservatives, but surely they didn't need to keep it.

His father shook his head. "Too risky, the army is riven with factions. The only thing we can do is mobilize, and hope Miro backs down."

"And there's not much chance of that," his grandfather said. "Donald, I just wanted to thank you."

"My pleasure, Grandfather."

"It was well done."

"You better get some sleep," his father said, resting a hand on Donald's shoulder. "You look dead on your feet. I'll walk you back to the suite."

His mother was waiting for them at the suite, and seeing Donald's state immediately packed him off to bed. Exhausted as he was, Donald didn't bother to argue and was asleep as soon as his head hit the pillow.

***

When he emerged again he found his mother making a cup of tea in the kitchen.

"Feeling better?" she asked.

"A bit," Donald admitted, pulling his dressing gown tighter. "How long was I asleep?"

"About eighteen hours. Want something to eat?"

"Thanks." He stifled a yawn.

"Your father asked to see you when you woke up," she said, putting some bread in the toaster. "He's with my father in his suite."

A servant walked through with some linen, placing it into a half-filled suitcase on the floor next to the sofa.

"You're packing?" Donald said, surprised.

His mother nodded. "We decided it would be better if I returned to Etu. The Perics are heading home as well. So who's this girl I understand you've been seeing?" she asked as she placed a cup of tea in front of him.

"How did you hear about that?" Donald said, surprised.

"From Isobel."

"My aunt! How did she hear? Oh — Margaret."

"And wouldn't it be better if I'd heard about her from my own son?"

"Her name's Matija Maras," he said, admitting defeat.

"So who is she?"

"She's a textile design artist. Her father's a professor at the university."

"Professor Maras?"

"That's right. Do you know him?"

"I may have met him at a Court function a couple of years ago. I've certainly read most of his books."

"Really?"

She smiled. "Have you forgotten I was undertaking a degree in comparative history when I met your father?"

He grimaced. He had forgotten.

"So is it serious?" she asked.

"What?"

"This relationship."

"I think so."

She nodded. "Good. Just remember I'd like to have grandchildren someday, and at the moment you seem to be my best chance for that. Here you are," she added, placing a plate of buttered toast in front of him. "You better not keep your father waiting."

As he left the suite he found himself thinking about his mother's comments. He hadn't really thought about it, but he probably was the best chance for getting the next generation of Clemhorns underway. Ivy was just starting her military career, he had no idea when Conrad was going to settle down and Arnold was, well, just Arnold.

Although the corridors were crowded, with piles of luggage stacked against the wall and a constant flow of servants and military aides filling the walkways, the city itself seemed strangely subdued as he made his way down to his grandparents' suit on the next level.

Donald found his father, grandfather, uncle, and four other World Leaders clustered around a table in the conference room. Hearing Donald's hesitant knock his father looked up and smiled.

"Mama said you wanted to see me?"

"Yes, I've got a favor to ask," his father said, drawing him outside and closing the door after them. "I was wondering if you could see your mother to the portal."

"Of course. Has something happened?" Donald asked in concern.

"Not yet. It's what could happen that worries me. There are troops crossing onto the Mainline from all over the Empire at the moment. If something isn't settled at today's Council meeting . . ." He shrugged.

"When are we leaving?"

"This afternoon. You're booked on the four o'clock flight. Once you've seen her to the portal you better get back to Charleston and settle your affairs there. I'll need you back here as soon as possible."

"And Arnold?"

"The doctors don't want him moved so we're leaving him in the hospital for the moment. He should be quite safe there."

Donald nodded, as he doubted anyone would want to risk an outright confrontation with Central Command. As split as the army seemed there was a real risk that any overt move by one side against the army's central base in Naisre would simply drive the entire army into the arms of the other side.

"Take care," his father said, giving him a quick hug.

Donald returned the hug, but he suspected his father's mind was already fixed on the question of troop movements and Council allegiances.

When he arrived back at the suite Margaret was just leaving it. His cousin was wearing traveling clothes; a tight, hussar style jacket and long riding dress. Her long red hair was pulled back into a single braid.

"I've just come from your rooms," Donald said. "Rajko didn't know where you were."

"We're just leaving."

"I know. I thought I'd missed you."

She checked her watch. "I've got to go. Our flight leaves in fifteen minutes."

He nodded, sensing the chasm yawning beneath their feet.

"Do I get a hug?" Margaret asked suddenly, tears in her voice.

He nodded silently, unable to speak.

She smelled of roses, and for a moment Donald thought she was trying to squeeze the air out of him. Suddenly she pulled away, and stretching up kissed him on the cheek, then without another word turned away. Donald watched her until she disappeared into the lift, before turning back to the suite.

***

Donald and his mother arrived in Lincoln at nine o'clock that night. The town was awash with the light blue of Clemhorn uniforms. There seemed something wrong with all that blue on the Mainline, though he was impressed with the job Conrad had done to get them there.

"Look after your father for me," his mother said, at the entrance to the terminal.

"I'll do my best," Donald promised.

"You better go if you're going to catch that flight."

He nodded, shivering with a sudden feeling of dread. "Take care Mama," he said, hugging her.

She returned the hug before patting his cheek. "Make sure you remember to eat."

"I'll try," he said, managing a half smile.

He watched her enter the building then turned and walked quickly back towards the car. His flight to Charleston left in half an hour, and he'd have to hurry if he didn't want to miss it.

As it happened the flight was delayed, and Donald spent the next three hours trying to make himself comfortable in one of the airport's ubiquitous bucket chairs. Boarding for his flight was announced at around one o'clock and Donald was finally able to stretch out on a couch in the observation deck. It was a smooth flight and he disembarked at Charleston around four-thirty, getting back to his flat just as dawn was breaking over the city.

The flat was freezing, and after turning the heat on Donald sat down on the bed to pull his boots off. The next thing he remembered was getting woken by the noonday sun as it arched in over the top of the curtains.

He blinked and shaded his face against the light as he struggled to free himself from the eiderdown, which had somehow tangled itself around his legs as he slept. His stomach growled and, after finally managing to unwrap himself, Donald swung his feet over the edge of the bed.

By the time he emerged from the flat the sun was hiden behind a thin layer of cloud. Charleston looked even grayer than usual and the few people on the street were all hurrying as though eager to get inside. Donald pulled his coat closer around him against the cold.

The corner store beckoned, warm and inviting, and James the shopkeeper looked up as he entered, his waxed moustache glistening in the overhead lights. Pulling off his gloves Donald sniffed appreciatively at the smell of pies warming on their trays.

"Mister Clemhorn," James said. "What can we do for you?"

"I'll have a pie, James. How are things going?"

"Quite well, sir. A bit of a shame about the Council though."

Donald's face must have shown his confusion.

"It's in all the newspapers," James said, waving at the stack on the counter as he pulled a pie out of the warmer. "There was some sort of fight last night in the Council and the army's declared martial law."

Donald's eyes flicked over to the papers, opening in shock as he noticed the headline for the first time. He quickly picked up a copy and scanned the main article for more information. Apparently, as he'd been arriving in Charleston last night, Council had taken another vote. From the report it appeared that the Dynand World Leader had moved to support Donald's grandfather and, with tempers already frayed from fifteen hours of debate, one of Miro's supporters had physically attacked him. A general melee had broken out, and when the army stepped in and dissolved the Council members of both sides staged a walk out in protest.

"Doesn't look good, sir, does it?"

"No," Donald said.

With the Council dissolved, there was little chance of a peaceful settlement.

"Fifty pence, sir," James said.

Handing over the money Donald took the pie in exchange. "I better buy this as well," he said, indicating the newspaper.

"So what do you think will happen now, sir?" James asked, giving him the change.

"God knows. The army's not powerful enough to impose a settlement. In fact, they're probably too busy trying to hold their own ruling body together to do anything constructive."

"It's a real pity about Treik, sir. If he hadn't died . . ."

"The world is full of what-ifs, James. The timelines even more so, but you're right. If Treik hadn't died we wouldn't be facing this now." He waved the newspaper to emphasize his point.

Outside, Donald folded the newspaper under his arm before taking a bite of his pie. The rich aroma of gravy flooded his mouth, and relishing the warmth, Donald turned and started towards the university.

It was three o'clock by the time he'd finished talking with Professor Dvorak, the Dean of the history faculty, and hoping Matija would be the College's library or in her studio, he headed downtown to the ivy-covered building next to the river. It was drizzling as he hurried across the grass towards the College library, the quadrangle deserted of students.

Donald found Matija in the alcove she normally occupied on the third floor. Although there were several books open on the desk in front of her it didn't look as though she was doing much studying, as she had her eyes closed and was leaning back in her chair. Her black shoulder length hair, spilling down her back, exposed the fragile lines of her neck.

"Hi," he said softly.

Her eyes flew open. "Donald!" she cried, throwing herself at him out of the chair. Her hug was almost painfully tight, and when she drew his lips down to hers and he responded ardently.

It was a while before she remembered where they were, and started to release him with an embarrassed smile.

"Got a moment?" he asked, refusing to let her escape so easily.

"Only a moment," she said, her face falling as she guessed what that might mean.

"I'm afraid so."

"Come on then," she said, picking up her files. "Let's go."

As he helped her pick up her files he couldn't help noticing the interested glances of a number of other people studying in the area, and one person doing his best not to smirk too broadly into the book he was pretending to read.

"How long have you got?" she asked, pulling his arm around her as they headed down to the ground.

"My flight leaves at ten tomorrow morning."

"And when will you be back?"

"I don't know," he admitted.

"Does the university know?"

He nodded. "I've just spoken to the Dean. To say he was unhappy would probably be an understatement, but he's promised to hold a position for me."

"Do you know where you're going to be?"

Donald shook his head.

"Not even in an hour's time?" she said, looking up at him with a sparkle in her eyes.

"With you?"

"I think the man can read the future."

He bent to kiss her but she pulled away quickly, looking around as she did so. "Come on, the studio's empty," she told him.

Later that night, cradled in each other's arms in a nest made of blankets on the studio floor, Donald became aware that Matija was crying.

"What's wrong?" he asked, alarmed.

"Nothing," she said, turning away to face the wall.

"Nothing doesn't make you cry," he said firmly, turning her back to face him. "Now, what's wrong?"

She rubbed eyes. "It's just you're going away."

"I'll be back."

"You better," she said fiercely. "Or I'll never forgive you."

"I'll be back," he said, laughing, sealing the promise with a kiss.

CHAPTER TWENTY

St. Paul — Mainline
December 1979 (95AE)

Swiveling in his chair, Conrad gazed out of the tower's window at the six massive airships tethered to their pylons outside. Searchlights played along their sides as troops moved forward to embark in long, sinuous lines that stretched off into the darkness of the terminal buildings beyond.

Pride warred with worry at the sight. Everything was taking too long. Someone coughed and he looked up to see Donald in the door.

"Come in," Conrad said, waving him in. "You took your time, I was starting to think we'd have to leave you behind."

"You almost had to; I was just leaving the flat when your telegram arrived. The airlines are chaos at the moment, so I ended up taking the train."

Conrad grimaced. "Everything's chaos at the moment."

"So what's happening?" Donald asked, dumping his kit by the door.

"We've been ordered to Europe, and the first Group's just embarking." He gestured towards the window.

"Europe? I thought we were concentrating on America."

"We were, but we've just about got everything sewn up here. Another day or so and we'll have finished sealing off any portals we still feel uneasy about."

"So what do you want me to do?"

Conrad gestured helplessly at the papers in front of him. "Whatever you can do to help. I've been boosted up to Corps Leader, but I haven't had time to set up any sort of proper Headquarters so the only staff I've got are what I can beg, steal, or borrow. You'll have to do the job of about four people."

There was a knock on the door, and Conrad looked up to see an aide standing there. "Yes?"

"The 'Fair Sky' has just finished loading."

Conrad glanced out the window to where the closest of the six airships was moored. The ground at its base was bare of troops and as he watched, the first of its huge propellers started to rotate. "Tell the Captain he can leave as soon as he's ready."

The aide saluted.

"So what's happening here?" Donald asked.

"My godfather got us six airships. We can fit just over one Group, with equipment, in each. That's without their mounts, but we're running up quite a bill on the portal just getting the men through, and I haven't got the transport to get them to Europe anyway. What I'm really worried about is the shortage of artillery, but I guess there's nothing I can do about that."

"Who are you taking?"

"The Rangers, and two Battlegroups of regulars from Maun. That's three flights each, say twenty-four hours for the lot."

"Who's holding the armory if you've got the Rangers here?"

"The 42nd militia. They arrived this morning."

"What do you want me to start with?"

"Coffee."

Donald looked at him, but Conrad was obviously serious, so he went to try and locate the kitchen.

Outside, the 'Fair Sky', its propellers blurring into motion, slowly maneuvered its way free of the ground. Then, as water poured from its ballast tanks, the airship surged skyward, rising quickly into the concealing darkness of the night sky.

"One down, seventeen to go," Conrad remarked quietly to himself.

***

Twenty-eight hours later the airship carrying Conrad and Donald followed in its wake. It was an uneventful flight and they arrived in London to be greeted by a heavy, pea-soup fog.

"Gods, I wish I was back in Mexico," Conrad said, turning the collar of his greatcoat up and pulling the peak of his kepi down as far as it would go. The air stank of stale coal and sulfur.

"I thought a pea-souper was damp," Donald said, surprised, as he peered out into the haze. "The air's actually quite dry."

Conrad grunted.

Raincloud, who had come across with the first flight, suddenly loomed out of the fog. "Leaders," he said, a wide smile creasing his face. "Welcome to England."

"How long is this going to last?" Conrad asked shortly.

"The fog? Forecast says for another couple of days."

"Hi Jon," Donald said.

Raincloud acknowledged the greeting with a nod.

"Sorry Jon," Conrad apologized. "Just got a lot on my mind. Where have you got us?"

"The Majestic," Raincloud said. "It was the only place I could still get any rooms. The rest of the Corps is all over the place."

Conrad noticed Donald's expression. "Make the most of it," he said. "It will only be for a day or two at most."

"Oh, I will," Donald assured him. "Six star elegance here I come."

Conrad winced.

Shepherding them towards the terminal, Raincloud moved everyone inside to pick up their kits, tendrils of fog following them in through the door. It didn't take long; a couple of staffers (nominated by Raincloud) called out the person's name as their kit was brought in by trolley, and they moved forward to collect it.

"It was chaos the first time, when everyone got their own kit," Raincloud explained. "It took us ages to sort out the mess."

Kits secured, Raincloud ushered everyone out the front to where the buses waited; Troop and Force identifiers plainly indicated on their front windscreens. The fog had started to lift slightly, and a chill, damp wind now swirled around the vehicles urging everyone on board.

"So what's been happening?" Donald asked Raincloud, as he helped stow their gear in the overhead racks.

"Not sure," Raincloud said, shaking his head. "Apparently there's another two Corps in England somewhere, but I haven't actually talked to anyone from them, and haven't the foggiest where they are." He looked at Conrad.

"Don't ask me. All I was told to do was to get these three Battlegroups to London, organize transport for them, and get them ready to move onto the continent as soon as possible. And speaking of transport, how did you go getting the buses I asked for?"

"I've still got a couple of people working on it. I've managed to get about half of what we need, but we're going to have to take the rest out of service. And I haven't been able to get any mounts."

"I was afraid of that," Conrad said. "Keep trying though. We need those horses."

"Of course," Raincloud said, as the bus lurched into motion. London's outer suburbs extended almost as far as the airport, and it wasn't long before they passed the first of London's ubiquitous red bricked terrace houses. Soon, however, the terraces were replaced by the gray stone-faced buildings of the city itself. The fog had thickened again, obscuring the view of those inside the bus.

Suddenly the coach lurched as the driver changed down to first gear.

"I hope the view improves tomorrow," Donald said.

"From what I remember reading, this is the best it gets," Conrad said.

As though to contradict him though the fog suddenly thinned, and they found themselves on a bridge, the Thames flowing dark and sullen below them.

"Where are we?" Conrad asked.

"Vauxhall Bridge," Raincloud said, checking the map.

Conrad noticed a couple of people listening and jerked his head towards the back of the bus. "Want to speak up?"

Raincloud grimaced but stood up. "Apparently I've been nominated to act as tour guide for all of you who haven't seen London before."

"And who can't see it now," someone responded from the back. There was scattered laughter.

There was a jerk as the bus turned right into Millbank Road. "We are passing through Westminster at the moment," Raincloud said. "On the left, if it wasn't for the fog, you could probably see the famous Heritage buildings built in 1845 by the army, but presently used as flats by the people of the City of London. Following them is Westminster Abbey, and on the right we are now passing the Houses of Parliament." The bus lurched again and Raincloud almost lost his footing.

At Admiralty Arch the driver ground his gears again as he turned left into the Mall, Raincloud balancing himself cautiously on the balls of his feet as he did so. Slower now, the bus passed into a long, tree bordered street, each tree looming out of the fog over them as they passed. The streets were empty of traffic, but despite that they were moving at a speed little more than a crawl.

Raincloud consulted his map again. "On your left," he said, as the bus ground its way up a low hill, "should be Buckingham Palace."

Conrad craned to see out of the window, but of course everything beyond the front gate was hidden by fog. He did glimpse two of the guard on duty; their distinctive bearskin helmets recognizable even through the fog.

A sudden gap in the fog showed them the statue of America that stood in the roundabout in front of the Palace. Thirty foot tall, she stood clutching the sword of liberty with outstretched arm, a small child gathered to her feet as she defiantly faced down the Russian bear.

After one circuit of the statue the driver drew off up Constitution Hill, before turning right down Piccadilly Road. They passed a car parked on the side of the road, their first sign of other traffic. Cautiously the driver edged left into Bond Street. A moment later he applied the brakes, and looking out of the window Conrad saw the Majestic's ornate facade looming over them out of the fog, its upper floors lost in the haze.

Inside the foyer a bright fire burned away the gloom. Conrad's boots sank deep into the oriental rug that covered the marble floor as he followed Raincloud over to the reception desk where the manager, in formal evening wear, stood ready to greet them. A series of large, luminescently beautiful English landscapes lined the wall behind the desk.

"They must have cost a packet," Donald said softly, looking at the landscapes.

"Why?" Conrad asked, wondering what he was missing.

"They're mosaics."

Conrad's eyes opened in surprise as he realized Donald was right, and the landscapes had actually been assembled out of minute slivers of stone. That would explain the vibrancy of their color, he thought.

"Leader."

Conrad looked round to find a Ranger wearing a signaler's flash holding a message slip out to him.

"From Naisre," the messenger said.

Conrad skimmed the message quickly. "Hold it everyone. Someone go and stop the coach."

One of the Rangers next to the door dashed out to hold the coach, while the rest stood by, wondering what was happening.

"We've been ordered to proceed with all speed to Calais," Conrad said finally, after reading it through thoroughly. "It seems things are starting to heat up. Raincloud, you're going to have to get those buses you were talking about. I don't care if you have to take them at gun point; I want to be in Calais this afternoon. We'll be taking the Maun, so you have to organize sufficient ferries for both of us."

Raincloud frowned, then nodded.

"We'll establish a temporary headquarters here until you're ready to move. There is a little spare time, but I wouldn't stand around waiting."

Raincloud started, then saluting quickly, turned and went into a huddle with three officers in the corner.

"Sir." It was the manager of the hotel. "If I could suggest the use of one of our conference rooms?"

Conrad looked round at the throng untidily filling the foyer and nodded.

"Thank you," he said.

It was a very informal headquarters that was quickly organized in the first floor conference room. Most of map boards and such like were still with the rest of the Battlegroup's heavy equipment at the airport, but within a couple of minutes members of the staff were organized enough to set about recalling units of the Corps which had been settled all over the city, and arranging for transport to get them on their way to the continent.

***

To Conrad's surprise Raincloud actually proved capable of accomplishing miracles, and they were at Dover before lunch. Once there, however, there was a couple of hours delay when it was discovered that the double-decker buses, which made up a quarter of the convoy, wouldn't fit into the two ferries Raincloud had hired. Conrad eventually solved the problem by requisitioning all the coaches of the local bus company, and when the Corps finally marched onto the ferries the hold was crammed with the green and yellow striped coaches of the South-East Coach Line.

Drizzle flattened the white tops that surged against the sea wall, and caused the ferries to rock uneasily in time to the swell. It was hot and stuffy inside the cabins, and as soon as they were underway Conrad went up on deck, where he found his brother staring out over the ocean.

"Penny for your thoughts," Conrad said.

"Just wondering if we've got everyone," Donald said, continuing to watch the drizzle drift slowly across the gray ocean. "I have this feeling there's a squad of Rangers still holed up in a London hotel somewhere. Snug and warm, with no idea they could be out on the Channel with us."

"Mired in the London fog." Conrad snorted. "How can people live like that?"

"I guess they're used to it."

"Yeah, but with all the lines calling out for labor?"

The two brothers fell silent.

"Did you ever visit Europe while you were at the Academy?" Donald asked.

"Hayden and I did a three week pub tour during a semester break in our second year. That was just before he started to see Mary."

"Trust you to do a three week pub crawl," Donald said with a smile.

"It was actually quite interesting," Conrad said defensively. "We ended up sampling over 315 different varieties of beer. I've still got the diary I was keeping the ratings in somewhere. And the pubs themselves had some pretty interesting histories attached to them."

"As much as you know how interesting I find beer I think it might be time to go inside," Donald said, as the drizzle threatened to turn to sleet.

Conrad lifted his head to feel the rain on his face and nodded. "Sounds like a good idea."

***

No one saw much of Calais, a city hidden behind a veil of sleet, because as soon as they landed they were ordered inland towards Lille. From there Conrad suspected they'd be moving south towards Paris, the center of Miro's European operations.

The rain had been replaced by the promise of snow as they approached Lille, the fading sun staining the western horizon blood-red as the fifty coaches of the convoy arrived at the outskirts of the city. A small detachment of soldiers waved them off the main road into a parking lot cordoned off for their use.

"Corps Leader Clemhorn?" a young Squad Leader asked, coming over to the coach. She had a strong Russian accent, and wore an off-white uniform that Conrad couldn't quite identify.

"Yes?" Conrad said as the driver turned the engine off. The sudden silence echoed disconcertingly in his ears.

"I've been asked to take you to Headquarters as soon as you arrived."

"Donald, you're with me," he told his brother.

He found his godfather in the temporary headquarters set up in Lille's Town Hall. He looked harassed, but still managed to give a smile when he saw them. His uniform was no longer the gray and maroon of the First Leader's Intelligence Corps, but rather the dark green of Notway. To Conrad the change seemed significant.

"Sorry for the confusion," he apologized, as he signed a chit a staff officer gave him. "We only got here an hour ago and every time we start getting settled something else goes wrong."

Conrad nodded. Confusion was an understatement; the hall was chaos. He stepped to one side to avoid a staffer. The noise of an autogiro practically landing on the roof made him look up, startled.

"Kristos, how are we going moving the giro-park?" his godfather asked a passing officer.

"I was told they'd finished half an hour ago."

"Then find out what that idiot was trying to do."

"Leader."

"Come on outside," he said. "It might be quieter."

In the relative shelter of the alley outside he paused to light a cigarette. "You've got three Battlegroups with you?" he asked, taking a puff.

"Yes."

"And transport?"

"Fifty coaches."

His godfather looked relieved. "There's a couple of fields set aside for you about a mile north of here. I'll get someone to show you where they are."

"Will the buses be all right?" Conrad asked. "The ground looked very soft coming in."

"Leave them on the road."

"And we've got no horses or artillery."

"Understood. Don't worry about it, a lot of the units coming in by rail don't have any transport at all. Here, hold on a moment." He stubbed the cigarette out and disappeared for a moment before reappearing with a member of the staff. "Jorgenson will show you where we're putting you. As soon as you're settled I want you back here though. I'm trying to organize a briefing on the situation in about half an hour."

"We'll be there," Conrad said.

"Good, I'll see you there then."

"What a way to run a war," Donald said, watching Lawrence's departing back.

Raising an eyebrow, Conrad surveyed the chaos now spilling out from inside the hall. "What do you expect? The largest group we ever exercise with is the Corps, and we've never even tried to transport that over any great distance in a hurry."

Donald shrugged. "I just hope the other side is as disorganized."

"Amen to that. If they're not this is going to be a very short war."

Conrad was pleased to see the field they'd been allocated was covered by a thin layer of stubble, which meant, he hoped, that it wouldn't immediately disintegrate into mud during the night. Another Group was already set up in the next field, their fires small beacons of lights against the gathering dark.

Disembarking, Conrad scuffed at the loose gravel on the side of the road, feeling the cold even through the two pairs of socks he wore. Thrusting his mittened fingers deeper into his pockets he hunched his shoulders against the wind. "You better go and see if there is anywhere to turn around," he told Donald. "I'll get everything unloaded."

"There's a widening in the road just around the next bend," Jorgenson volunteered. "But it might be best if you follow the road round because it bears back to the main highway. That way there's no risk of getting stuck."

"Thanks," Conrad said. "We'll do that then." He checked his watch. "I think we better be getting back if we want to attend that meeting."

"Did you want a lift?" Jorgenson asked.

Conrad nodded, turning to Running Bear, the Ranger's Battlegroup Leader. "We'll leave the buses here for the moment.

I'll be back as soon as I can, but in the meantime get someone to liaise with the Corps in the next field up and set up camp. I'll see what arrangements, if any, have been made for food and get word back to you."

Back at the hall chairs had been set out for the briefing. Most of them were already occupied, and taking two at the back they were joined a moment later by their father.

"When did you two arrive?" he said.

"About quarter of an hour ago. Weren't you told?" Donald said.

"No, but that's not surprising."

"Is there any possibility of getting some food to the Corps?" Conrad asked. "We didn't bring any with us."

"That's being taken care of at the moment. Or it was the last thing I heard."

Suddenly the buzz of conversation started to die down, and looking up Conrad saw that Grandfather had taken his place on the stage.

"Leaders," he said when everyone had settled. "We have just been informed that the 1st Corps has engaged, and destroyed two Battlegroups south of Bapaume, but is now facing a reinforced strength of two Corps."

There was a nervous rustle among those watching.

Conrad looked at Donald who shrugged. He didn't know where Bapaume was either.

Their grandfather waited for silence again before continuing. "Most of Miro's forces have already assembled around Paris, and would appear to be moving north in an attempt to prevent us from combining. We've still got a number of Corps moving up the Italian peninsula from North Africa and Greece, but most of our strength is already here. Accordingly it has been decided to reinforce the 1st Corps."

Conrad leaned over to Donald. "As soon as you can, get out and stop our lot from doing any more unpacking."

Donald nodded.

What a way to fight a war, Conrad thought tiredly. He couldn't see the troops being very impressed.

"Rations and ammunition will be available at Arras," the Notway World Leader continued. "We have a double track between here and Albert, but so does Miro. We've already started scheduling units to move and the first train leaves in half an hour." He paused for a moment. "The situation is not of our choosing," he said, his voice rolling out over the hall, "but this battle will determine the fate of the Empire. I would just ask you all to bear that in mind." He nodded and turned away.

"Now," Conrad said to Donald. "I'll follow as soon as I can."

When the meeting broke up about fifteen minutes later and Conrad followed his brother outside he found Raincloud waiting for him there. "What are you doing here?" Conrad asked.

"Donald thought you might want some transport."

"You've got some?"

Raincloud gestured at the lurid pink motorbike and sidecar combination standing in the shelter of the building, and grinned when he saw Conrad's expression. "War is hell, isn't it," he said with a smile. "It belongs to one of the local farmers. He was happy for us to take it off his hands. Apparently it used to belong to his daughter."

Back at the field Running Bear was peering over some maps with Donald. "So we're moving again," was the Battlegroup Leader's only comment when he saw Conrad.

"Afraid so. We just have to tighten our belts until we get to Arras. How long before we're ready to move?"

"About two hours. I'd sent scouts out to try and get us some food. I've recalled them, but not all of them have radios."

"Well, do the best you can. If necessary we can leave a bus behind for any stragglers, just so we get most of the Corps on the road."

Despite the obvious urgency of the situation it seemed to take forever for their orders to arrive. Finally, however, the coaches pulled slowly away.

"What's the time?" Donald asked, looking up from the book he was reading.

"Just after ten. We were sitting there for three bloody hours!"

"At least it gave us time to get all the stragglers back. Here, I got this for you," Donald said, reaching under his chair and handing Conrad a bottle of beer.

Conrad held the bottle, not recognizing the brand. He opened the cap and took a cautious mouthful. "Nice," he said. "Where did you get it?"

"Raincloud."

"What's the book?" Conrad asked, looking over his shoulder.

"It's a treatise comparing the idea of Historical Inevitability versus Individual Causation in the context of the Mainline. I'm thinking of doing something similar for Etu."

"Oh, and what's the difference between Historical Inevitability and Individual whatever you said?"

Donald smiled. "Individual Causation. That theory argues that history is shaped by the effect of a decisive individual. Historical Inevitability on the other hand holds that history, or the creation of separate 'timelines', is created by the effect of vast, impersonal cultural forces that eventually build up so much potential the line has to split."

"Which means?"

"There's research indicating that the pivotal creation point for the Mainline occurred in 1389 AD when the Serbian King crushingly defeated the Turks at the Battle of Kosovo, thus firmly establishing Serbian independence and the potential for a Balkan-based renaissance."

"As against, what — losing the battle and the renaissance occurring in France?"

"Most of the research on near lines seems to indicate it would have been an Italian Renaissance, but yes."

"So was it the effect of the Serbian King, or the effectiveness of the Serbian state?"

"Sort of, although you're over-simplifying the Historical Inevitability argument to the point of absurdity."

Conrad thought about it for a moment. "My money's on the individual." He held the bottle up. "Thanks for the beer," he added, and hoisted himself out of his seat to check with the Battlegroup Leader, leaving Donald shaking his head.

They arrived in Arras about midnight, to find that because of the delays in sending people off from Lille the situation was almost under control.

Disembarking outside the Town Hall they were each handed a five-day ration pack, before being ushered through into the main hall to get a hot meal.

There were no chairs and everyone had to eat standing up, but after eating his first proper meal in over a day, Conrad finally started to feel a little more confident about the coming battle. There was something else he'd noticed as well, the Etu and Maun soldiers who made up the Corps had finally started to talk to each other. Admittedly their English was rather broken, and there was more laughter than any meaningful conversation, but the barriers had started to come down.

They were allowed fifteen minutes to finish their meal before a rather harassed Squad Leader herded them outside where they were issued with additional ammunition. Then once more ensconced on the coaches they were on their way again. This time, however, they were heading into battle.

CHAPTER TWENTY-ONE

Bapaume - Mainline
December 1979 (95AE)

Conrad jerked awake from an uneasy doze to find their vehicle pulling over to the side of the road. It was still dark outside, although the full moon provided enough light for him to guess they must have reached Bapaume. The coach door hissed open and cold air spilled into the coach as an officer wearing the rumpled uniform of light green jacket and red tabards and trousers of a Kleng Group Leader, a strip of white cloth tied around his right arm, climbed on board.

"Corps Leader?" the newcomer asked.

"That's me," Conrad said.

"Group Leader Brillow from the 1st Corps. You'll be acting as reserve for the rest of the army. Do you have a map?"

"Several," Conrad said. They'd been among the supplies requisitioned by the forage parties.

"Thank goodness, the last Corps didn't have any."

Someone passed the map to Conrad and he passed it over.

"Station your men at Le Sars," the Group Leader said, marking a point on the map with his finger. "That's about four or five miles up the road from here, and about the same number of miles behind the line we've got set up along the road from Peronne."

Conrad nodded.

"What's happened so far?" Donald asked.

"We caught two Battlegroups when they were in a line of march just out of Albert and mauled them quite badly. Then they brought up reinforcements and pushed us back to Pozieres, that's where we are at the moment. We're trying to dig in on a line between Beaumont Hamel and Harcourt, but the ground is frozen solid." He traced the line with his finger. "It will be touch and go in the morning. The enemy have got a bottleneck at Albert. It's the only bridge over the river Ancre for miles, but they've already got more over the river than we have."

"Thanks," Conrad said. "Where's Army Headquarters getting set up?"

"In Bapaume. We've set up the Town Hall for them, but at the moment control is being exercised through my Corps. We're operating on channel 42; the secondary frequency is 51."

Conrad nodded. "So what's with the cloth?" he asked with a nod at the Group Leader's right arm.

"You weren't told?"

"What?"

The Group Leader swore. "We're all supposed to be wearing them. It's to identify friend from foe."

"Makes sense," Conrad said. With all the different uniforms around he was surprised they hadn't thought about it earlier. "So where do we get them?"

"You were supposed to get them at Arras." The Group Leader shook his head. "I can't believe this."

"We could use field dressings," Raincloud suggested.

"Sounds good. Raincloud, make sure everyone knows." He turned to Running Bear. "We'll disembark here, park the coaches out of the way, and move up on foot." The Battlegroup Leader nodded.

"I've assigned one of my staff to guide you into Le Sars," the Group Leader said. "Good luck," and with a nod he was gone.

The wind had died away and as Conrad climbed down from the coach his breath frosted up into the clear, cloudless sky overhead. It was a full moon, and in front of them the sixty foot artificial mound of Burtha de Harlen Court seemed to create a hole in the star-thronged sky.

Snow crunched noisily underfoot as Conrad moved away from the bus to watch the Rangers shake themselves out into marching order and start down the old Roman road towards Le Sars. Behind him the first of the Maun regulars in their khaki field uniforms and heavy greatcoats were already preparing to follow the Rangers.

A Troop of mounted infantry, the white strips of cloth on their right arms identifying them as friendly, clattered down the road from behind them, forcing the Rangers off the road. Behind them came four light horse artillery units. There was some good natured cursing as the units passed, then as the road cleared the Corps started off once again.

Despite the weight of the extra ammunition they were carrying there was little grumbling, and as the lead Group started up a marching song the words were quickly picked up and passed down the line.

The first units of the Corps marched into Le Sars shortly after midnight. It wasn't much of a village; just fifteen derelict houses and an old church — another casualty of the Decimation.

"We'll set up the Corps Headquarters in the church," Conrad told Donald when they arrived. "Raincloud, I want a situation report from each of the three Battlegroups as soon as you can get it."

"Leader."

"And make contact with the three Corps to our front."

Raincloud saluted, and started away to see to his orders.

"Now, let's see what we've got," Conrad said, referring to the building.

It wasn't too bad, he thought, as he peered around. The roof had held up and most of the windows were still in place. He ran his fingers lightly down the wall, the surface coming away under his touch. Someone brought a lantern, and in its flickering light they were able to see the debris that covered the floor, mostly leaves and straw from the thatch.

"Right. We may as well have this room," Conrad said, dumping his pack on the ground as he looked round the small room that had once served as the sacristy. "We'll set up the command post in the main room. Donald, want to see if you can get a fire lit?"

"Sure."

"Leader?"

Conrad turned to see one of the radio operators. "Yes?"

"A message from Headquarters. They've arrived in Bapaume."

"Thank you."

Outside, small fires, created from the debris of the village, sprang up everywhere as the Corps settled itself into position for the remainder of the night. It was getting colder, and Conrad shivered as he took a moment to look out over the snow-covered deserted fields that surrounded them. Even his breath seemed reluctant to leave the warmth of his body, and he readjusted his scarf over his mouth. Jamming his fingers deeper into their pockets he turned back to the meager warmth of the small fire that

Donald had managed to get going.

He woke in darkness, to the smell of roasting bacon.

"What's the time?" he called out softly, unable to make out even his watch in the darkness.

A dark hump in the corner stirred, and someone came to the door. "Quarter past six," said a voice Conrad recognized as Raincloud's. "Stand-to is in twenty-five minutes. Would you like a cup of tea?"

"Thanks," Conrad said, wriggling out of his bag. "Where's the toilet?"

"Out the back. You can't miss it, it's being guarded by a Troop."

"Guarding it?" he queried.

"Well, that's what it looks like."

When Conrad came back he found the rest of Headquarters awake. Grabbing a cup of tea he checked his watch, then put the Corps on stand-to. As the order was passed on men rolled out of their bags, and holding their rifles, stared out over a darkened countryside, waiting for the enemy who was, they hoped, only doing the same thing.

Gradually the eastern sky lightened, returning color to the day. More snow had fallen during the night, hiding all signs of the Corps' passing. Now the virginal fields stilled themselves for the sun's first appearance. Ensconced comfortably against the doorframe, mug of tea in one hand, bacon sandwich in the other, Conrad watched the sun rise slowly over the distant hills.

"So what happens now?" Donald asked, disturbing him. Raincloud was with him and Conrad made room for them both in the doorway.

"We wait," Conrad said.

"What do you think are our chances?" Raincloud asked.

Conrad looked round, but no one else was listening. He shrugged. "Fifty-fifty I guess. Miro's got more troops than us, but we might have got the drop on him. Whether that will last though . . ." he shrugged, then stretched. "Tell the Battlegroup Leaders to stand the troops down, it's light enough to see now."

He was outside, trying to hide his nervousness by taking a walk around the yard, when he noticed Raincloud sitting on the dry-stone wall by the back door, working on a letter.

"Who are you writing to?" Conrad asked.

"Ivy," Jon said, without looking up.

"You write?"

"Sure, got my A levels and everything."

"Cut the crap," Conrad said. "I meant you and Ivy."

"Every week."

"How is she?" Conrad asked, suddenly conscious that he hadn't written to his sister for over a year.

"Good. I got a couple of letters from her last week when the mail caught up with us at St. Paul. She's still settling in but it's going well. She's just met her third Troop Leader."

Every week! Conrad whistled silently to himself. That sounded serious. "I'll leave you to it. Send her my best, will you?"

"Sure."

About forty-five minutes later they were startled by the first hollow boom of artillery in the distance.

"Where do you think it's coming from?" Donald asked, looking over Conrad's shoulder at the map he had out in front of him.

"It's definitely to the south," Conrad said, looking out at the tree-shrouded hill that blocked their view. Suddenly he heard something else and held up his hand for silence. Under the muffled cannonade could now be heard the shorter, sharp staccato of small arms fire to their front.

"Raincloud, tell the Battlegroup Leaders I want everyone ready to move out at a moment's notice. And I want the spare ammunition divided up; everyone's to carry some."

"Leader." Jon paused. "Could I ask a favor?"

"Sure, what do you want?"

Raincloud handed him the letter he'd been writing. "If anything happens to me, could you make sure Ivy gets this?"

Conrad looked at the envelope for a moment before accepting it. "Of course."

Raincloud nodded his thanks before heading back inside.

Conrad looked at Donald, who smiled warily back at him.

"Looks like this is it," Conrad said.

Donald nodded. "Good luck," he said, holding out his hand.

Conrad took it. "Look after yourself," he said.

"I will," Donald promised. "Try to do the same."

It was another hour, however, before their orders to move forward finally arrived.

"Here," Conrad said, passing the message to Donald to read. "I thought they'd forgotten us. It looks like the 1st Corp's suffered some pretty heavy casualties. We're to move forward and take some of the pressure off them. Raincloud, get a SitRep from each of the Battlegroups. I want us on the move in ten minutes." Five minutes later, however, a messenger arrived with a change of orders.

Conrad scanned the message and swore.

"What is it?" Donald asked.

"We've got to dig in."

"Here?" Donald kicked at the frozen ground.

"That's what it says. We're to dig in and let the 1st Corps fall back on us."

Donald took the map and traced out the line they'd be holding. "We're a bit thin on the ground," he remarked.

Conrad nodded. "One person every four or five yards." He sighed. "Let's hope Grandpapa can get us some reinforcements. Raincloud."

"Yes Leader."

"Tell the Battlegroup Leaders our orders have changed. We're to hold our present position. We've got about fifteen minutes until the enemy gets here."

Raincloud saluted smartly and disappeared back into the building housing their headquarters to see to the message.

The whistle of an incoming shell caused Conrad to duck instinctively. A moment later the building across the road exploded into a rain of rubble and fire.

"Get them out of there!" Conrad heard himself shout, as a squad rushed to clear the debris. Another shell whistled overhead, and Conrad threw himself flat. As he started to pick himself up another landed just behind him, the explosion hurling him to the ground again. Opening his eyes he was suddenly aware of the frantic pounding of his heart, and wondered if he was having a heart attack. As he struggled to his feet, however, he had only the one thought, to find his brother.

There was an eerie silence over the battlefield. Then abruptly, as though someone had turned the radio back on, sound rushed in on him from all directions; the crackle of small arms in the distance, the explosion of shells around him.

The stink and heat of flames from behind him caused him to spin, and he staggered back as he found the church a roaring conflagration of flames.

"Donald!" he called.

"I'm here," his brother said, suddenly appearing beside him. His face was blackened with smoke, and a small trickle of blood escaped from a cut over his left eye.

Conrad flinched as another two shells screamed in to finish demolishing the church.

"We've got to move forward," Donald told him, signaling to those watching to start moving. "If we stay here we'll be cut to pieces. At least if we close up they won't be able to use their artillery."

Conrad nodded. He peered into the conflagration to see if there was anything he could do to help, but the fire was already too hot, smoke and flames everywhere.

"Where's Raincloud?" Donald asked suddenly. Behind him those still on their feet had already started to move out of the village.

Conrad felt a sense of dread, and instinctively his hand felt for Raincloud's letter in his greatcoat's inner pocket. "Gods," he whispered, remembering that Raincloud had been in the church when the first shells had hit.

He flinched as another shell slammed into one of the houses a short distance away.

"Conrad."

For a moment Conrad found it difficult to focus his eyes.

"We've got to move," Donald said.

Conrad took a deep breath, and then nodded. Suddenly the sharp crack of small arms fire penetrated the fog that surrounded him. "We have to find out find out what's happening," he said quietly. "The Rangers' headquarters should be just over there." He pointed north.

Donald looked at the chaos around them. "And quickly."

They found the Rangers, but the headquarters unit had also been hit and there were bodies everywhere, some being tended by medics, others just lying where they had fallen. A Troop Leader was standing unscathed to one side of the devastation.

"What happened?" Conrad demanded.

The officer looked at him dumbly.

"Troop Leader, what happened?" Conrad repeated.

"We got hit by a shell, Leader," the Troop Leader replied listlessly.

"And the Battlegroup Leader?"

"Dead." He gestured helplessly.

"Do you know what's happened with the other Battlegroups?"

The man shook his head.

"Well find out," Conrad snapped. "And use runners. I don't want the situation picked up by the enemy."

"Yes Leader," the man said, starting to respond.

"I need a wireless operator," Conrad called.

One of those who'd been helping tend to the wounded straightened, wiping his bloodstained hands on the front of his tunic. "Leader."

"I want both of the other Battlegroups informed that this is now Corps command. Then tell Army Headquarters. Donald."

"Yes?"

"I'm promoting you — congratulations. You've got the Rangers." He looked around the devastation that surrounded them. "Not that I'm doing you any favors. You've probably got less than five minutes to sort out of your chain of command before all hell breaks out."

Donald nodded. "Take care." He snapped a salute and headed off to try and locate his Group Leaders.

Conrad rubbed his forehead wearily. What a start to the day. Now where was that Troop Leader?

The Troop Leader got back to him ten minutes later and Conrad, to whom the situation had looked pretty desperate, muttered a small prayer of thanks that things weren't as bad as they might have been. They'd lost only about forty people in that first, surprise barrage, and thanks to artillery support were now getting some counter battery fire. Unfortunately, a significant number of the forty had been officers, leaving an enormous hole in his command structure. He was still trying to establish a new line of command five minutes later when the remains of the 1st Corps were pushed back onto his line and Conrad's three Battlegroups found themselves in the thick of the battle.

Outnumbered three to one, the Corps was pushed slowly back over the ground it had marched forward so confidently over the previous night. By ten, Le Sars was now a mile in front of them, while behind them the Gallic burial mound of Burtha de Harlen Court was now almost included in the line. And with each step they were forced back Conrad could feel their line getting closer to breaking.

Around midday, however, the pressure slackened as the enemy pulled back to regroup.

Conrad was sitting on a stump, studying the map, when Donald came riding in on a horse.

"Where did you get that from?" Conrad asked, as Donald dismounted tiredly, his mount blowing gently from the ride up the hill.

"Just found it wandering around. It looks like an artillery mount."

Conrad nodded, his mind moving to the next problem. "How are your troops holding up?"

"They're tired, and ammunition's getting low."

"Well HQ has promised us some more ammo within half an hour. At least we're not the only ones running short," he said, nodding towards the enemy.

Donald nodded. "Ammunition's not going to do us any good if they attack in strength again. If they do, they'll just push straight over the top of us. The real problem is our lack of reserves."

Conrad thought about it for a moment. "Look, if we pull a couple of Troops back we can set up some proper defensive positions along here." He drew a line on the map with his finger. "That should give us some breathing space."

Donald looked at the map, then nodded. "If we pull back the first squad in every Troop they can set up positions for the other two. I'll get on it straight away." He swung himself back into the saddle, and urged his mount back down the hill. Sighing, Conrad looked around for a runner to let the two Maun Battlegroups know what was going on.

All three Battlegroups carried out his orders efficiently, which was just as well because within an hour the attack resumed with all its previous intensity. The Corps tried to hold, but was pushed back in a steadily increasing rush that was only halted by the troops dug in on the new line Conrad had ordered. The enemy, grown careless by the mounting ease with which they had pushed their way forward, were blunted by the machine guns dug into hastily camouflaged positions; and for a time the Corps was able hold, and even regroup.

By three o'clock, however, as Conrad climbed the stairs slowly to the second-floor room where Donald had set up his headquarters, he knew the line was stretched to breaking once more. They were running low on ammunition again, and had been pushed back onto the outskirts of Bapaume itself. It was only the fact that those attacking were also short of ammunition that they had been able to hang for as long as they had. But now it seemed they were hanging on with just their fingernails.

Donald looked round from the window that overlooked the main road into Bapaume as Conrad entered the room. Donald's face was gray in the dim light that came through the half-closed, heavy wooden shutters. His eyes were red-rimmed with smoke and fatigue, and there was a smudge of dirt on his right cheek. The rest of his headquarters team didn't look any better. Their appearance was in complete contrast to the room with its aura of reduced gentility; heavy window drapes and yellowed brocade wallpaper. From the look of the half-eaten meal on the table in the middle of the room the building's owners had been disturbed at their dinner by the arrival of the Rangers. He wondered where they were as he took the last drumstick, savoring the flavor of the cold chicken as it melted in his mouth, and made his way over to stand beside his brother.

Three soldiers in black uniforms, possibly Dontfrey but definitely unfriendly, were working their way down the street towards them. One of the Rangers, who'd been watching them carefully from the other window, finally squeezed the trigger of his rifle and the lead soldier threw up his arms and collapsed in a loose tangle of limbs.

"What's the situation?" Conrad asked, moving away from the window as the enemy returned fire.

"Not good," Donald said rubbing his forehead. "How long before we get more ammunition?"

"Another couple of hours."

"How many rounds have you got left?" Donald asked the Ranger who'd fired the shot.

The Ranger swore as a bullet smacked into the brickwork just above his head and crouched to remove the magazine from his rifle. “Three rounds, Leader,” he said after he’d finished counting them.

“Headquarters are trying,” Conrad said.

“Then you better tell them to try harder.”

A sudden outbreak of rapid firing to the east brought everyone’s head round in a rush.

“Donald?” Conrad snapped.

“I know,” his brother said with a tired smile. “Find out what’s happening.”

The firing intensified and Conrad realized that if he didn’t do something the Corps would break. His brain was numb, however, and all he could think about was having failed his father. There was a clattering of boots on the stairs as Donald returned. Behind him was a female Troop Leader in an unfamiliar light green uniform and matching bonnet, something like a tam o’shanter. Conrad tensed at the camouflage paint that masked her face then noticed the white strip of cloth tied around her arm.

“Leader Clemhorn?”

Yes,” he said. Her accent triggered memory, reminding him of Defella. Dynand? he thought.

“We’re your reinforcements.”

“Thank the gods. How many are there of you?”

“A Corps. We’re taking up position now.”

Conrad turned to the radio operator who had followed Donald back up the stairs. “Message to all leaders; Dynand forces arriving to reinforce. And don’t bother with code,” he added. “I don’t want anyone to start worrying about the extra firing. We’re hard pressed enough that anything could cause a crack.”

“It’s that bad?” she asked.

Conrad nodded. “How long before you can get into line?”

“We’re moving in now. Do you have a map of your position?”

Conrad pulled out the map he’d been using, now soiled and torn almost beyond recognition. “We should be along here,” he said, tracing a line west from Serre to Bapaume, and then south to Combles. “Unfortunately I can’t confirm it. We’re just handing on, and I haven’t been able afford any runners.”

“Don’t expect too much from us,” she warned him. “The railway was cut so we’ve marched nonstop since seven this morning to get here.”

"At least you got here. How's your ammunition?"

"Reasonable. Sixty, seventy rounds per person."

"Good. I'd appreciate it if you could arrange for some of that to be transferred to my own Corps. We're down to our last couple of rounds at the moment."

"Certainly."

There was firing all along the line now, but the Dynandian Troop Leader had been right about how exhausted her Corps was, and it was all they could do to move into line and hold.

Almost immediately, however, the enemy brought forward their artillery, and commenced a close range bombardment. Once again Conrad had to give the order to close with the enemy, and exhaustedly the two Corps moved to comply.

By five o'clock it seemed to Conrad that the battle had gone on forever; and even worse, would continue forever, both sides slugging it out like two stubborn boxers until both fell exhausted. The fighting had died down a little, but there was still the occasional desultory rattle of small arms in the distance to remind everyone there was still a battle to be won. His feet ached with the walking he'd done, and he wondered how those on the flanks had coped. Their cavalry boots had not been designed for marching.

The sudden sound of a fierce artillery barrage in the distance around Albert, however, signified some major change in the battle; and Conrad sent a runner back to Army Headquarters, now only about five houses down the street, to find out what was happening.

It was a nervous wait until the runner returned.

"So what's happened?" Donald asked, when he saw the smile on Conrad's face at the news the runner brought back with her.

"We've broken through," Conrad said, unable to stop grinning.

"Where?"

"On the left. Three Battlegroups of mounted infantry moved around the river and crossed it at Bray. They caught the enemy in the rear and opened up access along the river. That left Albert open to the left wing. Apparently they managed to capture some guns that were waiting to move up and they're using them against their own troops. That's what we're hearing at the moment."

Donald's face broke into an inane grin. "We've won?" he asked, not really believing it.

"It looks like it," Conrad said.

The battle dragged on for another twenty hours however, until shortly after one the following day; when surrounded, and without ammunition, the enemy commander finally surrendered.

For Conrad that second day had seemed like an endless nightmare. Again, and again he had to order his troops onto the attack, forcing the enemy back into a steadily smaller pocket. It seemed an exercise in futility, but at last the orders were received to cease fire, and the nightmare was finally over. It was only then that he realized he would have to write and tell Ivy of Jon's death.

CHAPTER TWENTY-TWO

Fort Larsa — Etu Line
February 1980 (96AE)

"Leader?"

Ivy looked up from the staffing report she was trying to make sense of. "Yes Pecos?"

"There was a letter for you on the packet." Pecos looked uncertainly at the mess that covered the desk, not knowing where to put it.

Ivy smiled and held out her hand for the envelope. She was expecting a letter from Jon, and was surprised when she failed to recognize the handwriting. Turning the envelope over she was puzzled to see Conrad's name on the back. "Thanks, Pecos," Ivy said, dismissing her as she ripped the envelope open. Conrad was hardly the most prolific of writers and she wondered what he had thought it was important enough to write to her about. Inside was another envelope with her name on it, and a page that had been torn from an exercise book. Unfolding the note she read,

10 December 96 AE
Bapaume, France
Mainline

Dear Ivy,

It is with regret that I have to inform you of Jon's death on the fifth of December.

She stopped, frozen, and for a moment it seemed as though the entire world held its breath with her. Slowly her gaze slid around the room, skimming over the flags and trophies that lined the wall before returning to the letter.

There was a battle here on the 5th. Jon was on my staff when he was caught in an artillery barrage and was killed instantly. I have tried to work out what I can say, how I can express my sympathy but there are no words, and if I was to wait for them this letter would never be written. I can only tell you that Jon did his duty and that I will miss him. Enclosed is a letter Jon asked me to pass on to you in the event of his death.

I remain your Loving Brother

Conrad

The words on the paper had blurred. Something was rattling; it was the letter on the table, her hands shaking uncontrollably. She tried to breathe, but there was no air in the room and for a moment she wondered if she was dying. Finally a sobbing rush of breath flooded her lungs.

The first tear coursed its way down her cheek and she felt a moment's conceit, knowing it was for Jon, that what she had felt for him was genuine. But now she would never be able to tell him and a tear-laden sob tore its way free of her throat. Another followed, then her restraint disappeared and she was crying in great sobbing gulps for her lover lost in a battle she had not even known about.

"Ivy?" Gradually she became aware that Daniels was standing just inside the door.

Embarrassed, she struggled to control her tears. Slowly her sobs died away into a muted series of hiccups, and wordlessly she held Conrad's letter out to Daniels to read.

"I'm sorry," Daniels said, when she had finished, placing Conrad's letter carefully back on the table.

Ivy nodded, avoiding Daniels' eyes as she attempted to find a handkerchief to dry her face. Silently Daniels handed Ivy one of her own.

"I didn't even know he'd died," Ivy said, wiping her face. "I should have felt something."

Daniels raised an eyebrow.

"Or perhaps not," Ivy said, starting to feel a little more in control of herself. She took a deep breath. It quavered in her throat, threatening to turn into another sob and she swallowed quickly.

"Did you want anything?" Ivy asked, realizing Daniels wouldn't have interrupted without a reason.

"It can wait."

"Are you sure?"

Daniels nodded. "If I can help in any way?"

"Thank you."

Daniels hesitated, but when Ivy failed to say anything else simply nodded and turned to leave.

"Daniels," Ivy said, as her senior Troop Leader reached the door.

Daniels paused, looking back.

"Thank you."

"I'll make sure you're not disturbed."

Ivy watched the door shut behind her, then got up and checked her face in the mirror above the mantelpiece. She looked awful, she thought. Her nose was red, almost glowing, her eyes were puffy, and there were tear tracks down her cheeks. Briefly she rubbed at her face, trying to make herself look more presentable. When she'd finished she turned back to the desk where she caught sight of the envelope from Jon, still lying there, unopened.

She felt the threat of tears start to well in her eyes again, and something caught in her throat. Damn, she couldn't run a fort if she was going to fall to pieces every five minutes. Taking a deep breath she released it slowly, then returned to her desk. Carefully, delicately, she opened her bottom drawer and took out a small wooden box about the size of a large cigar case. Retrieving the key from the chain she wore round her neck she unlocked the box and tenderly took out the sheath of papers inside.

This was all that remained of Jon now. She lifted the papers to her nose, but there was nothing there, no scent of her lover. Carefully she replaced the letters in the box, the unopened envelope on top, unable to face the thought of its contents for the moment. A small photograph slid out of the pile onto the floor and as she bent to pick it up Jon looked up at her, his smile lighting up his entire face. Her nose pricked and as a sob tore itself free of her throat she buried her head in her arms.

CHAPTER TWENTY-THREE

Naisre - Mainline
March 1980 (96AE)

"Arnold. There's a visitor for you."

Arnold opened his eyes and stared blankly up at the ceiling above his bed. It was a ceiling he was intimately familiar with, having lived with it for the last three months.

"Arnold?"

"Yes Herr Doktor," Arnold muttered under his breath.

"Your father's in the visiting room," Doctor Harris said.

Arnold considered the statement. Words were important. He knew that now. "Tell him I'm asleep," he suggested.

"No, I won't," Doctor Harris said. "You know you agreed to meet with him at our last meeting."

He remembered the discussion. He couldn't remember why he'd agreed. "Perhaps next week," he offered.

"He's here now."

It was always rush, rush, rush. "I'm tired," he said.

"Then you won't want Keating's Treatise on Comparative Religions," the doctor said evenly.

"It's arrived?" The skin on the back of his left hand suddenly itched and he scratched at it with his right hand. The right hand, the good hand.

"It came in this morning. But if you're tired you won't want it."

There was a funny taste in his mouth, sort of like buttered copper. Perhaps the book would make it go away. He knew something would. His eyes drifted to the religious texts stacked up on his bedside table; all he needed was to find the key and he could open the door. He remembered the promise he'd been made. He swung his feet slowly over the edge of the bed and pushed himself up to into a sitting position.

"Arnold," Doctor Harris prompted when he didn't do anything else.

"Rush, rush, rush," Arnold said. No, there was no way to avoid it.

He met the doctor's eyes and with a sigh pushed himself slowly to his feet.

The doctor led the way down the corridor, an orderly following closely. The smell of floor polish filled his nostrils, the linoleum shining like polished glass under the light of the overhead lights. Arnold walked slowly, refusing to hurry.

Doctor Harris was waiting by the door to the visitors' room when Arnold arrived.

"Hello Arnold," his father said rising to his feet as Arnold entered the room.

"Papa," Arnold said, making his way over to the table. Avoiding his father's eyes, he carefully lowered himself into the waiting chair.

"How are you?" his father asked.

Arnold thought about the question. There were complexities piled on complexities.

"Arnold," Doctor Harris prompted.

"Rush, rush, rush," Arnold muttered He took a breath. "I am getting better." He must have been getting better not to miss the questioning look Papa gave the doctor.

"Your mother gave me this to give you." His father handed him a small container of sweetmeats.

Arnold opened the lid and looked at the candied fruits. The green was the same color as spruce leaves. He stirred the fruits with his finger, memorized by the way the light glinted on the sugar.

"Is there anything you need?" his father asked.

Need? Of course there was. Everyone had something they needed. He considered the question further. "Some books on the Sun God?" Not that they'd be helpful, the Sun God had obviously not been the one he was seeking — else the Empire would never have seized Etu, nor would he have allowed his people to have suffered the effects of the Decimation. But perhaps the books might contain a clue.

His father looked up at Doctor Harris. Arnold missed Herr Doktor's response but his father nodded. "I'll have something sent through in a couple of days."

"Is that everything?" Arnold asked, when the silence seemed to have gone on long enough.

"Annette asked me to send you everyone from the commune's best wishes."

"The commune?"

"In New York."

Arnold nodded, uninterested. The commune was part of his old life. He had a new one now; all he had to do was find the key. His father looked at him, obviously unsure what to say next. Arnold stared back at him. He could wait. He wasn't going anywhere.

"I should go," his father said finally.

"Arnold?" Doctor Harris prompted.

Always rushing, Arnold thought. "Thank you Papa," he said, carefully replacing the lid on the sweetmeats container. "Thank Mama for the sweets." He got to his feet. "Please don't forget the books."

"Of course."

As he reached the corridor he heard his father sigh.

"How is he?" he asked the doctor.

Arnold slowed as he turned into the passage, paused, and bent to retie his shoelaces.

"Progress is slower than we would like. He continues to isolate himself from the other patients."

"That's because they're all mad," Arnold muttered under his breath.

No one was interested in helping him locate the key.

"We'd like to recommend electroconvulsive therapy. It's quite safe nowadays; we use a muscle relaxant to weaken the convulsions and lessen the likelihood of injury."

"And it works?"

"In seventy percent of cases. But perhaps we should discuss this further in my office."

Arnold finished retying his laces, stood up, and headed back to his room. It sounded as if the book was going to take a little longer than he had anticipated. Well, he could wait. His search would be rewarded; the promise he'd been given had been quite emphatic about that.

CHAPTER TWENTY-FOUR

Charleston — Mainline
March 1980 (96AE)

Donald's hand paused uncertainly over the last digit he was dialing as he looked at the phone. Decisively he punched the last number and waited. If she didn't want to speak to him then so be it.

"Matija?" Donald said, as the phone was picked up. The noise from the crowd in the airport lounge made it difficult to hear properly.

"Yes."

"It's Donald."

There was a sharp intake of breath. "Where are you?"

"At Charleston Airport. I've just got back from Paris."

"Why didn't you tell me you were coming?" she demanded.

"I didn't want to disappoint you if I couldn't make it. Things have been pretty confused recently."

"Everything's all right now though?" She sounded worried.

"Everything's fine," he reassured her. "I've just been demobilized."

"When can you get here?"

"As soon as I can arrange a taxi. Half an hour or so?"

"I'll see you then," she said, and hung up.

Donald couldn't stop grinning as he headed outside to find a taxi.

The taxi had only just drawn up outside Matija's house when the front door slammed and Matija came flying down the path. Her long, raven black hair tucked into an oversized cream knit beret.

"Go," Matija ordered the driver as she piled into the taxi.

"What's the matter?" Donald asked, as he reached around her to pull the door closed properly.

"Nothing. It's just some of my relatives are visiting, and if they see you they'll never let you go. So," she said, snuggling into his arms. "Aren't you going to say how happy you are to see me?"

"I was, when I'd caught my breath," Donald said hugging her tightly, the fresh lavender scent of her hair triggering happy memories. "I've missed you, you know."

"I should hope so," she told him. "And you've really been demobilized? I'd heard a number of units were returning to their own lines."

He nodded. "There's still no sign of the World Leader of Dontfrey, nor any of the other World Leaders who had made up the core of his support, but Council's agreed to Grandfather's election as First Leader and the army's thrown itself in behind him as well. Papa and Conrad are both in Naisre at the moment helping get things ready for my grandfather's inauguration in a fortnight." He paused. "I'm hoping you can attend the ceremony with me?"

She looked at him, surprised.

He shrugged. "I thought it might be one way of getting you to meet my parents."

"Can I think about it?"

"Sure, we've got a couple of days," he said, disappointed at her lack of enthusiasm.

She must have sensed his reaction because she stretched up and gave him a kiss. "It's a big step. Just give me time to think about it."

"All right," he said, partly mollified.

At the apartment Matija held his bag while he jiggled the key in the lock to get the door open. The apartment was freezing and as he stepped inside. "How long can you stay?" he asked.

She looked at her watch. "An hour? My relatives are going back tomorrow, so I can spend more time with you then."

Donald's stomach rumbled hungrily, and he looked apologetically at Matija. "Would you mind getting something to eat from the Chinese takeaway next door while I get the heat on?"

"Of course not," she said. She kissed him quickly on the cheek, handed him the bag and headed back to the street.

By the time she got back the apartment had started to warm up, and while she hung her coat up Donald finished laying the table.

"Dig in," he said as she joined him at the table, waving his fork at the containers spread out in front of them.

"I'm not really hungry," she said, seating herself demurely next to him.

"This is good," he said a couple of minutes later, pausing in his assault on the food to ladle out a second portion. "You sure you won't have some?"

She gave him a small smile. "I'm sure."

He paused for a moment. "Are you all right?"

She started to say something but Donald had already returned to his food, so instead she merely shrugged.

"Right," he said, when he'd finished. "Talk."

"What about?"

"Something's bothering you."

She considered him for a moment. "It can wait. Come on," and pulling him after her, she headed for the bedroom.

***

He was whistling happily to himself when he answered the phone later the next day. He'd finished arranging to return to his university duties in a week's time, and had just booked a table at the restaurant for eight that night for Matija and himself.

"Donald, it's Conrad," his brother said as Donald picked up the phone. "Grandfather's dead. He's been shot."

Shot. Grandfather was dead! For a moment Donald sat shocked, unable to believe what Conrad was telling him. He heard something faint coming from the telephone and realized he had allowed it to drop away from his ear.

"What did you say?" he said, putting it back.

"Papa wants to know when you can you get here."

"Tomorrow sometime, I suppose," he said.

"Good, try and get here as soon as you can."

"Was it Miro?"

"It looks like it."

Donald put the phone back on its hook slowly. Pausing, he took a deep breath, closing his eyes against the reality that threatened to overwhelm him. Grandad was dead.

He was surprised when he opened his eyes to see that everything still looked the same. Taking another deep breath he reached for the phone to book his flight booked, then once that was done he phoned Matija.

"Matija, it's Donald," he said as she answered the phone. "I've got to go to Naisre. My grandfather's dead - shot."

There was silence for a moment. "What time's your flight go?" she asked finally, her voice sounding very small and far away.

"In about six hours."

There was silence from the other end.

"Are you all right?" Donald asked.

"I think so," she said. "We need to talk."

"Of course."

"No, I mean really talk. Can you meet me in the park next to my house?"

He looked at his watch; it was just after three. "Sure. Give me half an hour. I still have to pack."

Matija was waiting for him next to the pond near the park's entrance, a solitary figure rugged up against the cold occupying the park's sole bench.

"So, what did you want to talk about?" Donald asked, as he seated himself beside her on the bench. A lone duck came over to investigate hopefully. Despite the cold, spring had finally arrived in Charleston, and in the dark, freshly turned garden beds the tips of bulbs were breaking free of their winter prison.

Matija nervously twisted her fingers, avoiding his eyes. "How do you feel about children?"

"I don't know. Why?" Donald asked, the skin tightening along his spine as he wondered where this was leading.

"Because you're going to be a father."

"How?" Donald asked dumbly.

"How do you think?" she snapped. "I'm pregnant."

He thought about it for a moment. "How long have we got?"

"Five months."

He thought back to the way she'd sent him off to Europe four months ago. And now he was to become a father. A father! Elated, he kissed her soundly.

"What was that for?" she demanded, pulling back from him.

"Because I love you. How did it happen?"

She looked at him surprised. "You really don't know?"

"Of course I know that. Weren't you taking any precautions?"

"There wasn't time. I have since though."

A child. He started to grin again.

"Stop that," she told him crossly.

"Sorry." But he wasn't really, and the grin leaked out again.

"So what happens now?" she asked.

"We get married," Donald said.

"You don't have to, you know."

"Of course I do."

She sniffed.

Donald had the feeling he wasn't handling this quite as well as he might have done. Getting down on his knees in front of her he took one of her hands into his.

"Matija, it would give me the greatest of pleasure if you would agree to marry me."

"Oh sit down, you're making a fool of yourself," Matija told him, trying to pull her hand free.

"Not until you say yes."

"Yes," she said. "Now sit down."

"Not until you smile," he said.

She pulled a face at him, then smiled in spite of herself.

"That's better," he said, getting up and sitting down beside her again, sliding an arm around her shoulder.

"What will your parents say?" she asked.

He shrugged. "It's none of their business what they think." Then he realized what she meant. "Oh, it's fine, Mother has already given her approval."

She looked askance at him.

"Margaret, my cousin, was grilling me on Dontfrey about you. She told her mother, who told mine. What about your father though?"

"I don't know."

He frowned at her. "And what does that mean?"

"It means I don't know."

She'd turned her face away from him, and carefully he turned her back to face him. "What's wrong?" he asked.

"I'm scared."

"There's nothing to worry about," he said hugging her. "I love you, and you love me. It's all perfectly natural."

She nodded into his chest.

"Come on, let's go and tell him together."

"No," she said, pulling herself together. "I'll tell him by myself. There isn't time before your airship leaves, and I'd much rather just have you to myself."

"Here, you better have this," he said, pulling off his signet ring. "At least until I can get a proper one."

She took it and tried it on a finger. It was much too big, but she closed her hand over it protectively.

"Feel better now?" Donald asked.

"A little," she said, allowing her head to drop back against him. "I wish you didn't have to go."

"So do I," he admitted. "Let's hope it's for the last time." The weight of her head on his shoulders was soothing, and arranging his arm more comfortably around her shoulder he settled back against the support of the chair.

"You better go," she said finally, as dusk started to descend on the park.

He checked his watch; six o'clock. "You're sure you're going to be all right?"

She nodded quietly. "Go on. Be off with you."

For a moment Donald was tempted to call Papa and tell him he couldn't leave, then he realized he couldn't, that his father had asked him to help.

"I'll phone as soon as I get there," he promised as he stood up. "Take care."

The news of his grandfather's assassination was already out by the time he reached the airport, but there was little other meaningful information to be had so he boarded the airship knowing as much, or as little, as he had when he'd first received the call from his brother.

***

Conrad met him as he stepped off the airship at Naisre, two security officers in tow.

"Glad to have you back, just wish it had been under better circumstance," Conrad said, taking his arm to escort him through reception.

"Yeah, sure," Donald said sourly, thinking that personally he'd much prefer to be in Charleston with Matija. "So what happened? The news report only said Grandfather had been shot. Was it Miro?"

Conrad looked around to make sure they wouldn't be overheard as he led them towards the lifts. "We can't be sure it's Miro, although the odds seem to be stacking up that way. We got the assassin though; he seems to be from a new line we haven't contacted before."

Donald missed his step.

"What's more," Conrad said, lowering his voice. "It's an advanced line."

"The Edict."

Conrad nodded. "Yes, either someone's broken the Edict, or a line has independently discovered the time-front. Either way — bad news."

"So what's happening now?"

Conrad shrugged. "Papa is trying to hold things together until he can call a full Council meeting. He wanted to see both of us as soon as you arrived."

"How is he?"

Conrad shrugged.

Their father was in the First Leader's office, deep under the central core of the city. There were guards at every door, and they were stopped at least four times to have their credentials checked before finally being ushered through to the elevator which took them down to the First Leader's suite. To Donald it seemed rather like a case of closing the stable door after the horse had bolted.
"Donald," their father said, rising from his desk to greet them.

Lawrence McArthur, who'd been sitting in the chair across the desk from him, followed him to his feet.

"Papa," Donald said, taking his hand. "Lawrence."

His father gestured for them to sit down. "Have you heard from Paris?" he asked when they were settled.

"No."

"There was an explosion at the University of Paris's portal research facilities last night. Thirteen people were killed, perhaps a hundred injured. I've imposed a news blackout, but I wasn't sure how successful it was."

"I hadn't heard a word," Donald assured him.

"Why the blackout?" Conrad asked.

Lawrence sighed and rubbed the bridge of his nose tiredly. "One of the leads we were investigating in relation to Miro's disappearance was the possibility that he had used the University of Paris's research facilities to establish a portal through to an unauthorized line. Now, well we've got the local police shifting through the wreckage but I don't think they'll find anything."

"No idea of the line's coordinates?" Conrad asked.

Lawrence shook his head.

"So what do you want us for?" Conrad asked.

"I need you both in Constantinople," their father said. "I need you to talk to Kaito."

"His new portal?" Conrad asked. "How's it going?"

"He's had a full-scale model operating for three weeks now."

"I didn't think he would in a position to do a full-scale test for another nine months or so," Conrad said, remembering the last conversation he'd had with Kaito.

Donald shook his head. "I spoke to him last week. Apparently things went better than expected. So far they've cycled the prototype through ten repetitions without a single problem."

Lawrence groaned. "So much for security."

"And what do you want us to do?" Conrad asked.

"Three things," their father said. "First of all there's another test I want you to arrange for Kaito to undertake." He handed Conrad a sealed envelope. "This envelope contains the coordinates to a line I hope Miro is not aware of. I want the test portal, generators, the whole thing taken through to this line and a stable portal generated back to the Mainline. Your grandfather had already arranged for a Notway Engineering Group to assist. They should be arriving there within a day or so."

Donald shot a glance at Lawrence. Just what was this all about?

"Secondly." He held out an unsealed envelope to Conrad. "I want you to get Kaito to start work on churning out more of his new portals. This envelope contains the necessary authority to access whatever funds you need to accomplish that task."

"And thirdly?" Conrad asked, accepting the second envelope.

"I'm worried about security, as it turns out for very good reason." He glared at Donald then shrugged. "Langley's research is hardly secret, and we've confirmed that some of the funding that the University has been attracting has been funded through a research trust fund administered from Dontfrey, so undoubtedly Miro knows of it. All we can hope is that he isn't aware of how progressed it is.

"Just in case he does know, however, we're boosting security there. I've arranged for the 48th to be transferred in from Etu. The first Group should be arriving in Constantinople in about three hours. I'd have preferred the Clemhorn Rangers but they won't be back to full strength for another couple of months. I've also arranged for a Dynand Battlegroup to be flown in, so you should have enough to handle any eventuality."

Donald winced at the thought of the 'eventuality' that might require two Battlegroups.

"When are we leaving?" Conrad asked.

Their father looked at his watch. "Your flight leaves in an hour and a half." He stood up and held out his hand. "Good luck."

"Thanks," Conrad said, taking it.

"Donald."

"Papa," Donald said, taking his hand in turn.

CHAPTER TWENTY-FIVE

Constantinople - Mainline
March 1980 (96AE)

Through the window Donald could see the fresh earth that marred the smooth green perfection of the playing field outside the laboratory as a squad of Dynand worked to reinforce the trench connecting the two fire-pits dug in on its southern edge. On the field itself a Lacrosse team from the 48th had an impromptu game underway, watched by a number of students. Donald didn't know what people made of the sight of Clemhorn and Dynand troops in full combat gear digging in around the university, but there wasn't any way they could hide what they were doing. They couldn't close the university, and even if they could it would probably only create even more talk.

Behind him, Kaito was checking the melding of the first of the new batch of substrates in its liquid bath. The bath was a large, open metal tank that took up about half the room. Pipes of various sizes twined themselves round its side, while inside the bath the dark amber of the saturated solution gleamed in the sunlight.

Donald sighed, running his fingers round his collar before checking his watch. Matija should almost be up by now. "I'm off," he said to Kaito, turning away from the window. "I'll see you tomorrow." The substrate was pretty, but watching it form was no more exciting than watching grass grow.

Kaito raised his hand absentmindedly.

Outside, Donald paused for a moment to take a deep breath of the sharp, salt laden breeze drifting up the cliff from the Bosporus below. In the distance, rising above the haze that always seem to blanket it, were the thousand spires of Constantinople - the 'City of Churches'. After its capture by the Serbian Emperor Uros III in 1451 AD the city had served as the cultural center of the Balkans' renaissance that had so shaped his world. In another day or two, if things continued the way they were going, he'd be able to take a day off and actually have a look at it. Matija had asked him every time he'd phoned her if he'd been into the city. It would be nice to be able to finally report that he had.

He was halfway down the path to the parking lot when he remembered he'd forgotten to remind Kaito of tomorrow's breakfast meeting. He paused indecisively for a moment before starting back to the lab. If he didn't remind him he knew for a fact Kaito wouldn't remember. He'd just entered the lab when a loud explosion from outside the room caused him to instinctively drop to the floor.

The explosion was followed almost immediately by the sound of automatic fire. Damn, that sounded close, Donald thought worriedly, struggling to undo the strap to his holster.

"What's happening?" Kaito demanded from the other side of the tank where he, and the other four technicians who'd been in the room, were also hugging the ground.

"I don't know," Donald said. There was something coming through on the radio clipped to his belt, and he held it up to his ear.

"We're under attack," he said, trying to make out what the harried voice of the radio operator was saying over the sound of gunfire which now almost drowned it out. "They must have managed to set up a portal within the cordon."

A moment later Conrad's voice came over the set, giving crisp instructions for several Groups to turn inwards and try and locate the portal before they managed to get any more forces through.

"Stay down," Donald said, checking the magazine on his automatic before he started to crawl towards the window.

"I have absolutely no intention of putting my head up," Kaito told him tartly as Donald cautiously peered over the sill.

The flower beds just outside of the window had been flattened by the explosion, and there was a gaping hole into the room opposite. He saw a number of people peering cautiously around the opening, and even as he watched two of them climbed out of the hole and started towards him. He didn't recognize their uniform, which was a dark, almost black, blue. They were wearing strange, mottled colored helmets, with wide chin straps and darkened visors that covered most of their face. He frowned as he tried to work out what they were wearing over their chests - it looked like some sort of heavy body armor, although it was festooned with equipment and straps. One of them started to raise what looked like a rifle towards him and instinctively Donald's finger clamped on the trigger.

Both of them hit the ground; it was even possible he'd hit one of them, but as they did so someone opened fire at him, bullets striking the wall just to his right, and he dropped to the floor, swearing.

Jamming his finger on the transmit button he raised the microphone to his mouth. "Headquarters. This is Donald Clemhorn. The substrate growth section is under attack. Can I have some support?"

"Understood," came the reply.

"Out!" Donald barked to the technicians, jerking his head back towards the door.

Without waiting to see if they had moved Donald edged cautiously farther along the window, his boots crunching noisily on the broken glass that littered the floor. The sound of automatic fire seemed to come from all directions now. Carefully he'd started to raise his head to look over the sill when a sudden percussion of noise drove him to the ground and the wall on that side of the room disintegrated about him. Stunned, Donald clung to the ground as bullets tore through the wall above and around him, filling the room with dust and the debris of exploding bricks. There was a dull ache in his groin as he realized how close he had come to death.

The firing continued for ten seconds, but those ten seconds were sufficient to render the crystal substrate completely useless as dust and brick debris settled slowly onto the puddled remains of its bath, its container riddled with holes. Then, as though administering a totally unnecessary coup de grace, the lights suddenly went off, and in the dead silence left behind by the air-conditioners the rapid fire of automatic weapons echoed over the entire campus. Muttering a muffled prayer Donald started to wriggle backward towards the door.

Another burst of fire scythed into the room as he was halfway across the floor, and he increased his speed, knowing this second burst was probably to cover someone crossing the courtyard. Reaching the door he spared a moment to fire a burst back at the window before scrambling to his feet. Kaito and six others were waiting for him at the other end of the corridor, obviously uncertain about what to do next.

"In!" he said, shoving them through an open door into a small office.

"What happened back there?" Kaito asked as Donald pulled the door closed behind them.

Donald shook his head, too busy trying to contact someone on his radio to be able to explain. The only thing on the radio, however, was the hiss of random static. Seeing a telephone Donald picked it up and dialed nine to be put through to the switchboard.

"Donald Clemhorn here, could you get me the Corps Leader?"

There was a moment as the operator tried to locate him, then finally Donald heard his brother's voice, calm and unhurried.

"Donald?"

"Conrad, they've destroyed the substrate." The sudden explosion of a grenade from down the passage drowned out Conrad's reply.

"Out the window," Donald said jerking his head at the casement. Two of the technicians moved quickly to open it. "Quietly," Donald warned him, as another grenade went off on the far side of the corridor.

"What did you say?" Donald asked.

"I just said there should be a Force trying to get through to you, can you hold on?" Conrad said.

"No. I'll try and contact them outside." The last grenade had seemed awfully close, and as Kaito and the others were already on the far side of the window he decided it was time to join them.

Outside, however, Donald realized with a sinking heart there were at least fifteen yards of open ground to cross before they reached the cover provided by a series of waist-high raised garden beds. The beds were filled with roses, and a stray breeze brought the scent of their flowers drifting across the ground towards them.

"Any suggestions?" Donald asked hopefully.

No one said anything.

"We'll have to run for it then," Donald said. "Don't stop for anything. If anyone gets hit we'll come back for them later." A grenade blew out the glass in the window of the room next to them, scattering it over the grass. "Go!" he screamed, launching himself for the opposite side of the lawn.

He heard the sound of breaking glass behind him and swerved, almost colliding with Kaito. "Spread out," he yelled. Then there was only the running, adrenaline giving him energy he had not realized he had. The lawn seemed endless but already he was halfway across. Suddenly the stutter of a machine gun from in front of them surprised him, almost causing him to pull up, before he realized it was providing them with covering fire and he threw himself forward with renewed energy.

A sudden burst of fire from behind them stitched the ground at his feet, and he swerved, almost losing his balance, but recovering just as he felt the whistle of a bullet pass his ear. The lawn seemed endless, but suddenly he had reached the flower beds and threw himself forward into their cover. For a moment he could only lie there, gasping for breath, not even able to wonder how he had made it, or who else had managed to make it to safety.

Someone touched his shoulder gently, and Donald spun round, his finger already tightening on the trigger of his pistol. The Dynandian officer recoiled, and Donald shook his head ruefully.

"Sorry."

"Are you all right?" she asked.

He nodded, his lungs still heaving for breath. Kaito, lying next to him, was in the same position. Donald looked back at the building they had come from, surprised to find how close it actually was. Two figures lay sprawled on the ground in front of the window, blood staining the ground next to one of them. There, but for the grace of the gods, he thought.

"Can you move?" the Dynand asked.

"I think so," Donald said sitting up cautiously. He winced as the Dynand machine gun opened up almost next to his ear. She led them, crawling, until they were out of direct fire from the building opposite, then at a half crouch to where a small group clustered in the shelter of a brick stairwell.

The Leader of the group looked up, and smiled.

"Hello Donald."

It took Donald a moment to recognize Defella under the thick stripes of her black and green camouflage paint. Under the paint, however, she was still the starkly beautiful woman he'd met at Naisre.

"When you did arrive?" he demanded.

"About a couple of hours ago. Conrad sent me over to see if I could help."

"Well you've certainly done that," he said.

"Any idea where they came from?"

He came round to look at the map of the campus she was holding.

"Probably from near here," he said, indicating the building next to the laboratory they'd been in. "The first we knew about it was when they exploded a hole in this wall."

"That fits," she said. "We suspect they managed to open a portal into the gym." She turned to one of her aides. "Diayn, you better tell Headquarters."

Diayn nodded, and was gone.

"No radios," Defella said.

"I know," Donald said.

An autogiro came in from the west. It was keeping high, obviously trying to keep out of range of any ground fire when, without warning, there was a bright flash, and the giro exploded into flames. Smoke trailed out behind it as debris plummeted towards the ground.

Donald frowned, wondering if even two Battlegroups would be enough to hold the university. There was a soft droning sound from the direction of the labs, and peering around the side of the stairwell he spotted what looked like a miniature autogiro about the size of a football hovering a short distance away. No, not an autogiro he thought, as it didn't have any wings, but simply four rotors placed equidistant around its body. Donald's movement must have alerted it to his presence and it accelerated skywards, disappearing over the top of the building.

"What was that?" Defella demanded.

Donald shrugged. "I haven't the foggiest."

A moment later, however, a larger version popped up over the top of the building in front of them. This one had stubby wings protruding from its sides with what looked like two tubes suspended from the end of each wing - no, not tubes, Donald realized with a shock - rockets.

"Down!" he shouted, pushing Defella to the ground even as a gush of smoke emerged from the back of one of tubes.

A moment later the stairwell they were sheltering behind disintegrated, covering them with dust and the shattered remains of the structure.

Cautiously Donald raised his head, but immediately ducked again as bullets shredded the air above him. He swore, as the fire from those shooting at them from the laboratories split bone, flesh and brick with equal abandon.

“We’ve got to pull back,” Defella said.

Donald nodded. With the Dynands’ return fire having little effect against the armor worn by the enemy soldiers they didn’t have a choice. At least inside the building they’d be safer from aerial attack.

Ten minutes later Donald was at a window, trying to secure a target without becoming one himself when Defella crawled over to him.

“We’re going to have to pull back again,” she said. “Those flying things are just too dangerous.”

He nodded. The little ones were simply too difficult to hit, but they were letting the enemy know exactly where they were — and then the bigger ones would move in. Even inside the building they were taking damage. The Dynands had managed to destroy a couple of the bigger ones, but there seemed an inexhaustible supply of the things.

There was an explosion in the distance, and the constant random crackle from his radio died. Ducking down he held the radio up to his ear in time to catch his brother say:

“ . . .ten seconds, take cover and put your hands over your ears, take cover and put your hands over your ears.”

“Everyone down and cover your ears!” he yelled, wondering what Conrad intended. A moment later he found out as the whole world convulsed around him.

There was a ringing in his ears, and the world seemed to possess an eerier quality of silence as he carefully he pulled himself to his knees.

“What happened,” Defella asked, looking round, dazed.

“I’d say my brother called the air force in,” Donald said.

“A plane?” she said, stunned.

“Or two. Quite effective wasn’t it?” he said looking around. He wondered how fast it had been going, and how close to the ground. He remembered the pilot telling him their top speed was about Mach 4.

The radio crackled to life and Defella lifted it to her ear.

"Get your butts in motion," she said, switching through to her own Group's frequencies when it had finished. "We got their portal. We're counter attacking."

Donald levered himself off the floor, and cautiously looked out through the remains of the window. It seemed as though every window on campus had exploded, glass littering the ground like hail. The remains of two of the enemy's flying machines lay crumpled against a wall across the grass from him.

Even as the remaining Dynands with Defella moved onto the attack the enemy started to respond, but without their flying scouts their response was disorganized and uncoordinated.

Clambering into the shattered buildings on the other side of the lawn Donald noticed two of Defella's soldiers pause to replace their weapons with the enemy's heavier ones and nodded his approval.

Despite their disorganization, the enemy continued to fight fanatically, however, even beyond death. And after they discovered their second boobytrapped body Defella gave the order that troops were not to be searched, but simply shot.

Eventually Defella's Group was pulled back to reform and Donald, his ears still ringing with the explosion of grenades and small arms fire, as well as with the after-effect of the air attack, was ordered to report to his brother. He found Conrad in the administrative block, surveying the holes and shattered windows that had resulted from the fighting.

"Do we know what happened yet?" Donald asked.

"It looks like they set up a portal in the gym. Their radio jammer was right next to it so when our missile hit it we took out both the same time."

"So we're secure?"

"For the moment. We've got a bigger problem though. A message from Papa. The enemy launched simultaneous attacks on a number of lines, and at least eleven separate locations on the Mainline alone."

"Oh," Donald said, feeling as though someone had physically hit him in the gut.

Conrad nodded. "It's bad. We've managed to close off three of the portals, though my guess is that that's probably only temporary. So far on the Mainline we've already lost London, Brussels, James Town, New York, and Washington."

Donald grimaced.

"Papa's ordered us to prepare to evacuate through Kaito's portal."

"What about trying to pull back to Etu?"

Conrad shook his head. "That was one of the lines targeted in the initial attacks."

"Damn, do we still have the second portal?"

Conrad shook his head. "We lost it when the generator went down. Luckily Kaito's prototype is still working flawlessly."

"It's a pretty small bottleneck."

"I know." Conrad rubbed his neck fretfully. "We better start moving as much of his equipment through as we can. Can you to stay with Kaito, help him identify what he needs and get it moving through?"

"Sure."

"Thanks. I better see what I can do about getting some more supplies in."

Donald nodded. "How many did we lose?" he asked, as a stretcher went past, carrying a Dynand into the temporary hospital which had been set up in the building next door.

"Just over thirty dead."

Donald grimaced.

It was ten o'clock that night when a small convoy drew up to the gates of the campus. The news from the rest of the world had grown steadily worse, and as Donald made his way down the corridor to the conference room Conrad had requisitioned for the meeting, he wondered what Papa intended to do.

As he entered the room he found his father, surrounded by a small staff of officers in Clemhorn uniforms, sitting at the main conference table. Behind them empty window frames gaped onto the darkness beyond, light spilling into the pockmarked courtyard that lined the side of the building. Someone had done their best to clean the room up and the glass and other debris had been swept into the corner. All those present looked exhausted, and his father's uniform was crumpled and stained.

His father acknowledged him with a quick nod and smile that made it clear just how tired he was. "Take a seat. We're just waiting for Group Leader Hastings."

Donald looked uncertainly at Conrad.

"The Leader in charge of the Engineering Group setting up the base on the new line," Conrad said.

"Do we have any details on the line yet?" Donald asked, as he took a seat near the foot of the table.

"Nothing recent," their father said. "I'm hoping Hastings can tell us something. The last information we have on it was about 75 years ago. At that time it was at least early-industrial."

"Where did you get the coordinates from?" Donald asked.

His father gave a tired smile. "From some sealed records your grandfather stumbled across about five years ago."

"Sealed?"

"On the orders of Traek, the first First Leader himself."

"Why?" Conrad asked.

"The line was the first contacted by Traek after his conquest of the Mainline. This was before the Edict, and a small expeditionary force attempted to establish a base there. Unfortunately those living there didn't appreciate the attempt and there was a rather messy little battle that ended up with the base overrun and the expeditionary force destroyed. Traek responded with a biological strike, then ported a nuclear device through to destroy the base before ordering the line 'sealed'."

Donald grimaced. They tended to do things a little differently back then. At least the Kelsor Virus would give them immunity if the plagues hadn't burned themselves out.

A Group Leader in the dark green of the Notway Engineering Corps entered the room, and seeing the others seated at the table snapped to attention.

"Take a seat Group Leader," Conrad said, acknowledging the salute with a nod.

The Group Leader removed his forage cap and took an uncomfortable seat on the edge on his chair.

"So what can you tell us about the line?" the World Leader asked, leaning forward.

"Nothing much sir. There's no sign of radio traffic, and so far we haven't located any signs of human habitation."

"You've had scouts out for . . ."

"Just over twelve hours, sir. We've been concentrating on digging in around the portal so I can't confirm we haven't missed anything."

"That doesn't sound good," Donald said. The isthmus was a crucial site of human settlement in almost every line they'd contacted.

"It's too late to change our minds now," his father said. He checked his watch. "We've got less than an hour."

"What happens then?" Conrad asked

"I've authorized a signal of surrender to be sent. The other World Leaders, or at least those I can trust, have been told and most of those have already returned home."

Donald had started to suspect this was what his father had intended, but to actually hear it . . . He could feel the shock of those around the table. He looked at his father, but the World Leader's attention had already returned to the Notway Group Leader. "What's the status of the portal?"

"Stable and embrasured. We could probably run it for a month with the fuel we've got."

"And the camp?"

"Pretty well established. The tents are erected and at the moment we're simply extending and deepening the trenches."

"Good, we'll start moving everyone through right now then. Group Leader Clemhorn will act as your liaison officer with the 48th. Donald, I'd like you through the portal straight away to set up a secure perimeter. There's a Force waiting for you at the portal." Donald acknowledged the order with a nod. "Carry on Group Leaders."

Excused, the engineer leaped to his feet, causing his chair to flip over backward. With a mumbled apology he righted the chair.

Now there was someone uncomfortable with his seniors Donald thought, suppressing a smile as he followed him to his door.

Outside the conference room, however, Donald suddenly faltered, almost stumbling as he remembered that the telephones were still down and he couldn't phone Matija to let her know what was happening. He knew she'd be worried, and the gods knew when he'd be back, or even if he would ever be back.

Hastings noticed he'd stopped and looked back surprised but Donald just waved him on. To have to go without telling her. . .

"Donald?" It was Conrad, who must have followed them out. "What's wrong?"

Donald shook his head, unable to tell him.

"Matija?"

"Yes."

"We'll be back," Conrad said, reassuringly.

"You're sure?" At the moment it seemed a pretty forlorn wish.

"Absolutely, there's no way I'm going to let that snot of a Raputa think he's beaten a Clemhorn."

Donald gave him a small smile. "There is that."

"Course there is," Conrad said, giving him a slap on his shoulders that almost rocked him off his feet. "Do you need any help?"

Donald shook his head. "I'll manage. Thanks."

"Take care, I'll see you on the new line."

Donald grimaced. "Thanks, I didn't need to be reminded of that. Portals." He shook his head.

Now, in the university's main hall, he stared up at the blank holes that lined the wall where stained glass windows had glowed with life earlier that day, a silent reminder of the recent battle. The portal was about a yard from the north wall. It was smaller than Donald was used to, only six foot by four, and hung suspended a foot off the ground. A thick slab of wood had been laid underneath it to act as a step. The 2nd Force, 3rd Group, 48th Clemhorn Light Infantry were lined up against the far wall, most sitting, their heavy packs resting against the wall. The Force scrambled to their feet as he approached. Their heavy packs made getting up difficult.

"Group Leader Clemhorn," their Force Leader said, coming forward to meet him. "Force Leader Tsitsho. My orders are to accompany you and secure the outer perimeter."

"Thank you Force Leader," Donald said, returning her salute.

He studied the shimmering rectangle of liquid glass that hung disconcertingly in midair. Gods he hated those things, and this one was still experimental. "All right, let's get this show on the road." He spared a glance towards the east, and Matija, then stepped up and through the portal.

CHAPTER TWENTY-SIX

Charleston - Mainline
March 1980 (96AE)

Matija stared out of the kitchen window as her hands gently stroked her stomach and the new life it contained. Behind her the kettle had just come to the boil, temporarily drowning out the background noise of jazz coming from the radio. She'd been trying to work on the final sketches for a new tapestry, and in the past had always found jazz helped her to concentrate. Not this time though. All she could do was worry about Donald in Constantinople. Outside the garden reflected her mood as it prepared for winter. The single maple tree that made the small garden so shadowed and cool in summer had already taken on its autumn wardrobe and it wouldn't be long before her father was complaining about having to sweep its leaves up again. And by the time spring was here again, she'd be a mother.

After pouring the water over the tea leaves she found herself turning the signet ring Donald had given her round and round on her finger, dropping her hand quickly when she heard the key in the latch, and the sound of her father's voice.

"I'm in the kitchen," she called.

"Put the news on," he said as he entered the room.

"Why?" she started to ask, then stopped as she caught sight of his face. She started to reach for the radio dial but her father was already there.

"What's happened?" she asked.

We're being attacked - through the portals," he added at her look of bemusement.

"Who?"

"They don't know, but it has to be Miro."

The announcer's voice came on, reading a list of cities. " . . . London, Budapest, Constantinople . . ."

She sagged. Donald!

"Sit," her father told her, pulling the chair out for her. "Where's your boyfriend?"

"Constantinople," she admitted.

"Does he know?" he asked, nodding at her stomach

"How did you . . ."

"Matija, I'm your father. And really, getting woken at five every morning by one's daughter throwing up in the toilet . . ." He shrugged expressively.

She sagged again, her hand possessively covering her stomach. "Yes."

"And?" he asked, pulling up a chair to face her.

"He asked me to marry him." She flashed him the ring.

"That is better than I would have thought of for one of his class."

"Papa, at times you are such an inverted snob."

"And what else can you say about those whose existence depends on the continued oppression of the poor?"

She sighed. This was an old argument, and one she no longer enjoyed. "Papa, you are an extremely well paid professor of Temporal Metaphysics at one of the Empire's premier universities. You are neither poor, nor oppressed."

"Which doesn't stop me from pointing put the truth. And it doesn't change the fact that the Senior Families are so useless, they can't wipe their own arses without getting someone to do it for them."

She bristled. "Donald is not like that."

"No," her father agreed. "He actually seems a very nice young man. Even if he did get my only child knocked up."

They sat listening to the station anchors trying to make sense of what was happening for an hour until it was announced that they were crossing live to Naisre where First Leader Miro was to address the Council of Leaders.

"Not that there's many of them left," Matija said.

Her father snorted., and got up to boil the kettle again.

"Papa," she said warningly as the station cut to Miro's broadcast.

The professor turned the kettle off and resumed his place next to his daughter.

Matija twisted Donald's ring as she heard Miro's graveled voice begin to speak.

"Leaders of the Council," he began. "It is with the utmost respect that I attend today to inform you that the usurper, and those allied to him, are in full retreat. As of 14:00 hours today Kommando forces from Dontfrey, assisted by allied forces of the Etehad Sho'mali launched simultaneous across multiple time lines against the usurper's — "

"Arsehole," her father said, snapping the radio off.

"Papa!"

"Well he is. He's not just broken the edict, he's completely trashed it."

The thought that Miro would have broken the one truly intractable rule of the CT-E hadn't even occurred to her.

"How else could he just be sweeping in?" the professor pointed out. "He must have contacted an advanced line. Allies my foot!"

"Donald?"

"May already be dead. And if that fool who thinks he's in charge casts his mind to round up the rest of his family . . ."

Her hand went protectively to her stomach as her father looked at it significantly.

"What can we do?" she asked.

"Who knows about it?"

"Only Donald, and my doctor."

"Then I think we pack you off to my sister's in Rome until you've had it. You can hide among your cousins."

There certainly were enough cousins to hide among, she thought. "I'm not giving it up," she said, her hand cradling her stomach protectively.

"It would be easier if you did," he pointed out, then held up his hands. "But it is your decision, and I'll support you whatever you decide. All I ask is that you think about it."

She nodded, but she already knew she wouldn't change her mind. If this baby was all she had to remember Donald by then there was no way in all of the seven levels of hell that she was going to give it up.

CHARACTERS

Achicauhtli: Conrad's personal secretary at Cempoala, Etu.

Annette: A leader of the Anarchist Collective in Mainline New York in 95AE. Nedo's girlfriend.

Archos: A young Squad Leader at Fort Larsa, Ivy's first independent command. Archos is the son of a local chief.

Arnold Clemhorn: Second son of the World Leader of Etu. In 95AE was one of the leaders of an artistic commune in Mainline New York with his cousin Nedo.

Aris Arcaos: A Pegoni war leader. The Pegoni are a barbarian alliance centered on Etu's European Alps.

Brian Clemhorn: World Leader of Etu.

Cador Horsing: A Sergeant in Etu's armed forces. Born in Spain, transferred to Fort Larsa in 95AE where he first came under Ivy's command.

Clemhorn see Arnold, Brian, Conrad, Donald, Elam, Ivy

Conrad Clemhorn: Heir and son of the World Leader of Etu. Continental Leader for South America.

Constantine MacKenzie: Son and heir to the World Leader of Huis. A year younger than Conrad they were roommates at the Academy.

Cudomix: Clemhorn Corps Leader on Etu. Before returning to front-line service in 95AE he been seconded to Etu Officer's Academy where he had been Ivy's instructor on military history.

Daniels: Senior Troop Leader at Fort Larsa, Ivy's first independent command.

Dennis Domov: World Leader of Domov. His son Mark was one of Conrad's close, personal friends, he was also Mary's father and Hayden's father-in-law.

Defella Haratan: Daughter of a Continental Leader on Dynand, and when the story commences an aide to the World Leader in

Naisre.

Donald Clemhorn: Third son of the World Leader of Etu. Completed his PhD in Alternate History at Mainline's Charleston University.

Elem Clemhorn: Wife of the World Leader of Etu, and daughter to the First Leader of Notway (Griffin Windsor).

George Harnich: World Leader of Kleng.

Griffin Windsor: World Leader of Notway and leader of the progressive faction in the Council of World Leaders. Following the death of Manek in 96AE was contender for the position of First Leader.

Hayden McArthur: The second son of the World Leader of Clyde. A Continental Leader Hayden is a close friend of Conrad's, as a result of their period together at the Academy. He is married to Mary, daughter of the World Leader of Domov, and their eldest child, Felicity is Conrad's godchild.

Isobel Peric: Sister of the Brian Clemhorn, and married to Roland North American Continental Leader on Dontfrey.

Ivy Clemhorn: Only daughter of the World Leader of Etu. A career officer in Etu's armed forces.

Jon Raincloud: A Force Leader in Etu's Clemhorn Rangers. In 95 AE he was stationed at Fort Lanegan, 150 miles west of Leolie. A member of the Oneida tribe, one of the six founding nations of the Iroquois Confederacy on Etu.

Jules McKenzie: Force Leader in the Clemhorn 72nd Battle Group. Commander of Fort Perusia, where Ivy spent two years as a Troop Leader.

Kaito Langley: Inventor of the first re-usable portal. Shared an apartment with Donald during their time together at Mainline's University of Charleston.

Lawrence McArthur: Third son of the World Leader of Clyde, and a commander in the C-TE's Imperial Security. Conrad's godfather.

Leanne Daer: Designated heir of the World Leader of D'daer.

Lindsay Byre: Heir and son of the World Leader of Chikyù. A friend of Conrad's as a consequence of their time at the Academy together.

Louise Peric: Youngest daughter of Isobel and Roland.

Manek: First Leader died 96 AE. His death triggered the first war of succession.

Maras: Professor of Time-line Theoretics at the Mainline University of Charleston. Developed the unified theory of time at the age of twenty (see Matija Maras).

Margaret Peric: Eldest daughter of Isobel and Roland.

Mathilda: A Senior Troop Leader in the Clemhorn 72nd Battle Group at Fort Perusia, where Ivy spent two years as a Troop Leader.

Matija Maras: Studied textile design at the Rome Institute of Fine Arts (Mainline). Postgraduate student at the Charleston's Industrial College. Met Donald Clemhorn via her father, Professor Maras in 95AE.

Metztli (Governor): Etu's Military Governor of Neu Stuttgart / Western Europe.

Michelle Peric: Second daughter of Isobel and Roland.

Miro Raputa: World Leader of Dontfrey. Leader of the conservative faction in the Council of World Leaders, and following the death of Manek in 96AE contender for the position of First Leader.

Nedo Peric: Second son of Isobel and Roland. A close friend of Arnold, and a co-founder of the Mainline New York commune.

Nezahual: Tlatcani and head of Cempoala's City Council. Cempoala is the continental capital of South America. Father of Papanzin.

Papanzin: Conrad's lover at Cempoala during his time as Etu' South American Continental Leader. Their breakup in 95AE caused Conrad's early departure from the city.

Peric: see Isobel, Louise, Margaret, Michelle, Nedo, Rajko, Roland

Petro Raputa: A compatriot and rival of Conrad's as a consequence of their time together at the Academy. Heir to the World Leader of Dontfrey.

Rajko Peric: Eldest son of Isobel and Roland, and heir presumptive to the position of North American Continental Leader on Dontfrey.

Raputa see Miro, Petro

Roland Peric: North American Continental Leader on Dontfrey.

Romonav: World Leader of Neu-Moscow.

Running Bear: Battle Group Leader of the Clemhorn Rangers.

Shicowe: Battle Group Leader (retired) in Etu's armed forces.

Sitting Crow: Former head of the Etu World Leader's Intelligence Service and Ivy's mentor. He retired to take over his family's import and export business.

Treik: Son of the First Leader. Died 94 AE leaving the Empire without a designated heir. The death of his father set the Empire on the path of war.

Tsitsho: Force Leader in the 48th Clemhorn Light Infantry.

GLOSSARY

ACADEMY: The Academy was established by Empire's first, First Leader, Traek, in 25AE. The Academy provides 12 years of formal, military education to the heirs of world and selected Continental Leaders. Attendance at the Academy provides the First Leader with hostages, as well as a means by which the Empire's dominant culture is passed onto its next generation of leaders.

AE (After Empire): Measured from the creation of the Cross-Temporal Empire in 1884 CE (see CROSS-TEMPORAL EMPIRE).

AIRSHIPS: The predominant means of fast passenger transport on the Mainline before the First Trans-temporal War. A typical airship of the period was Her Majesty's Airship Britannia, which had the following statistics:

Length: 804 feet
Diameter: 135 feet
Gas Volume:7,063,000 cu. feet
Engines: Four 1200 hp diesel engines
Maximum Speed: 84.4 mph (136km/hr)
Lifting Gas Type : Hydrogen
Gross Lift:242.2 tons
Useful Lift: 112.1 tons
Crew: 40 to 61
Passengers: 50-72

When re-configured as a troop carrier, which was capable of being undertaken in under 24 hours, HMA Britannia could carry 180 infantry and their equipment, or a troop of thirty mounted infantry including their mounts.

ALERT STATUS: The Etu Line's security alert system. Created in 62 AE by Charles Clemhorn the system defines four levels of threats represented by four colors: yellow, orange, red, and crimson.

AUROCHS: A breed of early cattle now extinct on the Mainline. Aurochs are about 5.7 feet tall, while a large domesticated cow is about 4.9 feet and most domestic cattle are much smaller than this. Aurochs have several features rarely seen in modern Mainline cattle, such as lyre-shaped, horns set at a forward angle, a pale stripe down the spine, and sexual dimorphism of coat color. Males were black with a pale eel stripe or finching down the spine, while females and calves were reddish (colors now still found in a few Mainline domesticated cattle breeds, such as Jersey cattle).

CLASSIFICATION: Time-lines are generally classified by Mainline ethnographers in terms of their predominant culture. This is generally derived from religious, geographic or language groupings. For example, Aryan-Transpacific refers to an offshoot off the main Aryan-Oriental. In Aryan-Oriental speakers of the Indo-Iranian group of languages, who in most lines moved south and west, migrated east into China. In the Aryan-Transpacific subsector, some continued east, finally settling in America with their horses and cattle, and either exterminating or integrating the Amerinds into their own culture. (also see ***HALLOW SCALE***).

COUNCIL OF LEADERS: Supreme policymaking and administrative body of the Empire. It meets quarterly, or when summoned by the First Leader, and consists of World Leaders, or their deputies. It is often simply referred to as the Council.

CROSS-TEMPORAL EMPIRE: usually abbreviated to the C-TE. Established in 0 AE by Traek, former Historian of a Nayarit Research Station, and 2IC to Iapura who led the actual invasion. Its creation has remained a contentious issue between the two schools of Historical Inevitability, and Individual Causation ever since. The conquest of an entire line by only fifty-three people within a space of six months is worthy of note, however, by whatever school of thought one seeks to justify it by. It was not until 17 AE, however, that a second line was actually discovered and the term Cross-Temporal came into official use. After that the Empire expanded quickly, and by 46 AE included over 31 lines. Presently there are fifty-four World Leaders, although obviously many more lines have been discovered (see EDICT). The three dominant cultures of the C-TE are: British, Slavic, and Nayarit. The first two representing the dominant cultures of the Mainline immediately prior to the Nayarit invasion.

DECIMATION: the term used for the period 1 AE to 11 AE when a series of plagues devastated the Mainline, resulting in the death of over 65 percent of the world's population. The plagues continued to occur until 27 AE with reducing force; until sufficient of the population had been inoculated with the KVirus to provide the necessary level of protection (see KELSOR VIRUS). The successful establishment of the Empire on so many worlds has often been linked to the plagues which accompany the arrival of the Hraffor on a line, and which then leave them too weak to resist absorption into the Empire.

EDICT: An order proclaimed by the Council of Leaders. The most important was that proclaimed in 21 AE, which prohibits contact with a line once it is determined to possess a technology level of at least 6.4 on the Hallow Scale (see HALLOW SCALE).

EMPIRE (see CROSS-TEMPORAL EMPIRE)

ETU: Home World of the Clemhorn family, it was seised to Charles Clemhorn in 48 AE in exchange for support provided to the then First Leader, Treik. The main indigenous civilization (the Northern Lakes League) had arisen around the Great Lakes of North America several thousand years previously, but had remained static for much of that time. However, as a result of the introduction of horses onto the America mainland about three hundred years previously by League merchants trading across the Atlantic. the League had come under increasing pressure from the nomadic occupants of the Great Plains, and was no longer the static society it had once been.

FESTIVAL OF LIVAS: A native celebration of thanksgiving for the harvest among the inhabitants of the Northern Lakes League on Etu.

GATE: see TRANS-TEMPORAL PORTAL

HALLOW SCALE: a formula used to establish a particular culture's technology level against an open-ended scale. The formula measures over 200 variables, although quite often a key indicator may be used instead. For example: 6.4 on the Hallow Scale is generally taken to be the introduction of gunpowder.

HISTORICAL INEVITABILITY: a school of thought that holds that history is created by the effect of vast, impersonal cultural forces. In this theory the split between two lines is the result of the buildup over an extended period of a series of paradox that cannot be relieved in any other manner. (also see ***INDIVIDUAL CAUSATION***).

HOWTACHI LINES: A collection of three time-lines discovered by Howard Howtachi which split off early in human prehistory when a genetic mutation resulted in a prevalence to female births (one male to every ten females). There is no real explanation as to why only three lines have developed since the split, given the period they have had to develop.

HRAFFOR: A Nayarit term which translates as '*Soldiers of the Empire*'. The title also signifies the right of leadership through conquest. They have often been compared to the Mainline Conquistadors of Spanish and South American history.

INDIVIDUAL CAUSATION: a school of thought which holds that history can be shaped by the effect of a decisive individual. In this theory the split of two lines is dependent on the actions of one special individual (also see ***HISTORICAL INEVITABILITY***).

KELSOR VIRUS: also known as the KVirus, is a single stranded DNA synthetic virus created on the Nayarit time line during the early decades of the last Nayarit civil war. It was designed as a self-replicating nano-trap to provide enhanced resistance against viral attack vectors, a necessity once the Natrecyl Accord was breached and both sides escalated their use of biological weapons. Unfortunately, because the KVirus does not seek to identify and attack cells infected by attacking viruses, rather it simply attracts, traps, and destroys those circulating in the blood stream, viruses in a latent/dormant phase within a cell are able to avoid detection. An unintended consequence of this is the typhoid-Mary effect where those infected remained carriers, despite failing to exhibit any symptoms of the disease. Upon contacting a virgin population without the protection of the KVirus the consequences can be devastating with death rates of over 99% having been recorded. The use of this as an strategy to facilitate integration of a new line into the C-TE became the accepted modus operandi during the early years of the C-TE's establishment.

LEADER a translation of a Nayarit term, it is a designation of rank, and a title of respect used by any person to a superior. Within the Empire generally recognized civilian and military ranks are as follows:

Civilian
First Leader, Leader of the Empire.
World Leader, the person controlling a time-line.
Continental Leader, a person placed in charge of either a continent, or a major cultural grouping, on a line.

Military
Squad Leader, commands 9.
Troop Leader, commands 30.
Force Leader, commands 95.
Group Leader, commands 300.
Battlegroup Leader, commands 915 (Each Battlegroup is responsible for the recruitment, training and administration of its members, and over time tends to develop its own unique esprit de corps.)
Corps Leader, commands 2,750.

LINE: (see ***TIME LINE***).

MAINLINE: (*Romano — Balkan-Renaissance*) the seat of the Cross-Temporal Empire. Research indicates that the pivotal creation point occurred in 1389AD when the Serbian King crushingly defeated the Turks at the Battle of Kosovo, thus firmly establishing Serbian independence and the potential for a Balkan based renaissance. Immediately prior to the conquering of the Mainline in 1884AD (0AE) by First Leader Traek (a military refugee from the Nayarit cataclysm) the Russian and British Empires were on the verge of outright war.

NAYARIT: Little is now known of this line, following the total destruction of its ecosphere in 0 AE after 80 years of total war. A war which involved both biological, chemical, and nuclear weapons; and is now popularly referred to within the C-TE as the Nayarit cataclysm. The first trans-temporal portal was developed on Nayarit at Chiqu, a small training and research facility in the western foothills off the mountains that define the eastern boundary of the great central plains of the North American continent. The only survivors of the line were believed to be the fifty-three Hraffor who followed Iapura through the portal.

One of the three dominant cultures of the Cross-Temporal Empire (the other two being Russian and English). Its influence has become steadily more diffused with time. The language appears to have affinities with Mainline Nahuatl languages.

POISON GAS: Two main variants are used across the C-TE:

Geranium: so-called because of its distinctive odor, which has been described as similar to scented geraniums, but sometimes called by the name of its discoverer Dr. Phillipa Lewisite. It is an organoarsenic compound, specifically an arsine, and was developed by the British for use after the last Sino-British war as a vesicant (blister agent) and lung irritant.

Nerve gas: Developed by the Nayarit, and brought with them when they invaded the Mainline the gas is an organophosphorus compound with the formula [(CH3)2CHO]CH3P(O)F. It is a colorless, odorless liquid with a relatively high volatility relative to similar nerve agents. The gas is estimated to be over 500 times more toxic than cyanide.

PORTAL: (see ***TRANS-TEMPORAL PORTALS***)

SEAGUS: the Russian linguist who developed a simplified form of English consisting of just 1,000 key words. His work was used to create a 'First Contact Pack' of five picture books which were used by the Hraffor during the initial expansionary phase of the Empire to simplify the integration of multiple lines into its structure.

SYNCLAIR'S SYNDROME: a inevitably fatal reaction by the body's defenses against the KVirus.

TAHLTAN BEAR DOGS: the Tahltan Bear Dog is a breed of dog indigenous to Canada. Primarily black, dark brown or blue, with some white patches on the chest and sometimes the feet. They stand 14 to 17 inches high at the shoulder, with relatively large, erect pointed ears, and a refined, pointed muzzle. The glossy coat was of average length, with guard hairs covering a thicker undercoat. Paws are somewhat webbed and relatively large for the size of the dog. Foxy in appearance, they possess a peculiar yodel. Their main distinction among dogs is their novel tail. Short, bushy and carried erect, it has been described variously as a shaving brush or a whisk broom

TIME-FRONT: a term used to describe that point on a number of time lines which exist concurrently at the same moment of relative time. (see ***TIME LINE***)

TIME LINE: a multiple reality caused by time splitting into a number of component parts. It's creation is not fully understood. (see ***HISTORICAL INEVITABILITY*** and ***INDIVIDUAL CAUSATION***)

TLATCANI: the C-TE preferred to work through existing authorities when absorbing a line, simply superimposing their own authority over the top of the original. In Mexico, the Clemhorns found a culture that while loosely based on earlier Mayan social types was unique to the Etu Line, and based around individual city-states. Generally each city was administered by a council made up representatives of each calpulli or group of families. Each council would elect four members who would act as an executive council, with the four then choosing a Tlatcani, or council leader.

TRANS-TEMPORAL PORTALS: are a specific occurrence of a 'wormhole' or a Einstein Rosen-Podolsky bridge that link two non-contiguous space-time points between parallel universes (or in this case - time lines). The portal allows people and objects to pass through this gateway from one parallel dimension to another. The selection of the 'linked' time lines depends on how the quantum state of the exotic matter making up gate has been 'tuned'. Travel through a portal does not change the person's relative position in either time or space.

The first trans-temporal portal was developed by Tou Azulai at Chiqu - a small, secret research facility - during the last years of the Nayarit civilization. Azulai, an expert on string theory, had been attempting to create anti-gravity by means of the controlled application of dark energy to an underlying substrate of mono-planular-charhdian-silica (MPCS). Although the anti-gravity experiment failed, the exotic matter he had accidentally created resulted in the chance creation of the first trans-temporal portal. One of the more unusual characteristics of the exotic matter he had created was its ability to transmute normal MPCS into its exotic form when placed in contact with the substrate when in a complex, aqueous solution.

When operating, the portal requires a constant supply of electrical energy which grows exponentially with the number of simultaneous portals established between two lines. If the energy falls below a certain level the portal will collapse with a catastrophic shattering of the underlying substrate. This weakness was addressed by Dr. Kaito Langley of the Mainline's University of Constantinople, who developed the first re-usable portal in 96 AE.

While operating the surface of a gate resembles the shimmering surface of a soap bubble due to thin-film interference. Due to random quantum effects within the event horizon, coherent energy cannot pass through the gate. This prevents electrical signals from passing through the portal. As a result, it became a necessity to place telex and fax machines in close proximity to the portal, allowing a physical representation of the message to be passed through the gate, before being re-encoded and passed on.

Despite the transfer being virtually instantaneous, the quantum effects previously noted above have resulted in individuals using the portal reporting auditory, visual, and other hallucinatory effects during the transfer. One portal traveler describing the effect as "being similar to being consumed by chaos, before being spat out the other end".

FIRST FAMILIES OF THE C-TE (95AE)

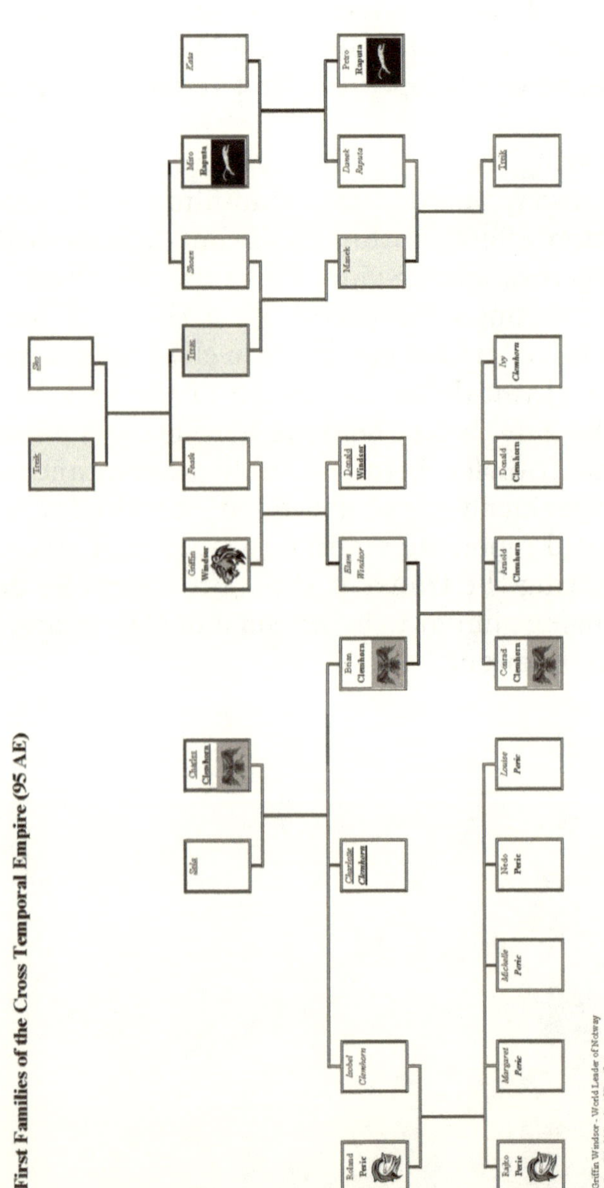

LINES OF THE C-TE (95AE)

Ah Kinchil
Ruling Family: Moyle
Symbol: Western dragon

Anhui
Ruling Family: Hefei
Symbol: Sea eagle

Atdhe
Ruling Family: Hoxha
Symbol: Olive tree

Chaac
Ruling Family: Polkinghorn
Symbol: Castle of Chaec

Changsi
Alignment: Conservative
Ruling Family: Treithick
Symbol: Californian Redword

Chikyù
Alignment: Progressive
Ruling Family: Byre
Symbol: Phoenix emerging from the flames

Ch'olan
Ruling Family: Couch
Symbol: Tiger

Chujean
Ruling Family: Medina
Symbol: A single flame

Clyde
Alignment: Progressive
Ruling Family: McArthur
Symbol: Sailing junk

Colletta
Alignment: Conservative
Ruling Family: Thompson

Symbol: Winged rifle

D'daer
Alignment: Progressive
Ruling Family: Daer
Symbol: Ruined city of Anphor Tor

Domov
Alignment: Progressive
Ruling Family: Domov
Symbol: The Ankh

Domovina
Ruling Family: Novak
Symbol: Thrush

Dontfrey
Alignment: Conservative
Ruling Family: Raputa
Symbol: The Raputa jaguar

Dynand
Alignment: Nonaligned
Ruling Family: Yanez
Symbol: Bhutan Cypress

Effling
Alignment: Conservative
Ruling Family: Ortiz
Symbol: Red Greek cross

Ekahau
Ruling Family: Poblete
Symbol: Coptic Ankh

Etu
Alignment: Progressive
Ruling Family: Clemhorn
Symbol: Double-headed Mayan eagle

Fitzmorton
Ruling Family: Stirling
Symbol: A round tower

Fujian
Ruling Family: Fuzhou
Symbol: Spinning wheel

Gansu
Ruling Family: Castillo
Symbol: Blue marble sphere

Guangdong
Ruling Family: Guangzhou
Symbol: Scimitar

Gwizhou
Ruling Family: Fuentes
Symbol: Griffin

Gwlad
Alignment: Conservative
Ruling Family: Morris
Symbol: Oak tree

Hainan
Ruling Family: Haikous
Symbol: Mace

Hocawi
Alignment: Conservative
Ruling Family: Ahler
Symbol: Southern Cross

Huis
Alignment: Progressive
Ruling Family: MacKenzie
Symbol: Ten-sided star

Ix Chel
Ruling Family: Borup
Symbol: Chinese dragon

Ixbalanque
Ruling Family: Ege
Symbol: Wolf

Ixtab
Ruling Family: Buck
Symbol: Coconut palm

Jerek
Alignment: Progressive
Ruling Family: Giesing
Symbol: Cedar tree

Kinich Ahau
Ruling Family: Han
Symbol: Eight rayed sun

Kleng
Alignment: Progressive
Ruling Family: Harnich
Symbol: Crescent

Mainline
Alignment: Nonaligned

Malac
Alignment: Conservative
Ruling Family: Espersen
Symbol: Yellowfin Tuna

Marke
Alignment: Conservative
Ruling Family: Boulay
Symbol: Blue star

Maun
Alignment: Progressive
Ruling Family: Lorge
Symbol: Zebra

Mawyhydi
Alignment: Conservative
Ruling Family: Phillips
Symbol: Tudor rose

Milawe
Alignment: Progressive
Ruling Family: Riendeau
Symbol: Yellow lotus

Nebo
Ruling Family: Turk
Symbol: Hand — palm outwards

Neu-Moscow
Alignment: Progressive
Ruling Family: Romanov
Symbol: Brown bear

Neydd Gymanwlad
Ruling Family: Morgan
Symbol: Chrysanthemum

Notway
Alignment: Progressive
Ruling Family: Windsor
Symbol: Cougar

O'Brien
Ruling Family: O'Brien
Symbol: Harp

Q'anjobalan
Ruling Family: Vannier
Symbol: Golden pearl

Rolfe
Alignment: Conservative
Ruling Family: Rolfe
Symbol: Red lion rampant on a black background

Styphon
Alignment: Conservative
Ruling Family: Morrison
Symbol: A single cannon

Velican
Ruling Family: Kos
Symbol: Four stars arranged on a circle

Vinogradov
Ruling Family: Morozob
Symbol: Single kernel of rice

Vorobyov
Ruling Family: Vazilyev
Symbol: Glass crown

Yucatecan
Ruling Family: Lachance
Symbol: Macaw

Yum Cimil
Alignment: Progressive
Ruling Family: Arthur
Symbol: Coyote

Yumil Kaxob
Ruling Family: Myricks
Symbol: Black lion

Zajendnic
Ruling Family: Krajnc
Symbol: Andean Condor

ABOUT THE AUTHOR

Andrew spent his high-school years in the school's library lost in the worlds of Andre Norten, Robert Heinlein, and Isaac Asimov. His first commercially accepted series of novels (the Garden Adventures) was originally completed to read to his two sons at night. Now his children have left home he lives in Perth with his wife, one dog, and sixty four gold fish. Andrew can be contacted at www.andrewjharvey.com.

In addition to writing, Andrew is also the Principal of Hague Publishing. Established in 2011 as an independent publisher of Science Fiction and Fantasy, Hague Publishing is registered in Western Australia, and publishes original work by Australian and New Zealand authors.

Previously Principal for the Davies Literary Agency, Andrew was also editor and publisher of The Western Australian Year Book for a number of years, in addition to being the editor and a writer for 'Afterlife - the on-line magazine for Atmosphere users'.

Andrew's first published short story (A Messenger to the Dragon) appeared in Aurealis - Australian Fantasy and Science Fiction in 1992.

A passionate reader of Alternate History Andrew is presently working on completing a series of trilogies based on the Cross-Temporal Empire, following the Clemhorn siblings and their cousins the Perics.

Look for the other books in this series:

Nadir and Sunrise

Look for more books from *Pike & Powder, LLC / Winged Hussar Publishing, LLC* and *Zmok Books* – E-books, paperbacks and Limited Edition hardcovers. The best in history, science fiction and fantasy at:

https://www. wingedhussarpublishing.com
https://www.PikeandPowder.com

or follow us on Facebook at:

Winged Hussar Publishing LLC

Or on twitter at:

WingHusPubLLC

For information and upcoming publications

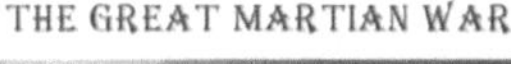

SCOTT WASHBURN

www.ingramcontent.com/pod-product-compliance
Lightning Source LLC
Chambersburg PA
CBHW030816020726
47499CB00006B/1944

* 9 7 8 1 9 4 5 4 3 0 6 7 1 *